BY PAPAL DECREE

When Belief Becomes a Weapon, No One Is Innocent

NORBERT E. REICH

SWEETSPIRE LITERATURE
MANAGEMENT

For Paul, my best friend.

What is a friend? A single soul dwelling in two bodies.

Aristotle

TABLE OF CONTENTS

PROLOGUE...1

CHAPTER 1 5

CHAPTER 2 8

CHAPTER 3 16

CHAPTER 4 25

CHAPTER 5 36

CHAPTER 6 46

CHAPTER 7 54

CHAPTER 8 60

CHAPTER 9 67

CHAPTER 10 74

CHAPTER 11 83

CHAPTER 12 97

CHAPTER 13 104

CHAPTER 14 109

CHAPTER 15 113

CHAPTER 16 121

CHAPTER 17 130

CHAPTER 18 138

CHAPTER 19 147

CHAPTER 20 155

CHAPTER 21 163

CHAPTER 22 167

CHAPTER 23 171

CHAPTER 24 176

CHAPTER 25 183

CHAPTER 26 192

CHAPTER 27 210

CHAPTER 28 223

CHAPTER 29 232

CHAPTER 30 249

CHAPTER 31 256

CHAPTER 32 261

PROLOGUE

The Syrian Desert

H E KNELT. HIS KNEES WERE BURIED in the sand; his hands tied behind his back. He wore an orange suit, which the prisoners at Guantanamo Bay wore. The sun was high. On the horizon, its rays show no mercy. He saw only sand, sand wherever he looked. There was no blindfold. He had been instructed to look straight into the camera.

The man behind him was dressed all in black with a mask to hide his face, but his hands were bare. In his right hand, he held a large knife, the knife that was about to take a life, the life of the man kneeling in the sand of the desert, the life of an American, a doctor who had come here to help the people in need.

When the camera began to record, the man in black started a short speech. Threatening all the infidels, he spoke directly to the president of the United States. He said that all infidels would die. His English was perfect, and his accent was clearly British. He raised his knife in a gesture intended to kill the man who knelt in front of him. The video stopped.

For the man from Britain, a self-proclaimed jihadist, it was his first kill. But he could not kill—not yet. Nonetheless, ISIS, the Islamic

The State of Iraq and Syria had asked him to be in the video. They wanted everyone to know that many nations supported their cause, and they needed recruits.

The man in black handed the knife to a young Arab, a man who would end the life of their captive. The young Arab, but a teenager, took the knife and expertly beheaded the doctor. He looked up, full of pride. He knew he had done well, had done what his grandfather wanted him to do.

The White House, Washington, DC

Monica Drew, the president of the United States, watched the coverage closely on her favorite television channel, CNN. The channel always supported her and seldom criticized her. It was a news outlet where she could do little wrong.

Even as she watched, she could not understand. The beheading of the doctor who had gone to Syria to save lives—Syrian lives— should never have happened. It had happened because the previous leader of the free world, the former president, her predecessor, had never understood the reasons for the war in the Middle East. He had never understood or accepted that it was a religious war. President Drew herself had no clue. The former president had been arrogant, rarely listened to his advisors, and thought he knew everything. It was a trait that seemed to come with the office.

Unlike the former president, Monica Drew knew a controversial health-care bill or a frail treaty with Iran to help solve nuclear proliferation in the Middle East would not establish a legacy for a presidency. She also knew that to make her own legacy as the president, she needed to act now. Her predecessor had waited too. Long had run out of options. She was not about to make the same mistake.

Monica Drew turned off the television set and leaned back in her comfortable chair in the Oval Office. Today, she was the most powerful person in the world, and she decided to use her power and all her resources to make peace in the Middle East. That was to become her legacy.

CHAPTER 1

Berry Islands, Bahamas

THE WAVES SPLASHED GENTLY AGAINST THE worn, light blue skiff that was drifting aimlessly in the calm Bahamian sea. The sun had not yet crossed the horizon, but it was about to do so. It was June. The waters were calm because there was no wind. The craft was carried only by the currents. The old wooden boat drifted toward the shores off Chubb Cay, one of the many Berry Islands in the Bahamian waters. The skiff slowly made its way toward the rocky shore. It had no motor, sails, or master. It was but driftwood, an old wooden boat that had seen better days.

The naked man inside the skiff run was barely conscious and hardly breathing. His skin was burned, the kind of burn seen after many days in the sun. The burns were red blisters, raw and oozing, the skin fried by the sun's rays. He lay motionless, about to die. The twenty-foot fishing boat was barely afloat in the gentle waves. It had no steerage. The sea was its captain as it drifted toward the shore, each wave helping it. Finally, the wooden boat found its resting place when a lazy wave pushed it between two coral heads. That was where it would stay. It would not—could not—go any farther. It had seen its end.

The sun entered the horizon, illuminating the water, making it crystal blue, and then changing it to turquoise. It lit the sky and shone on the waves, breaking softly on the shore. The sun rose quickly, generating much warmth. Soon it was blistering, emanating all its power. Then came the wind, and with it, a squall. It carried heavy, menacing gray and black clouds, but was just a bark without a bite. All Bahamians knew it would rain. All knew it would not last.

By midmorning, a heavy shower flooded Chubb Cay, briefly saturating the marina's grounds, grass, and gravel walkways.

It also flooded the skiff, the boat that had drifted ashore and was now anchored between two coral heads just a half mile from the docks. The rain drenched the man at the bottom of the old boat. His body was prone, and his breathing was still labored. He was severely dehydrated. The cool rain pounded his almost-lifeless body, and the bottom of the boat slowly filled with cool water from the sky. As the water reached and covered most of his body, his body temperature gradually returned to normal. Life crept back into the motionless being. The first movement was the tongue; it exited the mouth, searched, and found the fluid he needed so much. The rainwater, the water at the bottom of the skiff run, the water from the sky, saved his life.

It happened slowly. He had no control, acting only on survival instinct. He gathered the fluid, the fresh rainwater. He gained strength—not much, but enough to tell him he was still alive. The rain lasted for less than thirty minutes. It was a heavy downpour typical for the Bahamian islands. Two to three inches of the precious liquid had accumulated in the old boat. He took the water in slowly; instinct told him it was what he should do. He rolled over and took a deep breath. He lifted his right arm and touched his forehead and chest. He wanted to be sure he was alive, not just living. A dream.

Touching his body was painful because the sun burned his skin for several days. He did not mind—not now that he was still alive.

He continued to examine his body as he lay on his back in the boat. Suddenly, he felt a sharp pain. His hand had touched his belly just below the left side of his rib cage. That was where the bullet had passed through him, he now remembered. The bleeding had stopped long ago. The saltwater had helped to irrigate the wound, but the wetness had not helped heal it. It was still raw and open, but there was no push: it was clean.

He turned his body in the skiff run and took another drink of the precious fluid. As he did, he saw his cross. It was a reminder of his grandfather—a gift, Grandma had told him—given to his grandpa by his best friend, a renowned artist and devout Catholic. It was a gift his grandfather had worn around his neck when he had shot himself.

The wooden cross was floating, drifting in the rainwater that had saved man's life. Adam Bergman reached for it and retrieved it. He brought it to his lips, kissed the cross, and silently prayed.

CHAPTER 2

Berlin, Germany

THE CHURCH BELLS OF THE JESUS Christus Kirche in the fashionable suburb of Dahlem rang and filled the air on this beautiful, warm summer morning. Adam heard the sound. And was reassured. He had come here as soon as he could after hearing the unforgettable message: "To be certain, your pastor is next and thank the pope." His small wooden cross had also told him to come. Now the sound of the bells made it sure. Only here could he find the answer as to why someone had tried to kill him. And what did his pastor have to do with it? The bells continued to ring, calling for him. He stood up from the park bench he had sat on to reminisce. A few hours ago, he arrived in this city and went directly to the small park adjacent to the church. He had sat on one of the benches overlooking the pond covered with water lilies. The pond was not as he recalled it. It was smaller now than it had been years ago when he was a child. Then the pond was more like a lake. He and his friends had often played there. He recalled playing ice hockey in the winter, and in the spring, they had played the daring game of floating on the pieces of ice as they melted. Whoever stayed the longest was the winner. Not once had he lost.

He stretched and straightened his trousers. He was a handsome man with green, soft eyes that made you feel at ease, and a relaxed and reassuring smile. Curly, dark-brown hair almost touched his shoulders. His movements were fluid, relaxed, confident, and athletic. He was a man who stood out and was sure of himself. His six-foot-two-inch frame and muscular body barely fit in the gray, pin-striped suit he had bought on his brief stopover in Frankfurt. He did not know why he had bought the suit, but he had known he had to come here.

Adam left the park bench and followed the sound of the church bells. He knew it was coming from the tower that he and his older brother had climbed years ago while attending Sunday school. The bell tower had been responsible for his fear of heights. Ever since first climbed it at six, he had had nightmares of being chased by a pack of vicious dogs and falling off the tower.

It was here that he had first learned about a new world. He was six years old when his brother had taken him along. He had always followed his older brother, whom he adored. His brother had hated every Wednesday, the day of Bible school. But Adam loved Wednesdays. That was when the pastor talked to all the kids about religion, Jesus, God, and peace on earth. His brother hated these sessions. He wanted to be out on the soccer field, chasing the ball or the girls in the park. But Adam loved to hear the stories about Abraham and the baby Jesus. Most of all, he loved to hear about God, the almighty Father. That was when he had first heard about the Holy Land. He had learned that most people there believed in what Abraham had preached centuries ago: there is but one God for all people and humankind.

Adam left the park and entered the square in front of the church. The bell tower was to his right. The red-brick square appeared cold and larger than he remembered. It was not as intimate, not as familiar. But he knew it had been years since he would last stand here— years that had changed his life, perceptions, and outlook. Years that had changed everything about him. Those years, however, had never changed his core.

The large wooden doors to the church were wide open, and well-dressed parishioners were making their way into the sacred walls of the house of God. Adam did not join them at once. He stood for a moment, recalling many years. Then he joined the crowd and entered the house with which he was so familiar.

Adam did not listen to the sermon; his mind would not let him. Instead, he remembered. He recalled all the Sundays his family had come to worship, all the holidays, festivities, and plays he had always participated in as a child. He looked at the large wooden cross above the altar and smiled. Now he remembered being a child of five or six years of age. He had been the baby Jesus in a Christmas play, and he had been the main attraction.

That was when the pastor had given him the wooden cross, the cross his grandfather had worn, the cross that had been given to his grandfather by his best friend, a world-renowned artist. Adam's grandfather donated the cross to the church in his will. And his grandfather had made it clear that the pastor had complete discretion to award the cross to someone. He had asked the pastor to decide the right person to receive the cross. When Adam had won the prize for being the best of the flock, the pastor had given him the cross.

Once the service was over, the people left slowly. They enjoyed their Sunday morning in church. They respected their pastor. He stood proudly at one of the large wooden doors leading to the square.

As his flock left his house of worship, he shook many hands. He had built a large foe and was one of Berlin's most successful parishes.

Adam Bergman did not move. He stood erect in the last row of the church. He did not pray but stood silently and stared at the large wooden cross above the altar. He showed no emotion as he stood and stared, his gaze fixed on the large, plain wooden cross high above. Then his right hand reached for the necklace around his neck. It was a replica of the cross he was staring at. Gently, his fingers caressed it. It was the wooden cross that had given him the will and the faith to live.

He continued to gaze at the cross above the altar, the cross he had known about since childhood, the one he trusted, the one that had saved his life. Suddenly, his gaze shifted, and he noticed an older man strolling with assurance and dignity. The man had come out of one of the two doors adorned on both sides of the altar. He still wore his black-and-white robe. Adam did not react, but he noticed every move. He saw that all was quiet. There were no other people in the house of God, not even in hiding. There was only himself, the pastor, and God.

The pastor was much older now. He walked slowly and with care. He measured each step. He had to because his vision was beginning to fail him. He had been told to use a cane, but he had refused. He would need no help to find his way in the house of God. He had walked the path many times, and he had always walked it with God. He was dressed in his Sunday dress, the simple robe Adam remembered well. Adam recognized the smile as the holy man approached him and extended his hand in greeting. He saw the dimples, the curled lip, and the flicker in the older man's eyes. None had changed in more.

For more than twenty years, Adam took the pastor's hand, gave it a firm shake, and looked him directly in the eyes.

"It has been a long time since I was here last. I am sure you do not remember me."

"Yes, I do," the answer came. The voice was much stronger than Adam had expected. "You and your family worshipped here for many years, many years ago. And I recall you. You always participated in our plays, Easter, Christmas, you name it—you wanted to be part of it. And not just part of it. As I recall, you always had to be the star and have the leading role. Tell me, does my memory serve me correctly?" He said it with a smile, fully knowing he was right. He was not only a servant of God; he was a diplomat.

"Yes," Adam replied, humbled, and embarrassed. "Yes, your memory is perfect."

"Thank you," God's man replied. "Thank you for being honest. As I recall, you always were. You were not always on your best behavior, but you were always honest. That I do remember."

"Well, I tried," Adam responded. "That was how I was taught to be. That was what my parents wanted me to do."

"You had the best parents," the man of the cloth said as he put both hands on the other man's shoulders.

The pastor reminded Adam that he had known the young man's mother well for many years. He had confirmed her and had performed at the wedding ceremony when she had married Adam's father, Daniel. The wedding had been a bit unusual in those days, he recalled.

Daniel Bergman, an American, was the son of German immigrants. and a Jew. He had been an assistant professor of history at New York University. When he had published his first book, a text of the Bismarck era, he had become an instant success in academic circles. Many universities had offered him a position, and he had chosen the Freie Universität in Berlin. He had wanted to return to his roots—for a while.

Soon after arriving in Berlin, he fell in love and married. The pastor had many meetings with the couple. They discussed at great length the differences in their beliefs and religions. His wife had insisted on raising her firstborn as a Lutheran. Her husband had not objected. He always said that belief in Abraham's teachings, the belief in only one God, was all that mattered.

The pastor reminisced that they had had a wonderful marriage. Adam and his mother attended church each Sunday, and he had always been eager to participate in the church's functions. On most occasions, his father had attended. Daniel was proud to be Adam's father.

"I am glad you came back. It honors me. It tells me I do have a loyal flock."

"You do. Yes, indeed, you surely do," Adam responded.

The pastor smiled. "Now, tell me why you are here? We are in God's house. Here, we have no secrets. With me, you can share all your troubles and all your dreams. Then it is up to God; only he can decide."

But the pastor knew full well why Adam had come. He had received a message from the Catholic bishop of Berlin. It was a very unusual request, but the bishop had assured him that the pope had made it. He had asked that the pastor meet with a man who would come, who had once been part of his flock. Only he and the pastor should meet, and no one was to know about the meeting. The pope wanted the pastor to pass on a message to the man—a message he insisted could make peace between all religions—and the pastor had agreed without hesitation.

Adam felt nervous and unsure. He reached for the wooden cross that hung around his neck with his right hand.

And touched his hairy, muscular chest. He rubbed the cross gently between his thumb and index finger. He always used this gesture when nervous or unsure of what to do. He recalled that he had decided to come here to find answers. Why had he been shot? Who had done it? The decision had not come easily. He had thought about letting go, starting a new life, forgetting about the past. But as he had lain in the skiff, slowly regaining consciousness in God's rainwater as it filled the boat and gave him new life, he had known there was only one path for him. He had to go back and find answers.

And he knew that the servant of God now standing before him held the key. At least, that was his best guess.

"I don't know where to start," Adam said. "Actually, I am not sure I should have come. I do not know any questions I want to ask. Some voice inside told me to be here, to be with you." But Adam remembered the message. He could still hear the voice on the yacht as it had left the Miami Beach Marina: "To be certain, your pastor is. next, and thank the pope." He would never forget it.

"That, my son, is how God leads the way. He leads mysteriously. No mortals will ever know the way, but we all play a role. We all have a purpose. We all need to serve him. I know that is his way."

"Father, please, I have traveled long. More importantly, I have struggled over whether I should be here. I do not know. I need directions. I need purpose. I am adrift. I need God."

"Son, you made the right decision. Rome called me, and your God has chosen you for a mission. I waited long for God's chosen one to arrive, knowing through my prayers that he was a lost soul who used to be one of my flock. When I saw you today, I was certain you were the one. I saw the wooden cross around your neck and knew my God had spoken."

The pastor again stepped forward. Both men were standing in the last row of the large Protestant church. The sun was shining through one of the mosaic windows, casting a holy light—a halo—above them.

All the wooden benches were empty, and the candles barely burned, but the large wooden cross above the altar was alive.

"There is not much I need to tell you, my son. Go there. Go there in peace. God will always be with you. You are one of my flock. If you need sanctuary, you now know where to seek it. God bless you. God will be with you." Then the old pastor handed the man a small piece of brown paper. He leaned forward and placed his hands on the taller man's shoulders. He kissed him on both cheeks.

"I am glad you came. Now walk with God."

CHAPTER 3

Berlin, Germany

THE BEIGE MERCEDES TAXI TOOK ADAM Bergman from his church in the suburbs of Dahlem to his moderately priced hotel in the middle of town. It was a convenient location too. I will be staying in Berlin, Germany's capital. The hotel was located just off Oliver Platz, convenient to many critical Berlin destinations. As he entered the cab and sat, he looked at the brown, irregularly shaped paper his pastor had handed him. No doubt, it had been torn off in haste. The handwriting confirmed that the message had been prepared quickly. He could hardly read it, but not because it was in German. He was fluent in that language. No, it was the writing itself. He thought it had been done in haste, even in panic. There was but an address on the paper, along with three digits. Part of a telephone number? A room number? He could not be sure. But he did recognize the address. Strange, he thought. It was the address of the fashionable Hotel Adlon on the Pariser Platz in the center of Berlin.

He put the brown paper back into the breast pocket of his suit and leaned back in the rear seat of the taxi. He needed time to think. He needed to go back to his hotel, take a hot shower, lie in his bed, He covered himself with light down comforters and relaxed. He needed to know what God wanted him to do.

Adam lay back in the king-size bed in his room at his hotel on Oliver Platz. He recalled the events of the last few weeks. Again, he tried to remember the journey. It had begun at his home in Miami Beach and had taken him to the Bahamas and then back to the city of his family, Berlin. There was a party at the Setai Hotel in Miami Beach. A friend had invited him on a weekend cruise to Nassau on a luxurious yacht. The yacht, a one-hundred-twenty-five-foot Palmer Johnson, had been docked at the Miami Beach marina less than a few hundred yards from his condominium.

He had walked from his apartment past the small park along Government Cut, the artificial shipping channel between Miami Beach and Fisher Island. He had walked past the small beach club, La Piaggia, next to the Murino Grande, a large high-rise apartment. The paved walkway was lined by tall palm trees, which waved lazily in the soft breeze coming off the open sea. The walkway was well-lit and busy with pedestrians and people riding skateboards, walking dogs, and jogging. Soon he heard the music from the band playing at Monty's, a bar and restaurant on the docks. To his left was the marina, filled with boats of all sizes, both sailboats and motor yachts.

Beyond the break wall of the marina, he noticed the large cranes at the port of Miami. When he had first moved here, he had thought the cranes took away from the charm of the waterfront. Now he felt different. The cranes, the large freighters, the magnificent cruise ships docked along the waterway—all defined the Miami waterfront. They made it all come alive. The marine traffic never stopped. Often, he sat on his balcony overlooking downtown Miami. The channel to the ocean, and the port of Miami with all the cranes and freight boats. He had spent hours watching the marine traffic from his apartment on the eighteenth floor. That night, a bright, full moon had illuminated all.

He saw the yacht docked at the end of Pier F on the break wall as he strolled along the well-lit, palm-lined walkway. The Palmer Johnson was a sleek ship. It had been built in Wisconsin, but it had the lines of an Italian race car. It looked like a Ferrari, he thought as he walked toward her at the end of the dock.

The ship was engulfed in light. He saw several people on the flybridge next to the hot tub. When he boarded the yacht, he noticed the open glass door between the salon and cockpit. This made it a single space, allowing the night to enter the ship. The salon had been decorated with natural colors, light oak, soft leather, and stainless-steel appliances. Adam knew the yacht had several staterooms and was anxious to see them all. He loved boats. He particularly loved the big yachts. He had even thought about buying one.

Adam was surprised that the party was small, twelve or fourteen people. He was greeted by the host, a gentleman dressed casually, who had a trim shape, dark complexion, and an outgoing smile. He had a full black beard and piercing black eyes. The man was muscular, stood almost six feet tall, and had the features of a man from the Middle East. He was older than Adam, forty or forty-five years of age. The man handed him a glass of champagne, shook his hand, and asked him to feel at home. Curiously, he now recalled that the yacht had left the dock as soon as he embarked. At the time, he had paid no attention to it. He had been preoccupied with meeting the host and some other guests, most young, beautiful women. Again, he had made a mistake. It was a mistake he had made before. He had allowed women to distract him. He was a professional, a trained assassin. He should not have let it happen.

The yacht left Government Cut, the narrow channel leading into the open ocean. Fashionable Fisher Island was to its starboard, his condominium to its port. The channel was well marked. He stood on the yacht's aft deck, chatting with a wonderful young woman. He pointed out the sights to her as the ship left Miami. She asked him about the restaurant along the waterfront. He told her they served the best pork shank he had ever tasted. She told him it was one of her favorite dishes. They agreed to have dinner there when they returned.

Soon, he could no longer see the skyline of the city. He knew the yacht was heading toward the Bahamas, toward Nassau. He often took the trip in his boat, which was docked at the same marina. No longer did he need a compass or a GPS. He knew how to navigate like the Bahamian fishermen did. The sun and stars showed him the way.

Adam strolled around the luxurious yacht, meeting several beautiful women. He had another glass of champagne. He was enjoying the party. Many of the young women were attractive and interesting to talk to. Then his host walked up to him on the yacht's aft deck. He did so just as a bell sounded to alert the guests that dinner was being served in the dining room and salon. He asked Adam not to join the rest of the crowd. "Not yet," he had said. "Let us enjoy a cigar before dinner. Let us skip the cocktails." And he handed Adam another glass of champagne and a cigar. They were standing on the aft deck near the steps that led to the large swim platform of the boat. The host reached into his suit pocket to retrieve a butane lighter. He asked Adam to turn and face him to block the wind as he lit the cigar. As Adam leaned forward, close to his host, he heard, "To be certain, your pastor is next and thank the pope."

Then he had felt the bullet enter his body. He remembered thinking there was not much of a sound—obviously, a silencer. And he recalled the bullet existing his body. He had heard the thud as it hit the passage door behind him, which led to the yacht's swimming platform. He had felt light-headed and thought he would lose consciousness. Seconds later, he had hit the water.

The water had awakened him and saved his life. The yacht quickly moved away, and it was not long before he lost sight of her. He began to swim toward the northeast. He estimated that they had gone past Bimini and were heading toward Nassau. He had no pain. The initial trauma acted as an anesthetic. He did not appear to bleed much, as he saw no blood in the water.

It was getting dark. He knew he had to conserve energy, so he mostly floated on his back. He gazed up at the beautiful sky filled with stars he could touch. He felt relaxed. He had no fear. He had read somewhere that this was a person's state of mind when death was imminent, just before entering the portals of heaven. But Adam knew he was not about to die.

"To be certain, your pastor is next and thank the pope." These were the words his assassin had spoken. Strangely, Adam thought as if he floated in the blue water. He had once had a pastor many years ago. But now he was Jewish. Did the man mean his old rabbi in Brooklyn?

At sunrise, God reached out his hand in the form of an old, blue wooden skiff. It bobbed up and down in the gentle waves. The boat was only a few hundred yards away, and Adam swam there quickly, climbed into it, and was pleased to see two wooden oars lying in it.

Adam was almost naked. He had removed most of his clothing during the night to float more easily and wore only his underpants. As the sun rose, it beat mercilessly on his body. Now he regretted his decision to remove his clothing. And then his steerage, the two old wooden oars, broke as he tried to row. The wood was brittle, dried by the sun they had been exposed to. Without the oars, he had no way to propel the old skiff. He was at the mercy of the Bahamian sea. After two days, his skiff found its way to Chubb Cay, one of the thirty days of the Berry Islands. Adam has come here often. He was an avid fisherman, and the islands, located about sixty miles east of Bimini, were close to his home in Florida. Chubb Cay is the southernmost of the Berry Islands, only twenty miles northeast of Andros, the Bahamas' largest island. Off Andros lies the third-largest barrier reef in the world, known as the bonefishing capital of the world. Twelve feet of water covered the reef, but suddenly the sea depth plunged to six thousand feet. Record catches were made in these waters for mackerel, blue and white marlin, and sailfish. Adam loved to fish and often came here to enjoy sport.

A local conch fisherman had seen the old boat trapped between two coral heads as the waves splashed gently against the worn, light blue skiff. He was the one who had taken Adam to Marcus, the harbormaster at Chubb Key. Marcus immediately recognized the man who had come to Chubb Key often on his own boat. Marcus had visited Adam in Miami. They had become friends.

Adam was barely alive. Marcus and his pregnant wife took him in. They cared for him and took care of his wounds. He recovered quickly because he was young and strong. As he recovered, he would jog along the dirt road to the small airport on the island. Then he would head for the pristine beach next to the marina. First, he would take laps in the saltwater pool adjacent to the beach and swim for a mile in the protected, calm ocean.

After his swim, he would lie in one of the hammocks stretched between palm trees on the beach. The beach was always empty. The few cottages that lined the bay were hardly ever occupied. He had stayed in these cottages on previous fishing trips and loved every minute. He did not mind that no one was there. He liked the solitude and peace, the wind whispering to him, the soft splash of the waves as they gently touched the white sand. He wanted the setting sun, giving only light. Adam let his body dry as he watched the sun fall into the deep waters, into the "tongue" of the ocean, as the locals called the sea here. He never brought a towel, preferring to stay on the beach and let the sun dry him. Often, he thought he wanted to stay for good.

But he was also determined to get back on his feet and be as fit as he had been. He took most of his meals with Marcus and his wife. But as he recovered, he wanted to eat out, to no longer eat only fish and chicken. During his last weeks on the island, he took Marcus and his wife to the quaint restaurant at the marina and to the semi-private club where Adam was a member. They had breakfast there daily, and Adam asked for bacon and eggs. Each evening, they also enjoyed dinner in the restaurant. It was always a treat for Marcus and his wife.

Adam loved Chubb Key, and he loved Marcus and his wife. He liked the simplicity of life here and had thought many times about staying. He had enough money. He could be busy himself, go fishing, help Marcus at the marina, draft a book, do whatever he wanted. Each day, he struggled, unable to decide. Each day, he lay in one of the hammocks on the beach after his swim in the ocean. He loved the solitude, the peace, the calmness of the sea, the soothing blue sky. His emotions told him to stay here, to be at peace and forget his past.

But Adam made a different decision. He knew it was only a matter of time before his assassins would find out that he was still alive. Adam needed to change the game. He had to become the hunter rather than the hunted. Fortunately, his enemy had left two clues: the yacht in Miami and his pastor in Berlin—although he was unsure about the pastor. Had the assassin meant his old rabbi in Brooklyn? No, he decided, the man had clearly used the word *pastor*. Adam knew he had to pursue both leads; his pastor was the priority. After all, his enemy had threatened to kill the holy man, so there was no time to lose. But he also had to find out all about the yacht in Miami. Who owned it? Was it a charter? Adam decided to fly back to Miami immediately and catch the next plane to Berlin, Germany. Since he lost his cell phone in the deep Bahamian sea, he used Marcus' phone to place two calls.

First, he called his housekeeper in Miami Beach to let her know he would be arriving in a couple of hours. He instructed her to pack a small carry-on with a few clothing items and money.

Adam always kept several thousand dollars in his apartment, and his housekeeper knew where to find it. His second call was to his secretary, whom he instructed to make his flight and hotel reservations. He also told her to find out about the yacht he had boarded in Miami Beach, the 120-foot Palmer Johnson called *Tranquilo*. He had noticed the yacht's name while walking up to her at the Miami Beach marina. *Tranquilo*. Calmness, he thought with a smile. She had been all but that.

Adam stepped off the plane that had taken him from Chubb Cay to the small private airport at Okeechobee, only minutes north of Miami. The car driver, whom his secretary had hired, handed him his housekeeper's cell phone.

"There is a message for you," the driver said as he opened the rear door of the limousine. The message was from his secretary, and he gave him all the travel information. She had also checked out the yacht. A prominent Cuban American businessperson in Miami owned it. The yacht's captain had taken her to a local boatyard on Thursday, the day before Adam had boarded the ship—for minor repairs. A guard at the yard reported that a small crew had boarded the yacht Friday morning to take her for a sea trial. The captain had informed the guard that the boat owner wanted to be sure that no additional repairs were needed before his cruise to the Bahamian islands. It was routine, the guard understood. When the guard returned to work early Monday morning, the yacht was again securely docked at the boatyard. It had been the guard's weekend off. Adam's secretary had also contacted the owner and the captain of Tranquilo, who were surprised, as neither knew of a sea trial. It was clearly a dead end, Adam thought. His opponents were professionals. Now his only hope was his pastor, and he had to see him while he was still alive.

Adam Bergman, an assassin who had barely survived the Bahamian seas, turned over in his bed, enjoying the firm mattress and the soft down comforters in his room at the hotel on Oliver Platz in Berlin. Again, he picked up the torn piece of brown paper he had placed on the night table next to his bed. He stared at the words written on the old, brittle paper: "Hotel Adlon." Adam knew the hotel well, for he had stayed there on a previous mission. The three numbers still puzzled him. He did not think it was part of a phone number. A room number was more likely. He would find out soon.

CHAPTER 4

Berlin, Germany

THE PASTOR OF THE GERMAN LUTHERAN church smiled. Today, he gave another good sermon. His flock liked him, and he had more parishioners than he could accommodate. And they kept coming.

Then, of course, *he* had come, just as predicted. The pastor had always known he would come. It was just a matter of time. He thought he had handled Adam poorly, but he was not sure. Indeed, he had known him when he was young. Even then, the boy had been an enigma—always a loner, always sure of himself, independent. He could not be controlled or directed. Adam was complex.

The pastor was not sure what made him tick. He had been different from all the other children and had kept to himself. The other kids had followed him and respected him. He had been their leader, and when he had decided to become active in all the church's activities and plays, the pastor had been thankful. Now, he had a flock to follow God's way.

The pastor turned toward the altar after everyone had left his church. He looked at the large wooden cross. He bowed his head, used his right hand to form the sign of the cross in front of his chest, stood, and walked past God's stage.

The holy man's living quarters, a beautiful house adjacent to the church, and a splendid park were only steps away from the house of worship. As he left the church and walked toward his home, he reminded himself how well he had done. He lived in one of the best suburbs of Berlin, and his church had been successful. Indeed, the liberals from the Freie Universität had given him a run for his money. But he had persevered. He had given in some, but that was God's way. He would give more if needed, for he knew how to play the game. He knew how to keep a flock.

The young man he had met earlier had a different mission. The pastor had not been told much. He had been instructed that the mission crossed all religious barriers and that all of Christianity was at stake. He had been told to forget all things Catholic, Lutheran, Episcopal, or Baptist—to forget them all. The appeal had come from the Catholic Church, an appeal made by the pope. The pastor suspected it had to do with the Middle East. He knew all the churches had become more concerned and more outspoken about peace in the Middle East. He had read the speeches of the church leaders. He had noticed all their declarations, including those of the presiding bishop and primate of the Episcopal Church USA, the Methodist Church, the bishop of the Evangelical Lutheran Church, the senior pastor of Foundry United Methodist Church, and many others. He had also read all the statements issued by the Catholic Church. All called for an end to violence in the Middle East. All called for prayers to make everlasting peace.

The older man strolled toward his comfortable brick home. He measured each step because his gait had become unsteady over the last few years, but his mind had not. He knew as he approached.

On the front steps of his home, he knew that the problems in the Middle East needed more than prayers. He also knew that the only way to resolve the issues, the differences, was through faith, through the one belief they all had in common: one God. Only through God could there be peace.

As the pastor entered his two-story brick residence, he again wondered. He did not understand what was going on, did not understand the mission. All he knew was that one of his flock had a vital role. He smiled at the idea that the Holy Father in Rome had called on him.

That was when the bullet hit him. It came from a .22 mm Beretta at close range. The assassin had opened the door for the pastor. The holy man had no time to greet him, to extend his blessings. Four more shots were fired into the dying body of God's man. The assassin did as he had been trained to do. It was instinctual. It was the Mossad way—one shot to the head, four more into the body. The Mossad, Israel's secret intelligence agency, took no chances. But the kill was too late. The message had been delivered.

Rome, Italy

Carlo DeFino, a young priest at the Vatican and the pope's closest confidant, received the phone call from Berlin in his office at the Vatican. He did not wear robes, but he wore a pin-striped dark-blue business suit. Soon, he had to attend a luncheon outside the Vatican. He was going to dine with several vital industrialists. The traditional robe of the priesthood was not called for. His long, black hair was tightly combed back, and his dark eyebrows were neatly trimmed. The expensive tailor-made suit accentuated his slender body. His manicured hands gently held the phone receiver. He stood as he listened, he realized everything had been going according to plan. The man had arrived on schedule and as predicted, had gone to his church. His old pastor had spoken to him and given him the address there. He would follow the lead. No need to worry was the message from Berlin to Rome. All is as anticipated. All is in our control. All is how God wants it to be.

Berlin, Germany

ADAM HAD A SLEEPLESS NIGHT. He tossed and turned and thought about drifting aimlessly in the blue Bahamian waters, about Marcus and Chubb Cay, his pastor, and most of all, about her.

He had reached out in the middle of the night, hoping to touch her, but she was not there. Would she ever be next to him again? He rolled over in his bed, caressing the soft down comforters. His naked body was wet with perspiration as he stepped out of his bed. Meeting his pastor and returning to the church, which had meant much to him when he was a child, had caused him to be anxious. Missing Nicole made him feel emotional. It was not the way he had been trained. The moment did not last long; his mind would not let it. He needed to focus on what lay ahead. The past, with its fond memories, was gone. He could not let these emotions linger. And he knew how to control them. He had been trained to do so.

Once more, he picked up the small paper his pastor had handed him. Once more, he looked at the address written on it in German script. There was no need to study it again. It had been etched in his mind the first time he had read it. He did it out of habit because he always wanted to be sure. He sat back down on his bed and reached for the book of matches next to the candle on the night table. He lit the match and set fire to the holy man's paper. It burned rapidly. It was dry—a piece torn from an old Bible.

Adam walked toward the bathroom to the right of his king-size bed. He stepped into the shower and let the hot water soothe his body. He spent more time in the shower than most people did. He brushed his teeth, shampooed, shaved, and manicured. This was his time to relax, his time to be with himself.

Adam stepped out of the bathroom with a towel wrapped around him. Now he was a different man, no longer relaxed or at ease. Now he was what he had been trained to be—cautious and focused, a cold-blooded killer. Never had he thought he would be in this position. He was an idealist. That was why he joined the US armed services and became a member of the Navy SEALs—the sea, air, and land forces that had evolved from the combat divers of World War II.

After only one year of serving with the regular SEALs, which were called "white" or "vanilla," he had become a member of the SEALs' Black Squadron, Team Six's sniper unit. SEAL Team Six was the elite of the SEAL units, and only 50 percent of SEALs who tried to make the unit succeeded. It was also the most secretive arm of the US military. Everything about Team Six was shrouded in secret, and the Pentagon did not publicly acknowledge the name.

Then he went to law school at Georgetown University. This was where the NSA had recruited him. He was the best they had, the cream of the crop. Then they had asked him to infiltrate the Mossad, Israel's famous intelligence agency. The NSA knew it would not be easy, so it had to be planned carefully and take time. Months earlier, the National Security Agency had learned that a small, private, boutique Wall Street investment bank, the Ross Bank, was a front for Israel's intelligence agency, the Mossad. The NSA decided this was how Adam would try to infiltrate the agency.

Adam enrolled in Harvard's MBA program and was eventually courted by all the major Wall Street firms, for he had graduated in the top 3 percent of his class. The Ross Bank, although small and private, only recruited top graduates from Ivy League schools. Mr. Ross, founder and CEO of the bank, personally interviewed Adam, as he did all potential candidates. Mr. Ross immediately liked Adam, for he met all of Ross's requirements. Adam was brilliant, well-educated, good-looking, and charismatic. Most importantly, he was Jewish. Sidney Ross wanted Adam to join the Ross Bank at all costs, and so did the NSA.

Not long after Adam joined the bank, TSOMET, Mossad's recruiting department, approached him. Adam became a double agent. The NSA wanted to know the real game the Israelis were playing in the Middle East. They wanted to see about the game Mossad was playing in the United States.

Ha Mossad-Le Modiin ule-Tatkidim Meyuhadim was the Institute for Intelligence and Special Operations. The agency had been born in 1951 to be an intelligence agency independent of Israel's Ministry of Foreign affairs. Israel's first prime minister and minister of defense, David Ben-Gurion, was its creator. Although the agency was small—their personnel were about 1,200 in number, compared to the many thousands employed by the CIA—the Mossad was as good as it got. The Mossad relied on the loyalty of the Jews. When approached by the Mossad, few Jews refused to help. These helpers were called *sayanim*, and they were all 100 percent Jewish. They were not agents; they were volunteers. It was said there were more than two thousand *sayanim* in London alone.

Adam knew that a *katza* was different. A *katza* was a case officer who worked full-time for the Mossad. He had to be Jewish and Israeli— no exception. The training to become a *katza* was extensive.

It took almost three years later, a few candidates graduated. The institute did not care; they wanted only the best. They knew Israel had to be protected. The head of the institute, a man whose name and position had not been made public until a few years ago, had liked Adam the moment they had met. They had become close friends, and the head of Israel's intelligence agency was going to bend the rules. He wanted Adam to become a *katza*. But Adam refused. Instead, he joined the Mossad's assassination team, the *kidon*, or Bayonet.

It did not take Adam long to become disillusioned when he found out that the agencies of his beloved country, the United States, were abusing their power. Those agencies abused the country's status, which meant so much to many other nations. They abused what his country stood for: freedom of speech, freedom of choice, freedom to choose who you were. He revolted when he learned that these agencies' true agenda was to control everything and run the world. He wanted no part of it. He was a true American. He believed in all the values his country had been built on. He thought that all were one, one nation under God.

Now all that has changed. America had become a police state. The authorities said that the terrorists' attacks were responsible. Adam was not sure. Often, he asked who those terrorists were. How could terrorists do so much damage without help from the inside—the FBI, the CIA, or the NSA? Didn't it make sense to create chaos in their country, restrict citizens' rights, and gain ultimate control? Wasn't that what other demagogues had done? They had all taken advantage when their people were down. It was not a new concept. Was the president of the United States doing the same? Did he want to rule the world?

Adam had studied his former president. The man seemed insecure and could not make critical decisions. On foreign policy. He set "red lines" but never enforced them. His warnings were quickly ignored. Everyone knew he would only bark, never bite.

A smile came to Adam's face, and he almost chuckled. He remembered being at a restaurant on South Beach in Miami, Florida, only weeks before the president's first election. He and Nicole often went there, as it was one of their favorites. They had sat by the waterfront, watching the boats go by in Government Cut. They wanted to enjoy a quiet meal with a view and watch the sunset over Miami. But a group of Europeans was involved in a lively conversation next to their table. They were discussing the upcoming presidential election.

"There is no way the Americans will elect an African American president," one of them passionately proclaimed. "The Americans are not ready for it, not mature enough as a nation." The man was Italian, as his accent gave him away.

At first, Adam was irritated by the comment. He asked Nicole how mature Italy had been when it became a democracy. He was about to confront the man to discuss the issue, but Nicole stopped him. "Adam, please ignore it. Let us have a wonderful dinner."

He had obeyed. Looking back, he realized the man had been right. It was not that America had not been ready for an African American president. Instead, this African American president had not been prepared for America. And as could be expected, when a leader could not decide, all hell broke loose with screwups everywhere—Benghazi, the IRS, the NSA, the Middle East, and Ukraine, to mention a few. Adam believed that the former president had lost control.

Soon, Adam decided to leave the service of his government and the NSA. Adam knew that over the years, the United States had signed treaties to protect 25 percent of the world's population. When would it stop? Why did the president of the Russian Federation not have the same right as the United States to become involved in the

Syrian war? Because he had a different plan to resolve the conflict? At least Mr. Putin had had a plan. When would Adam's country realize that no nation had the right to control all? Adam believed in a free world that let each person decide their destiny—with no constraints, threats, or menace of power.

Adam Bergman stepped onto the balcony, still wet from his morning shower. A large towel covered most of his body. He glanced to his right and noticed his rented BMW parked where he had left it in front of his hotel. He would not use the car again. He would take a taxi to the Hotel Adlon.

The concierge at the Hotel Adlon was most accommodating. Adam did not know what to ask for, as he had only three numbers hastily written on his pastor's old paper. It was not a room number; the kind concierge informed him. It was a reservation box held for the hotel guests. The hotel man handed him the message left in the box. Adam took the envelope he had been given and sat at one of the tables in the hotel lobby. The lobby was busy, and Adam had taken the last table. The waiter approached him, and Adam asked for an espresso with a lemon rim. He opened the envelope after the waiter left. The message was brief. It was an address in Rome, and there was a telephone number. Adam put the paper in the ashtray, lit his cigar, and burned the message.

Adam asked for the concierge when the waiter returned to serve the coffee. He ordered a large Mercedes car. He loved to drive. Berlin to Rome was a trip he intended to enjoy.

Rome, Italy

SEVEN HUNDRED MILES TO THE SOUTH, a man sat on his balcony overlooking his city, Rome. He was their bishop. It was dark now, for the sun had left the horizon to the west. God's man bowed his head as lights began to illuminate his city. The stars and the moon made sure that the pope could see. He needed the light, for he wanted to see clearly and be sure. The full moon gave him the required light, support, and signal he knew God would send. He looked at the sky and crossed himself humbled before the omnipresence of his God. Then he kissed his ring and bowed his head. He had to make the most major decision, and he needed support. He required his God.

Suddenly, Pope Leo XIV received the answer—or he thought he did. Now he knew what to do, how to proceed. There had been no lightning, no parting of the waters. He just knew. The Holy Father stood up slowly, stretching his arms and legs. He was an older man, and he had arthritis. He also had a mission to fulfill. God had asked him to do this, and it rejuvenated him. The holy man knew he could do it even though many had failed. The United States was fighting its war against terrorism—or that was what they called it. The White House did not know the reasons for the conflict in the Middle East. It was not a political or military issue, not a secular problem. Most of all, it was a matter of religion and belief. No military forces would ever be able to resolve this conflict; history had proven that much. Only belief in one God had the power to do it. And God had asked the pope to make peace in the Middle East. That was the message.

In the past, some of the pope's predecessors, the heads of the largest body of religion in the world, had made appeals for peace in the Middle East. A previous pope had called for immediate renewal of Middle East peace talks in Vatican City before bidding farewell to ten thousand pilgrims at the general audience in Paul VI Hall. He had called for peace in the Holy Land during his Angelus audiences, in his address to the Chief Rabbis of Israel, and on many other occasions. He had also called for peace in many of his prayers.

But the current pope knew that all the speeches repeated the problems everyone was aware of. The prayers asked for hope or a miracle, but he knew his God wanted him to do more. Praying and preaching were not enough. He had to assume a more active role. He had to confront a problem head-on, be the leader, and unite the religions of Abraham. First, he had to get the religious leaders to meet and talk. Then they could all decide their destiny and the right path to peace.

The pope knew the mission of a lifetime would define his papacy, making him part of history. The bishop of Rome knew it would not be easy. He knew that many people did not want him to succeed, so he had sent for the man from the United States. He needed someone by his side to help him make peace, someone who understood the realities, someone who had served in the trenches, someone who understood the enemy who could eliminate them.

CHAPTER 5

Langley, Virginia

WILLIAM P. DAVIS—OR "PISTOL PETE," as he was affectionately called by his friends—the DCI, Director of the Central Intelligence Agency of the United States, sat in his large office in Virginia. He had been fortunate. His boss had resigned shortly after Monica Drew was elected the president of the United States. Rumor on the Hill said he refused to work for a female president.

Although William had been the head of the Directorate of Operations, the division that conducts human spying, for twelve years, he knew his tenure as DCI at the agency would be short. He knew that the new administration blamed his agency for the failure to control terrorists, the failure to show the world that the United States, with its vast military power, could dominate all. He knew that the information his agency gathered was inadequate—and not just inefficient. They were missing the point. The CIA did not seem to be well-informed. His agency, it appeared to him, had lost touch.

The DCI was a large man. He stood six feet three and weighed almost 240 pounds. He had a full head of brown hair, beginning to gray at the sideburns. He did not mind. His brown eyes were as young as ever, showing a youthful and friendly sparkle. William Davis was not obese, but much of the muscle that had once covered his body had become soft. Today it was hard to tell, as his baggy, pin-striped suit made him look fit.

William left his chair behind the large desk and walked to the small refrigerator below the elaborate bar at the corner of his rectangular office. He opened the door and chose his favorite beverage, Diet Coke. He popped the can open and returned to his desk.

The DCI knew that he had to save his agency's reputation. And now he was no longer competing only with the FBI. Now there was Homeland Security, the CTA, a counterterrorist agency, the NSA, and more. Homeland Security clearly wanted to take all the credit. He would not let this happen on his watch at the CIA. William would make sure his agency was always a step ahead. Surely, he would not tell the others all the information his men had gathered. He knew how to play the game, and there was no room for a mistake now. His reputation and the agency's destiny were at stake. The DCI looked at the dossier on his desk. He had read it many times. The brown manila folder was worn, having been handled by many people. William had asked for the best team, but he knew that even the best had little chance of succeeding. His agency had lost much time barking up the wrong tree. Yet only the best should try. He had not had time to design a plan. He needed more information and wanted to ensure his team had at least a slight chance. He wanted to believe that they could win. The CIA did not play to lose.

The DCI also knew that he had to act quickly. The CIA needed to become involved now. It could not afford to wait and gather more information. William had to put one of his field officers into the game. This would allow him a little time to assemble the right team. He had to pick the officer best suited for the mission, the best to find the American he had to win back, the man who could make the agency a player once more, the man who had once been one of them. To do this quickly, he needed someone already up on the learning curve, someone experienced in the field, someone who knew the man they needed to find, a CIA agent who knew how that man thought and could anticipate his moves. William had to choose someone who had been close to that man. He looked at the folder next to him and picked up the telephone.

"Send for Jefferson. Put her in charge of the Vatican affair."

Berlin to Rome

ADAM BERGMAN'S RENTED MERCEDES S550 WAS all he had expected— comfort, luxury, and performance. He loved the car; he now steered through the South German countryside into Austria. Soon, he would be at the Brenner Pass crossing into Italy. There was little traffic on the highway. The speedometer in his car read two hundred kilometers, just a hair over 120 miles per hour.

Adam loved to drive, relaxed, and enjoyed the trip, the car, and the views. He pulled up to the tollgate at the Brenner Pass and paid the fee to enter Italy. Now his mind stopped wandering, and he focused on what lay ahead. He knew he had to go to Rome. That was his destination: the address on the paper he had burnt at the hotel in Berlin.

Since it was already midafternoon, he decided to spend the night in Milan. There was no sense of urgency, no deadline to arrive at the capital of Italy. He picked up the telephone in his car and called the Four Seasons Hotel in Milan. Yes, he was told rooms were available. He asked for an executive suite, nonsmoking, with a king-size bed. Late arrival was confirmed.

Milan, Italy

THE ATTENDANT AT THE FOUR SEASONS Hotel in Milan showed Adam Bergman his suite. The tip he received was generous. As soon as the man left, Adam instinctively moved to check the slicks, the hiding places he had been trained to look for while working with the NSA and the Mossad, Israel's renowned and feared intelligence agency.

Adam knew he possessed unusual skills. He knew other people would pay handsomely for the expertise he had gained at the expense of the US taxpayer, and he intended to take advantage of it. He had become an independent contractor. Soon after he decided to go on his own, Rome had called. It had not taken long for him to agree, not only because of the price Rome was willing to pay but also for the cause he had been told of. And he remembered his pastor.

Milan to Rome

THE BLACK BMW 750 LI SEDAN was parked at the hotel's reception area. The driver, a young man clearly of Middle Eastern descent, had said he would be only a minute and had left the car idling. The valet at the Four Seasons Hotel in Milan did not object after the man had handed him twenty Euros. The BMW driver entered the lobby, where another man and a woman joined him. Then, the valet lost sight of them.

"Fredo, the large Mercedes, get it. The guest is leaving," the doorman shouted.

Adam Bergman walked through the door of the Four Seasons Hotel and waited for his car. It was a beautiful morning. He knew he would enjoy his drive to Rome. He settled behind the wheel. When he reached the Autostrada, he put his car under cruise control. He was now on alert. He knew he had to be more careful as he got closer to Rome.

Adam pulled off the highway soon after he left the hotel and entered one of the many rest stops. He did not need fuel for his car or to go to the bathroom, but he wanted to see if he was being followed. He was. Immediately, Adam recognized the BMW that had been parked outside his hotel. He got out of his car and entered the building. He went to the men's room, approached one of the urinals, and relieved.

The BMW had pulled up at one of the many gas pumps. A large man was refueling the car, or so it seemed. In fact, the large BMW needed no fuel. That had been taken care of the night before. The man with the BMW was not alone. He had a passenger sitting next to the driver's seat. The man was speaking on a cell phone as he watched the doors that led into the building at the rest stop.

Adam steered his Mercedes from the rest stop and back onto the Autostrada. A quick look in the rearview mirror told him his tail was still there. He expected no different. When the time was right, when he was on his playing field, he would find out who they were. There was no reason to disturb his drive through the beautiful Italian countryside.

South Beirut, Lebanon

ACROSS THE MEDITERRANEAN SEA, HASSAN NASRAL, secretary-general of Hezbollah, sat in his bunker deep in the ground in South Beirut. Rarely did he leave his bunker, for he feared the Israeli assassins and their drones.

Hezbollah had been classified by the US State Department as a foreign terrorist organization, but it was also a popular political party in Lebanon. Hezbollah, the party of God, had been created by the Shiite Muslims as an alternative to the Christian-Sunni government, which the Shiites loathed. Hassan believed that the pope's efforts to make peace in the Middle East were an American Israeli plot to deny Muslims the establishment of a caliphate, a political-religious state of their own, to become a world power once again. Hassan also realized that the true enemy of his people, his Shiite Muslims, was not the Catholic Church. He thought the pope had to stop making peace in the Middle East. The Israelis had no right to be here on their people's soil, and a peace treaty would only solidify their position.

Hassan's true enemy, however, was the Sunnis, his Muslim religious rival. Their terrorist group, ISIS, the Islamic State of Iraq and Syria, was becoming a more formidable force each day as they conquered more territory, grew their forces, and increased the brutality of their tactics. Hassan had watched the killing when the camera had zoomed in and out to the music of a prophetic lyric, a *nasheed*. He had seen the human fireball, the Jordanian pilot, dying. Hassan knew it was *quisas*, the principle of equal retaliation under Islamic law.

Despite this brutality, thousands of recruits from all over the world crossed the border from Turkey to Syria to join ISIS's training camps. More British Muslim men had joined ISIS than were serving in the British Armed Forces. They were not the underprivileged or uneducated who joined ISIS, as the former president of the United States had proclaimed. Doctors, nurses, schoolteachers, technologists, and accountants all rushed to join the terrorist organization. Most joined because they were bored, angry, or frustrated. Some were students of martyrdom, who wanted to die as soon as possible and go directly to heaven. Many were women. The "Mother of the Lion," ISIS's most successful female recruiter, had many young girls join the fight. And now ISIS had extended its field of play with Boko Haram in sub-Saharan Africa and in Libya, Tunisia, Egypt, and Afghanistan. The black-and-white flag of ISIS was flying everywhere, thanks to all the US weapons it has acquired.

Hassan Nasral, the secretary-general of Hezbollah, put down his glass of attar, the alcohol-free drink made from musk oil that was popular with many Muslims, and leaned back in his comfortable Polo leather chair. Even though he lived in a bunker, he had all the comforts of a luxurious villa. Persian rugs covered the floor, and hundreds of candles illuminated the bunker. Hassan loved light. He loved seeing the sun rise in the desert and traveling all day to disappear in the sand again. He knew this was God's land. He had to protect it, for Allah had chosen him to do so.

Hassan stood and slowly paced his bunker. He was barefoot, for he liked the feel of the rich fabric beneath his feet. He strolled toward the old fireplace carved into the bunker's walls hundreds of years ago. Often, he threw papers into the fireplace, papers he wanted to discard. But the fireplace was never lit. There could be no sign of smoke, no sign of his hideaway. His staff always retrieved each paper and used a shredder to destroy it. He scratched his long beard, a gesture he always used when he was deep in thought. He knew his people were fighting two enemies, the Israelis and the Sunni Muslims. He knew that the Sunnis were the more formidable enemy by far. They represented most Muslim people. But Hassan was confident that the leader of all Shiites, the Ayatollah, the leader of Iran, would prevail. He would have nuclear weapons that would again make former Persia a world power. It was only a matter of time.

However, time was of the essence to stop the pope's plan for peace in the Middle East. Hassan smiled. He did not need a nuclear weapon to stop the pope. He requested his brother-in-law, Imad Mughdial.

Imad knew the game and was the best at it. He was the mastermind of most of Hezbollah's terrorist attacks. He had masterminded the bombings of the US embassy in Beirut in 1983, the hijacking of TWA flight 847 in 1985, the Khobar Tower bombing in Saudi Arabia, the kidnapping of Israeli soldiers, and more. Yes, Hassan decided that his brother-in-law was the man to stop the pope.

Imad Mughdial, Hezbollah's fearless and brutal enforcer, decided to follow the pope closely, monitoring his every move. Imad created several surveillance teams, all communicating via cell phones bought with false identification far from their base in Beirut, Lebanon. All phones were paid for in cash, most in advance. All Hezbollah assassins were instructed to work in groups, and each had a leader. Imad ensured that each member could not call the leader, but the leader could call each member. Never could they call each other. This method made it difficult, almost impossible, to trace his team.

Hassan was confident his brother-in-law would succeed. But Hassan never fully trusted anyone. When he was younger, he himself had taken charge, but later he had had to delegate as Hezbollah grew. However, he always had his finger on the pulse.

Hassan's body was old and frail. He was not only fighting age, but he was also battling cancer—and he was losing both battles. But his mind had not yet been compromised; it was as strong as ever. Hassan was afraid he was running out of time, that his body would not let him fulfill Allah's wish. Hassan needed help. He required his grandson. He was alone, as he often was, but he did not mind. He had a mission that his God, Allah, had asked him to complete. He knew he would, do it? He had to. It did not matter what the cost or how many would die. The infidels did not matter, for their lives were worthless. And his brothers would die with joy, knowing they served Allah.

The old Arab exited his chair, which had been placed in front of the fireplace. As a younger man, he had always sat on the carpet, but age had taken its toll. No longer could he rise from the carpet without help, but he liked to be alone with Allah. So now he needed the chair. The older man began to pace the large room of his underground sanctuary. He strolled toward the mahogany desk and sat down. Today, he wore his usual attire, the Arabian dress. The white cloth was his favorite. He hated the dress of Western men. He had to wear it more often than he wanted. Hassan had never understood the men from the West. He did not trust their beliefs, but he had learned what made them tick. It was always the dollar. He had studied in the United States and had received his MBA degree there. He knew that their God was the dollar.

However, the United States was no longer his real enemy. The Americans had tried to make peace, at first through diplomacy, and he had laughed aloud. They knew nothing about the Arab world and never bothered to learn. Then they tried force. Fools. Vietnam had not taught them a lesson.

Today, he had to deal with another, much more sophisticated enemy, which was the most dangerous. This enemy also believed strongly in God, but not his God. That did not matter. It was the enemy's firm faith that worried the old Arab. The frail man knew that a devoted belief in God made one a formidable foe. Yes, the Vatican was a foe like no other.

Hassan was a devout Muslim, believing in only one God, Allah. He knew that other faiths also believed in a single God, and they were all children of Abraham. The Jews and the Christians were not all that different. Of course, they believed more strongly in other prophets and celebrated different holidays. But they all believed in one God. He knew that the number of the pope's flock far exceeded that of Muslims, and to make it worse, his own people were divided. He was a Shiite Muslim, and most Muslims in the world were Sunni, not Shiite. Although the Sunnis and Shiites differed little in their fundamental beliefs about God, throughout Islamic history the two groups had been hostile. The issue that divided them, the older man reminded himself, was that it was so old that it should be let go.

In AD 632, the prophet Muhammad had died. Unfortunately, he had not named a successor. Most Muslims, who became the Sunnis, united behind Abu Bakr, one of Muhammad's close followers. A smaller group believed that Ali, Muhammad's son-in-law, should be the leader and that the leadership should stay in the family. Hassan had never understood why this minor difference in his religion had caused so much harm and bloodshed and the deaths of so many people—deaths not only in the past but today. Persecution continued even now while he was sitting in his bunker.

Surely this was not what Allah wanted. Surely Allah wanted all the Muslim children to live together in peace. That was Allah's wish, and Hassan would do all he could to fulfill it.

CHAPTER 6

Tuscany, Italy

SHE ONCE AGAIN CRIED OUT LOUD with pleasure as she had yet another orgasm. It had been more than an hour since he had first entered her after much foreplay. She felt completely satisfied, but he did not. He wanted to extend their lovemaking and make it last longer. He was enjoying every moment and wanted to do more. Then he lost control.

In a moment, it was all over. The bullet hit him in the back of his head, and he died instantly. Blood splattered across the room. Some of it hit her naked body. She threw the dead man off her and dove to her left. She reached for the Beretta on the table next to her, rolled off the bed, and fired two rounds into the chest of the man who had interrupted her lovemaking. The large man fell forward on top of her lover.

She knew others were nearby, on the staircase of the luxurious villa. She knew that her lover was dead, and she would be next. There was only one way to escape—through the wine cellar where her lover had brought her after dinner. That was when he kissed her. She remembered how dark the basement had been. It was filled with many barrels and thousands of bottles of precious wine. Her lover, the Colombian drug lord she had been assigned to follow, had told her about a narrow tunnel that led to the vineyard. He had suggested they walk there and make love in the vineyard under the star-filled sky. But she had wanted to make love in a bed—a wrong decision, she now decided.

She was still naked as she moved toward the window. She realized that the staircase was no option. She glanced down the two stories to where she knew the entrance to the wine cellar was. It was the only way she could escape. She grabbed the pants and shirt she had worn for the casual dinner with her lover. She did not bother to look for her underwear or sandals. There was no time.

She opened the floor-to-ceiling window and jumped. She hit the well-manicured lawn on her feet and immediately rolled. Then she bounced up and raced toward the outside entrance of the cellar. Her gun was in her right hand, her clothing in the other. The small wooden door to the basement was only thirty feet from the back of the house, concealed by several rhododendron bushes. She opened the old door, entered, shut it, and bolted it.

There was complete darkness now, and the air was filled with the smell of oak barrels. Using only touch, she slowly walked to where she knew the tunnel was. The coolness of the cellar caused her naked body to shiver. When she reached the tunnel, she bent down to enter it. It was only five feet high, but the passageway had no obstacles. This allowed her to walk more quickly, but she still had only her touch to guide her through the blackness. Suddenly, her hand hit an object in front of her. Using both hands, she traced the outline and found a handle. She lowered it, opened the door, and quickly entered the vineyard.

The stars above gave her enough light to survey the surroundings. Symmetrical, endless rows of vines lay ahead, disappearing in the dark. She turned to view the spot where she had come from, the exit of the tunnel. It was in a small gulley, lower than where the vines had been planted. Dense bushes were placed eight to ten yards from the exit on top of the hollow. She knew that running through the vineyard to escape was a mistake. She would be too exposed and had a long way to go. She made her decision. Offense was always the best defense. She would make the pursuer become the pursued.

Nicole Amy Jefferson quickly put on her pants and shirt. She raced to the tunnel door and turned on the light outside the exit. It did not give much light, but it would be enough. She rushed up the slight incline and hid in the dense bushes, lying prone with her gun cocked and ready in both hands. She would wait for her enemy to come to her. She would no longer run. The hunter had become the hunter.

Tuscany, Italy

THE BLACK SEDAN S_{550} MERCEDES SPED toward Parma on highway E35. The music of Mozart filled the luxurious cabin of the car. Today's destination was Firenze.

Adam Bergman was in no hurry. There was no timetable. Once in Florence, he would not take the direct route to Rome. Instead, he would head west through Siena and then drive through the beautiful countryside along Route 73 to the Autostrada, the highway that ran along the western coastline of Italy. It would take him right to his destination: Rome.

But Adam was not sure he was ready to go there. Not yet. He thought he would go farther south to Napoli, Positano, and Capri. He had visited these places before and had always enjoyed them. Capri was his favorite island, and he owned a small apartment there. Yes, he would go to Capri and stay at his home for a few days. He needed time to think. He checked his rearview mirror. The car was still there. Adam did not mind. He loved company.

South Beirut, Lebanon

HASSAN NASRAL, THE OLD ARAB WHO was secretary-general of Hezbollah, sat at his mahogany desk in his bunker. He had just been informed about the stranger. His people were unsure who he was and were checking him out. They did know that he had an appointment at the Vatican and that the pope wanted to see him. For now, they were tracking him, following him as he drove through Italy toward Rome. The Arabs assured their leader that he was not to worry. They had the man in sight, and they would handle him. They would not make a mistake.

The older man scratched his beard. He knew his men were dedicated. They believed in the cause and Allah, and Imad, his brother-in-law, were leading them. But Hassan was a careful man. He decided to have a plan B.

Hassan Nasral had only one grandson, heir to Hassan's vast riches. The older man was fully aware of the importance of this mission. He knew that his enemy was the most formidable one the Arab world had ever met: the Catholic Church. To win this war, he had to use the best people, and he decided to ask his grandson to meet the man who was to see the pope. The old Arab needed to know the Americans' mission and why the pope had sent for him. He was confident that he could arrange to have his grandson meet the pope's man. He knew Allah would prevail.

Vatican City, Italy

The Holy Father of all Catholic people, Pope Leo XIV, stepped off the balcony of his residence as the sun left the horizon to the west. He had said all his prayers, but his mind was not at ease. He continued to think about the mission his God had asked him to fulfill, his God's wish. But there was another God, not one he believed in, though many others did. He had to compromise, understand, and reach out. He had to let his God speak to all, including his adversaries. To make them listen was the pope's mission. Every hour, every minute, he struggled with how to do it. He asked his God how in every prayer, but the Almighty had not yet given him the answer. But he had sent a message, a missionary. The Holy Father anticipated his arrival.

Tuscany, Italy

Nicole Jefferson knew they would be there. She knew they would come through the small tunnel. The dim light she had turned on at the tunnel exit was all she needed. The two men did not disappoint her. They exited the tunnel in unison.

She fired only four shots, which was all she needed. She was not sure if others would come. Nicole dragged the two bodies into the bushes. Then she waited. She waited until the sun rose above the vines, and then she made her way south. She knew she should not return to her lover's house, where she had left her rental car.

Nicole had to speak to her boss, contact Langley, and talk to the DCI. She needed to know what was going on. She went through the woods to a small road that meandered across the mountainside and began jogging down the road. Soon, a small truck appeared, and the driver took her into the small town of Rosia. Nicole went to the first telephone available at the local post office. She called her boss.

Adam Bergman had planned his trip to Rome meticulously. He would not use Italy's main highway for much of the trip, the Autostrada. He wanted to enjoy his drive and reminisce, think about the past, and make sure he wanted to leave his old life behind. It had been a life he enjoyed very much, a life of leisure without intrigue or violence, the life on South Beach in Miami. Adam knew that to leave that life behind and once again become what he had trained to be, he had to make one more stop. Adam had to go to Rosia.

Rosia is a small town in Tuscany, southwest of Siena. He had not been there for more than a year. It was there that he had fallen in love with Nicole. Both had been on an assignment together for the CIA, and he for the NSA. Both had been instructed to use a safe house in the small town. Now he wanted—no, needed to sit once more at the quaint café in the city center next to the fountain where he and Nicole had held hands and kissed. He wanted his emotions to be free once more. He wanted to relive the past to make sure he was about to make the right decision. He fully realized that his life was about to take a different turn. But he needed one more day to understand his destiny, one more day to make sure.

Driving into the town center, he remembered calling his housekeeper on Capri. She had to know about his arrival and ensure everything was in order at his apartment. Adam went directly to the small post office to make the call.

And there she was. He had just opened the door to the post office when she rushed out and fell into his arms. She was as beautiful as he remembered her. No, he thought she was more attractive. Her black hair was tied in a ponytail, and he knew she liked to wear it that way. Her large blue-green eyes expressed surprise at first, but then they smiled. He held her lean, five-foot-eleven-inch body close to him. He did not know whether to kiss her, but she seemed to. She opened her full lips slightly and kissed him on the mouth.

"Nicole," he said as he steadied her. "You follow me everywhere. What are you doing here?"

"I once told you before that women follow you wherever you go. I am no exception."

"Be serious, please. Did the agency send you to keep an eye on me? Of course, they did. I do not believe it. Why you? Why not someone else—someone I do not know?"

"I guess the CIA likes to maintain relationships," Nicole replied. "And besides, we have never fallen in love."

She smiled as she said it, and her blue-green eyes looked directly at him. Falling in love in the spy business meant winning the trust of a person you wanted to recruit as an agent. Nicole was a CIA operative. Her primary role was to recruit people to help the agency in the spy business. Months ago, her boss, the director of central intelligence, had asked her to recruit Adam Bergman as an agent. She had been called off the job before she had been able to complete it. The CIA had been informed that Bergman was already working for the US government. He was working for the NSA, the National Security Agency.

Adam smiled. He released his arms and stepped back. What a woman! He thought. She still wore the black pants and white blouse she had worn when she had shot the two intruders who had killed her lover not many hours ago. And she was barefoot.

"I guess you know I no longer work for the NSA," Adam said. "I'm sure the agency knows that much."

"Yes," she responded. "I understand you are out on your own now and ready to save the world without the help of our country. Word at the agency is that you want to be like James Bond and save the world all by yourself." She smiled.

"It is not exactly like that. I know what they tell you back at the agency: that I am a renegade, a deserter, someone who would never agree. But it is not true. I just became disillusioned. I started to question some of our country's policies. I started to see the other side. That is why I left the NSA."

"Adam, we need to talk. I want to understand you."

"Okay, but why follow me? Let us travel together. That makes it all a lot easier."

She did not hesitate. "I agree."

Nicole Amy Jefferson, CIA officer, opened the passenger door to the large Mercedes sedan and sat in the plush leather seat.

"I'll be right there," Adam said. He walked into the post office to call his housekeeper on Capri.

CHAPTER 7

Tel Aviv, Israel

AZA SHAREF, THE HEAD OF ISRAEL'S intelligence agency, the Mossad, was reading his morning brief in his sparsely appointed office in Tel Aviv. He read the report every morning, always at 7:00 a.m. That was how he started his day. Today, he paid particular attention to the section headed "Vatican." He had been informed that the Vatican had sent for a remarkable man, a trained assassin. The head of the Mossad did not know why the holy church had called for this man, but he knew the man was the best, for the Mossad had trained him. The man had once been one of them.

The head of the Mossad also knew that others were interested in this man. Arabs were following him on the road, and the CIA had deployed a case officer to keep an eye on him. Maza knew that the EU, the European Union, had shown a deep interest in the man traveling to the Vatican. However, the Mossad surveillance team had not yet detected the EU's surveillance team. He smiled. *Of course, we have not*, he thought. *We trained those bastards. They know our methods and how to stay hidden. They know what to do.* And so did the man the Vatican had called. After all, he had been one of them, a member of Kidon, the Mossad's assassination team, not long ago.

Maza worried about the man and his mission. He did not yet know all the details, but he soon would, and what he did know troubled him deeply. He knew that the Vatican and some of the religious leaders of the Arab world wanted to create a settlement for peace in the Middle East. Maza trusted none of them. They did not want Israel to be involved at the outset of the negotiations. Surely Israel had to be part of it, he thought. How could there ever be peace in the Middle East without Israel agreeing to the terms of a settlement? He knew his country needed to be involved at the outset. Israel had every right to be part of the negotiations, for it was Israel's destiny that they were about to negotiate. Was the state of Israel to have no voice in the discussions? He, the protector of the children of Israel, could not allow this to happen.

Maza Sharef had tried to foil the plan twice. His man on the yacht in Miami had failed to kill the assassin the pope had sent for. Then his man in Berlin had killed the pastor, but he had been too late. He had killed a man of God, but the message had already been passed on.

The Mossad, the institute, was the national intelligence agency of Israel and one of the best in the world. But it was only part of Israel's intelligence community, Maza reminded himself. There was Aman military intelligence, Shin Bet, and internal security. Mossad was formed in 1949 at the request of then-Prime Minister David Ben-Gurion. For years, the identity of the head of the Mossad had been guarded as a close secret, but this was no longer the case. The current director is well known. Maza Sharef had taken over the role on January 1, 2011. He had been born in Tel Aviv to a family of Turkish and Serbian Jews. After his military service, he had joined the Mossad.

Maza Sharef was a thoughtful man and a history student. His father had been a schoolteacher and had always wanted his son to follow in his footsteps. Maza had disagreed. He had joined the Israeli army to defend his country, to claim what belonged to Israel. He had fought in the Six-Day War and the Yom Kippur War six years later. Although a fragile cease-fire arrangement had been established between several of Israel's enemies, including Syria and Lebanon, he knew that all Arab nations wanted to annihilate his country. The Gaza Strip and the West Bank were not just about territory. It was about religion.

The head of the Mossad always rose early, at 5:30 a.m. He showered, wore a sweat suit, and left his home with four bodyguards. He went to his favorite gym to work out. Breakfast had to wait. At 7:00 a.m. each morning, he met at the Mossad headquarters for his daily briefing. This was when he was brought up to speed. Maza always sat among his advisors, never at the head of the table. By then, he had already taken a second shower and was dressed in his official clothing: khaki pants, sandals, and a loose shirt, which was never tucked into his pants. He was a handsome man—muscular, six foot three—but he had the face of a baby with an innocent smile. "Let's get going," he said as he took a sip from the Starbucks coffee that one of his officers had given him, a routine that never changed. He only recently asked for milk in his coffee. For years, he had always wanted it black.

"People," he said," I know there is much on the agenda, but I must prioritize. I want to focus on what is happening right here—the war in the Middle East, ISIS. Please tell me all. And I particularly want to know about the efforts by the pope to make peace."

"Maza, let's face facts," began one of his advisors, the head of military intelligence. "No one cares about us. I am sure this peace will only come to the sacrifice of our country. We have one supporter, the United States, but how long do you think they will hang on? How long will they support us? Our support in America is strong but will not last forever."

"I agree," replied the head of Shin Bet, the internal security agency. "We cannot rely on America—or any other country, for that matter. We must protect ourselves. I understand that a new thought or movement—a spirit—is coming out of Berlin."

"What do you mean? Explain," the head of the Mossad demanded. "All right," his minister replied. "I am not sure what precisely the chancellor of Germany, the president of the EU, is saying, but the message is that religion is at fault. That religion is the cause of this war that makes the Sunnis fight their Islamic brothers, the Shiites. That religion makes all of them want to kill all infidels and eradicate us. The message we seem to get from Berlin is this: to stop. In this war in the Middle East, we must stop religion."

Maza Sharef always listened and paid close attention to his advisors. He was a rational man, and he respected their counsel. But he was also a profoundly religious man. He prayed every day, asking his God for guidance. Was it possible that religion was the culprit, that religion could be the source of all evil? His belief in God would not allow him to accept this.

Maza got out of his chair, reached for his Starbucks coffee, and began to pace around the mahogany conference table. Everyone was silent as they watched him. Finally, he spoke.

"We need to look at all possibilities, all options," Maza said. "We are a country constantly under siege, and we cannot afford to make a single mistake. Certainly, the president of the EU is no fool. As a matter of fact, he is a statesman like no other. Recall that he united Europe, countries that have fought wars with each other for centuries. Now they all make love." He chuckled. "Surely, we cannot ignore his message. You all know I am a religious man, and peace. For Israel, peace for my people is my priority." He addressed the head of the internal security agency. "Ben, all people need religion—not religion, but something in which they can believe. How does the EU president address that problem?"

"You are right, Maza," the minister replied." The EU president is aware of that fact. But as you know, belief is not the truth. It is not an actual state of things. It is a state of mind, not a fact. I am not sure of his answer, but there are rumors."

"What kinds of rumors?" Maza was anxious to know. He had finished his coffee, thrown the plastic cup into one of the wastepaper baskets, and sat back in his chair. He did not lean back but put his forearms on the large conference table, tilting his head toward his minister. He was curious. The whole concept intrigued him, and he wanted to know all about it.

"Well, the rumors," the minister responded, "imply that he is calling for the truth, for people to understand the difference between truth and belief. He wants all people to know that they are not the same, and that for centuries religion has tried to blur the difference." "We all know that in our lives we often need help—religious or spiritual help," the head of the Mossad interrupted. "If we get rid of religion, where is that help?"

"According to the rumors I hear out of Berlin, the help we seek now is false," the minister replied. "It is not based on fact. There is no fact, no proof that God exists. It is but a belief. The message is that belief must be replaced by truth.

"How do we do that?" Maza could not wait to hear the answer, and apparently neither could anyone else in the room. There was silence as no one spoke. No one even breathed.

"The EU president is calling for a new spirituality," the minister continued. "One that replaces religion—replaces belief—with truth.

The president calls for a meeting and wants all the religious leaders to meet. I do not know any more, and I do not know the details." Maza Sharef needed time to think and understand all the ramifications of the information he had just received. No more religion? He called for a recess. All would reconvene in two hours. Usually, during hours of stress, he would go to his synagogue to pray and ask for advice. Strangely, today he did not. Today, he decided to catch fresh air and take a stroll. As he walked to his favorite park, accompanied by his four bodyguards, he thought about all that had been said at the meeting. It troubled him. The president of the EU was brilliant, a man he respected very much. Could his reasoning be correct? Was there no God? If there was no God who had promised his land—the land of Israel—to the Jewish people, then his people had no right to the land. Was all the bloodshed defending Israel in vain? Should he continue to believe, or should he seek the truth?

Maza Sharef, the head of the Mossad, decided to go to Berlin to speak with the EU president and participate in the meeting.

But Maza was also concerned with the item in his morning briefing labeled the "Vatican." Maza knew about the man the Vatican had sent for—an assassin. And he was not just an assassin. He was the best, a former member of his own assassination team, the kid on. Although Maza and his intelligence agency had been unable to determine why the Vatican had sent for the man or what his role was, Maza had given the directive to stop all the Vatican's attempts to make peace in the Middle East. He could never allow any peace attempt without Israel's involvement. Twice, his men had failed to stop the man the Vatican had sent for. The Mossad agent on the yacht in Miami Beach had failed, and then the Mossad agent in Berlin had been too late. He had killed the pastor, a man of God, but the message had been sent on.

CHAPTER 8

Wannsee, Berlin, Germany

THE PRESIDENT OF THE EU AND Germany's chancellor, Prince William von Hohenzollern, was relaxing in his private home, a fashionable yet modest villa on Lake Wannsee, one of Berlin's most beautiful lakes. It was a beautiful evening, filled with silence. He sat on his porch, which overlooked the lake. He always sat in the dark-green rocking chair his wife had bought him at a Berlin flea market. His wife loved to shop at flea markets, and there were many in Berlin. She also knew that he loved rocking chairs and that his favorite color was the dark green of British racing cars.

Prince William was a fan of Formula One racing, though dark green was no longer part of the circuit. Yet he still loved the color. Now he supported all the German drivers—Vettel, Rosberg, Hulkenberg—but deep down he had always wanted Lewis Hamilton, the British driver, to win. He never really knew why. It was not that he drove a Mercedes, a German car. It was something else. Over the years—when he had been an ambassador at the UN, and during the process of uniting Europe—he had learned to put nationality aside. He just wanted the best to win. And he thought Lewis Hamilton was the best.

Prince William was drinking a glass of his favorite beer, Charlottenburger Pils, which he could only buy in Berlin and at the Schildkroete restaurant near the Kudamm, Berlin's major thoroughfare. A keg would be delivered to his home on demand. William lifted the glass but did not take a drink. He wondered who had created the beer. There were so many breweries in Germany. But who had held the belief that their beer could be the best? What was the truth?

Then he thought about belief and truth. He tried to recall the definitions he remembered from the years he had studied philosophy and political science at the Freie Universität in Berlin. He recalled that the word *belief* had many definitions, "the state of mind in which a subject roughly regards a thing to be true," or "a mental attitude of acceptance toward a proposition without the full intellectual knowledge to require the truth." Prince William von Hohenzollern knew that many people *believed*. He also knew that most did not see the difference between *truth* and *belief*. For centuries, theistic religion had made it its mission to blur the difference, to make it all one. And for centuries, religion had succeeded—and still did. It preached that truth and belief were one. But by definition, the EU president knew, they were not. *He knew truth* was a verified fact, reality, and absolute certainty. *God* was not.

He leaned back in his favorite rocking chair and began reminiscing about how his belief in God had changed during his formative years. As a young boy, he had been raised as a religious man, a devout Protestant. He remembered that he had always been inquisitive as a child, wanting to know the reason for everything. It had not taken him long to ask his tutors about religion, its origin, its purpose, and why people believed. He had been taught that religion in its strict sense meant belief in a creator, that people. He needed to believe in a God for sorrow, security, and escape from hopelessness. But he had never understood because he suffered from no such anxieties. When he had asked to see God and speak with him, he had been disappointed to learn that there was no proof that God truly existed.

When he had reached adolescence, his father had decided that his son must become fluent in the French language, and a renowned French philosopher was hired. It was this philosopher who had changed his mind, his belief, the prince recalled. He had taught William that a wise man was a man of action and strong, someone who lived in the present and only sought what *is*, not what one hoped. Hope would only disappoint because one could not control it, yet most people needed hope because they were weak.

But how could people live without religion, without believing in a creator who could give them hope? The prince had asked his tutor. Many people had already done so, and the tutor had replied. They were the Buddhists, the Taoists, the atheists, agnostics, and more.

That was when William began to no longer believe in God. That was when he had become an atheist. Funny, he thought, remembering. He had felt freed, freed from two thousand years of fantasy. He felt more at ease, and everything appeared more open, simpler. He felt like he had finally entered the world of truth.

Prince William took another large drink from the glass of the Charlottenburger Pils. Religion had deceived humanity for centuries. Why had their leaders embraced it? Overall that time, the motives had to have changed, didn't they? The true motive, he thought, was always survival, and survival was made easier by fighting in a pack, with people joining forces and banding together. Strength lay in numbers. To have people rally in support, one needed. A cause and religion have become the most potent causes, with Jesus Christ and Mohammed as the foremost motivational leaders.

Some nations had used nationalism to dominate—or, according to Darwin, to survive—and had failed. His country had been the most recent example, Prince William reminded himself of. Even today, most major powers—the United States, Russia, and China—are using nationalism as their reason to dominate. The United States called it democracy, a concept that had died with Alexander the Great and had been perverted by the United States.

Nationalism was no match for religion as a cause. Nationalism had boundaries; religion did not. Religion metastasized, crossed all barriers, and spread across national borders and continents. If uncontrolled, the prince was convinced, it would destroy all of humanity. Already, the cancer was growing in the Middle East, killing women, children, infants, and innocent men; causing mass destruction; and displacing millions of people.

The prince rose from his chair, now clearly understanding his mission. He had to put an end to theistic religion to remove the cause that had been responsible for so much damage to humanity. He slowly walked toward his boathouse at the edge of the lake. The walkway was all gravel and lit by low lights along the way. William had not turned on the lights, for tonight the full moon gave all the light he needed, illuminating the path. The moon showed the way as it kissed the lake, painting a picture of calmness and peace.

When the prince reached the edge of the lake, he walked onto his dock, where he kept a small fishing boat he had bought years ago when he had had time to go fishing. Then there had come a time in his political career when the boat sat idle. He had had no time for fishing. But now the small boat saw much use again. His grandson loved to go fishing, and the prince liked to sit in the boat, be on the water and hear the waves as they gently splashed against the wooden hull. He loved being with nature, the water, the moon, and the stillness of the night. Prince William von Hohenzollern loved peace.

The prince knew that to make peace in the Middle East, he had to remove the cause of the conflict. To have much of humanity ceased to believe in a creator appeared to be an impossible task, yet hundreds of millions of people have already done so. In his own mind, he had never understood how one could believe in a God who was witness to so much evil on earth—the genocides, rapes, murders, and even sexual abuse by God's own disciples. Despite this, more than a billion people still believed in the Creator. Prince William was determined to change it all. He would show all the believers what he had seen first as a teenager, what he still saw today: a world free of more than two thousand years of fantasy, a world more open, more at ease, and simpler world not of belief but of truth.

Prince William leaned back into the stern of the small fishing boat and reached into his pocket to retrieve the cigar he had taken from his humidor before he had left the house. He did not smoke often, but when he sat at the lake, surrounded only by peace and Mother Nature, he enjoyed it. His small fishing boat now bobbed gently up and down. A slight breeze had come from the north, the open end of the lake, creating small waves.

The rocking motion of the boat reminded Prince William of his political career. It had not been easy, for many others had tried to win the office of chancellor of Germany, and later the presidency of the European Union. William was a descendant of the Hohenzollern family, but other royal families had also tried to regain control. The royal families continued to believe they were the ones chosen to lead the world, and he also believed that to be true. But to win, he needed more than belief; he needed money, for money controlled all. He had always known this. And he had made it his business to win over everyone who controlled the flow of money. It was not destiny that had gotten him the job of president of the EU; it was the people with money.

But now Prince William faced a new challenge, one like no other. His true ambition, his dream, was to make peace in the world. He was obsessed with this mission, though he did not know why. Often, he thought it was the guilt he felt, or should feel, for what his country, Germany, had done during the world wars. He knew that history showed that his country had not been the only culprit, but surely it had played a significant role. No matter. He wanted to make it all right. He wanted peace.

The prince understood all the ingredients necessary to make peace: truth, belief, cause, and religion. He recalled what Confucius had said: "By nature, all men are nearly alike; by practice, they get to be wide apart." And it was the practice of belief versus truth that divided humanity. But the truth would prevail—the truth of no heaven, no God, no seventy virgins waiting, and no place where all would be forgiven.

The prince stepped out of his small fishing boat onto the dock next to the boathouse. He leaned down and straightened his trousers, which he had rolled to his knees before stepping into the boat. His wife had instructed him not to soak his pants in the water, particularly if the water had the smell of fish.

William strolled back to his house on Lake Wannsee. At the end of the gravel walkway leading to the house, his wife had planted an oak tree over thirty years ago. Beneath it, she had placed a wooden bench; it was her favorite place to sit and relax. Rarely did the prince sit there by himself, but tonight he did. He had not yet finished his fine cigar—a Padrón torpedo anniversary edition.

As he took another draw on his favorite cigar, he recalled the information he had received from his cousin, Prince Albert. The pope had sent for a man from America, a very unusual man, a trained assassin, a killer. The man had been trained by the best—the Navy SEALs, the Mossad, and the NSA—but now he had become an independent. The American was not a Catholic. In fact, he had been born in Germany and raised as a Lutheran before converting to Judaism. Prince Albert also had informed him about the man's rabbi in Brooklyn and about the pastor in Berlin who had been shot only days ago. The pastor had confirmed the American in the church and had performed his parents' marriage. The rabbi had taught him the Jewish faith.

Prince William decided he needed to know all about the man and why the Vatican had sent for him, and he knew his cousin, Prince Albert, could get all the answers. William took another large drawer on his cigar, stabbed the butt of it against the trunk of the large oak tree, and tossed it into the woods. He picked up his cell phone.

"I need everything on this guy the pope sent for. Something is coming down. Get on top of it, Albert."

He did not wait for a response. It was getting late, and he knew his wife was waiting for him to have their favorite dinner, Wiener schnitzel.

CHAPTER 9

Tuscany, Italy

THE TWO ARABS FOLLOWING THE LARGE Mercedes sedan was tiring. They had not been told this would be just a surveillance mission. They were itchy. They wanted to strike. They wanted to kill. But their imam had told them to hold off. Follow the car; that was the order. The men tried to keep busy. They cleaned their guns. They drank the drink forbidden by Allah. They dreamed of victory. They dreamed of dying and the seventy virgins promised to each of them when they died for Allah.

Their leader was a deeply religious young man. As a teen, he had fought for al-Qaeda. He always followed orders, but he thought he could fight better. He thought he should lead, give the commands, and decide when and where to strike. And his men agreed. No longer did he follow al-Qaeda's plan. Now, he was in charge. He would win the *jihad,* the holy war.

His group was unlike many other splinter groups of al-Qaeda. They all thought there was a common cause, and they all thought it was religion. Yet most of them did not understand the religion they were so willing to die for. Most of them had never read their bible, the Koran, and if they had read a few of the passages, they did not understand them. But their leaders had told them this was a religious war, a war in which the enemy fought against their faith, against Allah.

This young Arab wanted to die for Allah. He tried to defend his faith. But most of all, he wanted the seventy virgins promised to him when he went to heaven.

Rosia, Tuscany

Adam left the post office and got into his car. He smiled at Nicole, sitting in the passenger seat. "I really want to take some time off," he said. "I am in no hurry. I want to go to the Amalfi coast and then to Capri. I have a small apartment there. I guess I do not know your diary. Well, that is not true. I do know. How about it? Are you ready to join me?"

He turned to her as he drove the Mercedes onto the highway. "I am game. Take me to wherever you want to go. I am alone for the ride."

"Great. Let us go to Positano, and then to my place in Capri. Nicole, I know you work for the CIA. How come the agency is so interested in me?"

"Are you kidding?" she responded. "You cannot be serious. You are the hottest item on the CIA list since you left the NSA and became independent. People do not usually leave government spy agencies to spy on themselves. And if that was not enough, you got a call from the Vatican. The CIA heard that the Pope himself wants you to run an assignment. And you wonder why the CIA is interested in you?" "I am overwhelmed. I cannot believe all the attention I am getting. You know, the pope never called me. It was only an emissary of his. And I am sureit iss one way down the totem pole. So, you people at the

Agency are overestimating the importance of all this. But you always do. This time I do not mind. I like to spend my time with some of the CIA officers, particularly the one with blue-green eyes and black hair pulled back in a ponytail. I want to show her all the beauties of Italy. I want her to learn how the Italians live. They live for the joy of life. They live to enjoy food and *amore*."

"*Amore* sounds good to me. But Adam, something continues to trouble me. Why did you leave your job? Why did you leave your country?"

"I never left my country. I am now closer to my country than I have ever been. I now understand its values. I understand what we stand for and what our forebears meant when they talked about freedom for all, the right to choose, be free, vote, and live in a democratic society. But today we must put their ideas, ideals, and vision into perspective. No longer is there just one country. Now, there is the world in which we must be involved. I know it changes things, but not all that much. We can still apply our forebears' wisdom. We can still have a world at peace. The fundamental difference is religion. It always has been. That was how our country started, but our current leaders do not see it that way. They do not understand. But there is a man who does. He is the Holy Father of all Catholic people, the Pope. I believe in him. I believe in his mission. That is why I am driving toward the Eternal City. That is why I will see the pope."

Adam pulled the car onto Highway 323 to Grosseto and checked the rearview mirror. The car was still there.

"Adam, please tell me why you left the National Security Agency. Why did you leave them to go on your own?"

"Nicole, there is no easy answer. I thought about it for a long time. I wavered. I could never make a definitive decision. But when

I read and heard about all the prisoner abuses in Iraq—that was when I decided. I know we are not perfect. As you do, I know we use unconventional methods not always sanctioned by all. Hell, we all do. But in Iraq, we went too far. Everyone got too desperate— no weapons of mass destruction and all. I now believe that the only way I can make a difference is to be on my own. There are too many parties involved, all with their own interests. I know mine. I like to keep it simple."

Adam smiled at her as he again checked his rearview mirror. The car was still there—just one car. He knew there should be more. He was driving a particular vehicle behind him. He never worried much about them, for they were not true professionals.

Their methods were crude and predictable. He worried more about the people he did *not* see, the Mossad, and the men from the EU. He knew they were in the hunt. They all knew the Vatican had called for him.

He also worried about the Americans, about the woman sitting next to him. They had taken a different approach to surveillance. They had put one of their cases officers right next to him in his car. That was the American way, he thought. That was ballsy. He smiled at the thought.

Adam decided to stop in Rome for the night. In the morning, he would go to Capri to his apartment. There he would relax for a few days before returning to the city of the Vatican. Then he would start his assignment. He entered the GRA, the Grande Raccordo Anulare, the beltway that encircles Rome. Marking on this highway was confusing, but he knew his way. He drove to his favorite hotel, the Hotel Hassler, at the top of the Spanish Steps. He had called to reserve one of the Hassler suites. He loved the terraces and the view.

Rome, Italy

Adam stood on the terrace of his hotel as the sun left the Eternal City. He wore only the Hassler Hotel robe. He had showered and was now waiting for Nicole to join him. He had placed the champagne glasses on the table next to the appetizers that room service had brought to his suite. He held the bottle of Cristal champagne in his hands. He wanted to pop the cork the minute she stepped onto the terrace.

She walked out of the suite and onto the terrace as the sun put its last glow over the Eternal City. She wore a white gown. Her black hair covered her shoulders. She looked as if she had come from heaven. All he could do was stare. Then he remembered the champagne. He fumbled with the bottle.

"This is a beautiful night," she said, wrapping her arms around him.

He did not answer. He put the bottle down and held her close as he kissed her. Soon their tongues met, and he pulled her into his body. He ran his right hand over the backs of her thighs. Then he stepped slightly away from her. He was still kissing her as his hand moved between her legs. She moaned. He lifted her and carried her onto the king-size bed. He gently put her on her back. He spread her legs and lay on top of her. He entered her as her fingernails dug into his back. He did not mind. They made love for two hours, the best hours of his life.

Tel Aviv, Israel

The Mossad knew it all. They even knew about the lovemaking. They knew how long it took, knew the appetizers the man had ordered, I knew the bottle of Cristal had never been opened. They realized the man was much more important than all the other agencies had anticipated. The Mossad was watching him closely. They had installed video cameras and listening devices in his suite just before his arrival. The room service personnel had been hand-picked. The hotel's owner was a *sayan*, a Jew who was always ready to help the State of Israel.

Maza Sharef, head of the Mossad, paced back and forth in his small office in Tel Aviv. He was not happy. He had to know more, but his people had no answers. He needed to know all the details of the pope's plan. He wanted to understand the entire game; only then could he make the right decisions. He also understood that things never worked that way. The puzzle never fell totally into place. There were always pieces missing. That was when the fun and games started. That was when his agency, the Mossad, was at its best. Each time it happened, it was a challenge. Each time, he wondered if they would succeed. This time, he felt very uneasy. This time, the enemy was one of their own, one they had trained, one of their best. No, he reminded himself, not just one of their best. He was the best Mossad had ever trained.

The Mossad had tried twice to stop Adam Bergman. Their man on the luxurious yacht had failed and so had the man the Mossad had sent to the pastor's church in Berlin. Maza Sharef, the head of the Mossad, had used up two strikes. Three strikes, and you are out, he had learned in the United States.

South Beirut, Lebanon

The general secretary of Hezbollah, Hassan Nasral, sat in his bunker, deep in thought. The leader of all Catholic people, the bishop of Rome had asked him for help to make peace in the Middle East. Hassan smiled. Peace in the Middle East, peace with Israel, should never be. He knew Allah's wish was to kill all infidels, a mission he was determined to complete. Yet the pope's invitation intrigued him. Often Hassan had sat in his bunker, wondering how he could fulfill Allah's wish. Many times, Allah had confirmed that all infidels must die. Hassan had contemplated many strategies for accomplishing Allah's wish, but he thought none would be effective.

But tonight, Allah had given him the answer: deception. After all, deception has always been one of the most powerful tools that all religions use. Now Hassan would use it again. He would agree to help the Pope make peace in the Middle East. He would attend the meeting the pope had planned. Only there could he learn all the details. Only there could he learn how to kill all the infidels.

CHAPTER 10

Brooklyn, New York City

THE OLD RABBI SAT ON A wooden bench in a small park in the Garden Heights section of Brooklyn, New York. It was midafternoon in July, and the sun was showing no mercy. It was hot and humid. There was no breeze. He had gone to the bench under the large oak tree to escape some of the heat. He had come here often since childhood, and every day since his bar mitzvah celebration had taken place here. This was his home. The neighborhood has changed over the years. Now it was a melting pot of races and religions— Caucasians, Hispanics, African Americans, Jews, Muslims, and Christians. They all lived here and survived together.

Each day, he came here to pray. Each day, he prayed for his grandson, the boy who was not a child born into his own family. The old rabbi had met and married a woman in Miami. They had fallen in love at once. The woman had a grandson. The rabbi loved the young man, and when his wife, the young man's grandmother, had died, they had become even closer. With the tragic loss of his wife, the rabbi felt he had gained a son, a grandson.

Each day, his prayers also turned to his faith. He worried about the survival of his own religion. He was a descendant of Eastern

Europeans, an *Ashkenazi* Jew. He knew the name *Ashkenaz* had been given during the Middle Ages to Jews living along the Rhine River in Germany and France. Later, the term *Ashkenaz* had become identified with descendants of German Jews. His people had lived in Christian, Eastern European lands. The old rabbi's family had come from Eastern Europe in the late twenties. They had come to New York and Brooklyn and been there ever since.

He always sat under the large, old oak tree. It had two massive trunks. One leaned toward the east, the other toward the west. Both were like large umbrellas, their leaves shading beneath the majestic tree. The tree gave him shade to escape the sun and reminded him of his religion, with two branches leaning their own way, two branches giving shade and protection.

He knew the other faction of Jews came from the Iberian Peninsula—Spain and Portugal—and were referred to as Sephardim. The word came from the Hebrew term for Spain: Sepharad. The difference between the two factions was once been ceremonial— different music, dances, and dress. Today, however, tensions had grown because of the poor treatment the *Sephardim* received and the difficulties these Jews had in approaching equality in Jewish society.

The old rabbi knew much work needed to be done within his religion. He wanted to have peace among all the Jews. He knew it could only be done if they all united under a single leader, but there was no single leader. There was a joint chief rabbinate, represented by the *Ashkenazic* chief rabbi and the chief rabbi of the *Sephardim*. His religion could not decide on one religious leader. How could they make peace in the Holy Land when they had not been able to make peace within their own religion? The older man knew that peace would never come from within the boundaries of the Holy Land. The Arabs and the Jews had too much housecleaning to do. They first needed to get their own acts together. Only someone from the outside, a miracle man, could make peace in a land where peace was unknown.

He stroked his gray beard as always when he sat on his bench, ready to read the script and say his prayers. Each day was like the last. Nothing had changed in more than thirty years. But today was different. There had been a telephone call just before he had left the house. It was most unusual. The call had come from Israel. He had been unable to answer it, for he had been in the shower.

The message on his answering machine left a telephone number he would call as soon as possible. He had not called at once as the message had asked him to do. The old rabbi was a methodical man who liked to think things through. Never did he overreact. Even when he was much younger, he had never been impulsive. He had always been pragmatic. He had not memorized the telephone number, although he could have. His memory was still sound. Instead, he punched the phone number into his cell phone.

The rabbi reached under his black robe and pulled out his phone. He did not receive many calls, and none from Tel Aviv. He looked pensively at his phone, not knowing whether to call the number to make the overseas call. Finally, curiosity got the best of him.

He made the call and let it ring. There was no answer. He pressed the *end* button on his cell phone and put it back into his pocket. *Strange*, he thought. *I feel relieved.* Little did he know that the telephone call would change his life.

Tel Aviv, Israel

The *Katz* at the Mossad in Tel Aviv knew the rabbi had called the number, the number of a small restaurant in Israel's capital, the A restaurant that would not open for several hours. But now he knew the rabbi in Brooklyn would cooperate, and he knew his cell phone number. Soon, his agency would contact the holy man.

The Mossad wanted to know all about the man who had grown up in the old rabbi's neighborhood, the rabbi's adopted grandson who had grown up to be an assassin and work for the US government. That man now works on his own as an independent. The Vatican had sent for him, and now the man was traveling at his leisure through Italy, arousing the attention of the security agents of the European Union. He was being followed by Arabs and accompanied by a beautiful woman, a CIA officer.

Ira, the Mossad case officer, *Katz*, picked up his phone and called his boss. He had to report to the head of the Mossad and needed direction.

"Yes," Maza Sharef responded in a husky voice at the other end of the line.

"The old rabbi in Brooklyn returned our call as you predicted. I have his phone number."

"Good. Call him back. Set up a meeting. Please go to Brooklyn, meet the rabbi, and bring him to me. I need to know all about his grandson, the guy the Vatican is so anxious to meet."

"It's done," the response came back without hesitation. "Anything else?"

"Do it quickly!"

Maza hung up the phone in his bathroom. He had just stepped out of the shower when his *katza* had called him. His body was still wet and naked. He reached for the large white bath towel and wrapped it around his lean body. Although he was almost forty-five years of age, his body looked like that of a much younger man. He exercised daily and ate the right food.

Maza removed the towel and began to dry himself. He stood in the center of the small bathroom, which was part of his office in the Hadar Dafna building in Tel Aviv. He wished he could still work in the field. That was what he had enjoyed the most. He loved to be in the middle of the action. But he also knew his country needed him to head its intelligence agency. He, after all, was uniquely qualified.

He had received the best education. First, he studied at Oxford and then Harvard. He had received his law degree from Yale. After he had spent time in the Israeli army, the State sent him to work with MI6 in London, England's renowned intelligence agency. He also spent time at Langley, where he learned more about the spy business. He knew how to protect his country. Israel had made a wise choice. Maza Sharef would always protect the children of Israel, for he had learned his trade well. But he also had instinct. He knew when trouble lay ahead. He could always smell it. He smelled it now.

Tuscany, Italy

The two men in the car had been told to follow the large Mercedes. Their imam had not told them much more. They did not know how to react when the man in the Mercedes picked up the woman. They had been told to follow the car to the Vatican, where the man was supposed to go. Now they were confused. The Mercedes was heading south. It never entered the city. The car was not heading for the Vatican. The car's two passengers were heading for a vacation spot.

The Arab in charge of the pursuit smiled. The man in the large Mercedes was obviously married and had picked up his lover on the way. His team was on a wild goose chase. It happens far too often. He recalled the last time. It had been in Scandinavia. They had followed a young couple in a Volvo for two weeks, only to find out it was the wrong car. In the meantime, the real target had infiltrated one of their camps in Eastern Europe and exposed it. This had caused much damage to their cause to win the *jihad*, the war against the infidels.

Now he knew better. He learned from his mistakes. He decided to abandon the chase of the large, black Mercedes and go for the heart. He decided to head for Rome. He wanted to be close to Vatican City. There he would wait.

Adam Bergman was surprised. Once more, he checked his rearview mirror. The car that had followed him was no longer there. He had last seen the car pull into a rest stop. He had been sure his pursuers would fill their vehicle with gasoline and continue the hunt, but it did not happen. He never saw them again.

It did not matter to Adam. He knew he was constantly being followed. When he saw the enemy, he felt comfortable. It was the enemy he did not know that he feared most. Or was it the enemy so close he could touch it? He looked to his right and smiled at the beautiful woman beside him. He knew she was a spy, a CIA officer. He did not mind, because that was his world. That was what he had chosen to do. These were the games he liked to play.

They left Rome and entered Highway 148. Traffic was heavy now, and it would be that way until they reached Positano. It was early afternoon, and Adam decided they would stay in Positano tonight. The next day, they would take the boat to Capri. Adam intended to spend several days at his apartment on the island. He had no fixed plan. He knew they would take a day trip on the gondola, go to the grove, go swimming, go shopping, relax, have two-hour lunches in the sunshine, have dinner as the sun set on the beautiful blue sea, sleep with the windows wide open as the ocean winds freshened the air, and listen to the rhythmical sound of the waves.

But Adam also knew he had an agenda—places, dates, and times he had committed to, a meeting in Rome, a meeting with a man from the Vatican. He knew she could not come with him. He would ask her to stay behind at his place in Capri. He would only be gone for a day, two. He really did not know how long the Holy Father needed him. But first he was going to enjoy his stay at Positano and Capri. He wanted to show her all the sights, enjoy all he knew, go to the restaurants and bars, take the boat trip into the grotto, and be with her all day. He longed for her companionship, for he was a lonely man, and he needed the company of a woman before he began a new mission. He did not know why. But it gave him peace, a peace he needed before he went into war and became what he had been trained to be: an assassin, a cold-blooded killer.

Capri, Italy

They honestly thought they were in love. The last three days on the island of Capri had been all Nicole had ever wanted. They had spent each minute together, laughing, crying, dreaming, being one. They strolled through the beautiful streets, shopped at all the fashionable stores, and dined at the excellent restaurants. They took the gondola to the grove and walked hand in hand through the town. They stopped, laughed, and kissed. He was gentler than she had thought he would be. Man could ever be. He always parted her hair with his left hand as he kissed her on her lips. Then he would whisper into her ear how much he enjoyed her touch, warmth, and body. But best of all, he always told her he loved her intellect and how they always talked.

That was when she stopped him and said, "Enough. Kiss me. I want to make love." And they did. It was the best lovemaking both had ever experienced, for it came from the heart. They loved each other.

Adam Bergman awakened as the early morning sun illuminated his bedroom. He stepped onto the large balcony of his apartment and listened to the waves. He was naked, for he had not bothered to put on his robe. His lover was fast asleep in the bedroom. Adam looked at the sea and listened to the breaking waves. He thought about his life. He had more than ever aspired to a home on Capri, a flat in London, an apartment in Miami. And now he had a woman he thought he really loved.

He stared at the water as the sun gave its first light. He touched his chest and then his abdomen. He felt the scar, but he did not need to. He would never forget it. And he remembered the words of the man who had shot him on the yacht in Miami Beach. He knew he had no choice. It was his destiny to find out—not just to find out why he had been shot, or why his pastor had had to die, but why he had been called to the Vatican, why the Holy Father of all Catholic people, the bishop of Rome, wanted to see him. He knew that was why he had survived the Bahamian seas, why the skiff had been sent to him. He knew his God wanted him to help the Holy Father. He knew his God had called him to fulfill a mission.

Geneva, Switzerland

The G8 had another summit. All the political leaders met for another economic summit of all the world powers. They met to discuss economic policies, but this time, world peace was the priority issue. Yet few leaders, if any, understood how to approach world peace. Many—no, most—thought world peace was an economic issue. Some thought it was a matter of balance of power. Others—the more narrow-minded—thought it revolved around oil, nuclear power, and a country's military strength. Nonetheless, diplomats and heads of government disagreed. They all thought world peace was a secular issue.

CHAPTER 11

The White House, Washington, DC

MONICA DREW, THE PRESIDENT OF THE United States, had been raised in the small town of Ashtabula, Ohio. She excelled in high school and attended Georgetown University in Washington, DC. There, she had met her husband, a man determined to make politics his career.

Her husband had joined the Democratic party and quickly rose through its ranks as a congressperson, a senator, and finally the governor of his home state. Twice, he tried to win the Democratic nomination for the presidency of the United States, and twice, he failed. But he was obsessed with power and urged his wife to run for office.

Monica Drew easily won the election to Congress in her home state of Ohio. She had been convinced then, believing she could make a difference. Then, she had been an idealist. But when she had run for the Senate, she realized that she had to make promises and forget her beliefs and convictions to win the public votes. She had to tell the public what they wanted to hear. Her husband had always insisted that she forget what she believed in, what she thought was right or wrong.

After a time, she no longer knew her real beliefs or for what she stood. She had made too many promises to gain votes, few of which she knew she could uphold. At first, this troubled her, but her husband had always assured her that it was what all politicians did. One had to tell the constituents what they wanted to hear to get the votes. Eventually, Monica Drew had become the best at informing the public what they wanted to hear, making promises, and deceiving them.

When the former president ran for a second term, he had decided that a woman on his ticket would assure him of reelection. He had been right, and Monica Drew had become the vice president of the United States. That her boss, the president of the United States, had been elected to a second term surprised her. He had made many mistakes and continued to do so. Yet she had to support him. She had to. Monica Drew wanted to be the next president of the United States, the first woman ever elected to that office. More importantly, her husband had made it his mission. During the campaign, her husband had known that his wife would face very difficult issues, issues he would have to downgrade. He would write his own rules, the Drew Rules.

The former president had exhibited poor judgment. He had been reluctant to listen to his advisors, who were all well-informed. The president's arrogance, his belief that he knew all, had resulted in many new terrorist groups springing up. Most were now encouraged by the former president's lack of leadership. Even groups he had called JV teams only weeks earlier posed a significant threat.

And then he made a blunder in dealing with Ebola. He had told all Americans that it was unlikely, almost impossible, for the deadly virus to arrive on US shores, but less than a week later, it did. Then there were many other blunders: the NSA spying on all Americans and their allies; listening in on cell phones, including that of German leader Angela Merkel and the leaders of France; the fiasco in Benghazi; the IRS targeting of his opponents; his lack of a plan to defeat ISIS; his ill-conceived health-care plan; his policy to halt Iran's nuclear efforts; his reluctance to work with Israel, the United States' closest ally in the Middle East; and his decision to release five terrorists in exchange for an American deserter.

Monica Drew had also been part of all the former president's failures. But she had had little choice. She was his vice president, and she had to support him. She knew that to win the next election and become president, her party had to be united and support the president's policies, no matter how wrong. Unity was what her opponent, the GOP—the Grand Old Party—lacked. There had not been a single candidate the GOP would rally around and support to win the election. And then, of course, there was her husband. He had all the knowledge and knew how to build the infrastructure to win the election.

Despite it all, Monica Drew won by the slightest of margins. Her predecessor had run and won on the slogan of change. Yet as president, he had failed miserably. But Monica Drew knew—no, she did not know, but her husband did—that the American voter had a short-term memory. America once again wanted change, even if the only change was the gender of the commander in chief: America, the land of opportunity.

The Vatican, Rome, Italy

POPE LEO XIV, THE BISHOP OF Rome, the chief bishop of Italy, the patriarch of the West, the absolute monarch of the Vatican City State, the head of the college of bishops and all the Catholic Church, knew he needed help. He did not need help looking after the pastoral needs of 2.6 million Catholics living in the diocese of Rome. He did not need help to rule over the 108.7 acres, his Vatican City, the smallest independent state in the world. But he knew he needed help to fulfill the new mission he thought God had given him.

He remembered the very first dispute in the Christian community, which involved the treatment of Gentiles. And he remembered more: the Reformation of the Papacy, the Protestant Reformation, and the fall of European monarchies. He was not just a student of his religion; he was a student of history. And he was an arm of God, the almighty Father. His Father had given him a mission to complete. The words had been direct and straightforward: His God had told him to create peace in the Middle East.

The man in Rome, the Holy Father, knew it would not be simple. He knew that many others had tried. The world's power, the United States, had failed and continued to do so. He understood that their approach was different; it was secular diplomacy. The Holy Father in Rome knew the solution was a religious one of belief, of faith in God. But he was a realist. He knew well that not everyone thought as he did, and he knew he would have many enemies when going to the Arabs to propose peace. But he wanted peace—peace under one God.

That was why he had asked the man his advisors had recommended to come to him to go to Vatican City. The holy man knew he was well protected but knew the enemy would change. He needed someone familiar with these new enemies' ways. He needed someone whom they had trained, someone trained by the United States and the Israelis, someone trained to deal with the Arabs. The pope knew the man he had sent for was not the final answer. Yes, the man could help, no doubt about it. But he and the religious leaders of Islam and Judaism had to agree. They had to make peace. Only then would there be peace in the Middle East.

The White House, Washington, DC

THE PRESIDENT OF THE UNITED STATES did not often meet with the heads of US churches, but Monica Drew decided it was essential to do so now. Her mission, she had decided, was to make peace in the Middle East. It would become her legacy. Unlike the former president, she understood peace could not be established without the church's help. Monica Drew needed to learn more about how the churches operated and the different religions. She believed in God, went to church every Sunday, and prayed, but she knew little of what divided the different religions. She had never had to—until now.

This morning, as the CIA director met with her every morning to discuss the presidential brief, a paper prepared by the CIA each day was presented to the leader. It contained all the essential information the president needed to know. The presidential brief on this day spoke of a threat to the United States, its eminence, and its position in world politics. The Vatican intended to invite all the important leaders of Islam and Judaism to come and meet with the pope in Rome to discuss peace in the Middle East. The president of the United States was not to be part of it. The leader of the free world would have no say on how there would be peace. Monica Drew surmised that someone else was trying to steal center stage. Someone else was trying to fulfill the mission she thought would make her the greatest US president and world leader in history. She would not let the pope, the bishop of Rome, make her come in second.

Like the former president, Monica Drew had been unaware that religion was the real cause of the conflict in the Middle East. Not until now had she understood that the Holy Father in Rome had the best chance to make peace. She intended to change the odds because she wanted to be the peacemaker. Monica Drew invited all her country's foremost religious leaders to Camp David. She needed a crash course on religion.

Capri, Italy

Adam Bergman, the man the pope had called for, was sitting in the blue water of his swimming pool on the Isle of Capri. It was midafternoon, and he was enjoying a cigar, a limoncello, the sun, and the beautiful woman beside him. They had arrived at his apartment on Capri late the night before. They had made love until the morning sun illuminated their room. Reluctantly, they had left their bed and showered. Adam's housekeeper had served lunch on the terrace. Then both he and Nicole plunged into the pool.

Nicole looked over her shoulder. "I can't believe the view," she said. The pool was built on a cliff overlooking the blue Adriatic Sea, two hundred feet above sea level, and the view was breathtaking.

"Nicole," Adam said as he sat in the pool, smoking his cigar. "I have a wonderful idea."

She approached him in the water, slowly swimming toward him. Once she reached him, she put her arms around him and whispered into his ear. "What is it?" Her head moved, her lips touched him, and she kissed him.

"Well," he said, "we seem to get along well. I mean, as professionals, in our business. Of course, we get along fabulously as lovers. But I am talking about the professional aspect."

She wanted to know, "Why now?" "Why now, while we are enjoying every moment?"

"You know I must leave soon—in a day or two. I hate to leave you behind. I would like to have you next to me. I enjoy your company. No, it is more. I do not really know. But I hate not being with you for a while."

"Why don't you tell me where you are going and for how long? Tell me why. Tell me all about it."

"I cannot. Nicole, you know the way it goes. You are not on my side. You are working for someone else. But why can't you join me? We could be a team. I do not know anything about my new mission. I have no idea."

"Adam, we are lovers. We have shared much but perhaps not enough. I still love my country. One day I will understand you. It is not today. I pray for you. Go with God."

It was 5:00 a.m. when Adam left Capri. Nicole was still fast asleep on his king-size bed overlooking the blue waters. Adam had made sure she would not be awake when he left. He had drugged one of her drinks. He hated to go, and he did not want to leave her. He thought he loved her. He had left a message on the down comforters: an envelope, a diamond bracelet, a single long-stemmed red rose, and a few words: "I saw love. Shall I see it again?"

The early ferry back to the mainland was almost empty. Adam Bergman had a cup of hot coffee as he stood at the stern of the boat and looked back toward Capri, his island, and his apartment where he had left the woman, he thought he loved.

He turned and looked to the east, where he was heading. Not long after now, he would leave the ferry at Positano, walk to the garage where he had left the Mercedes, and drive directly to Rome. He did not know why the Vatican had sent for him. Often, over the past few days, he had thought about it. He had considered several possibilities. He had always come to the same conclusion. It had to do with the Middle East. It had to do with Palestine, with Israel. It had to do with peace in the Middle East. He was sure of it. His instincts had never failed him in the past.

The Vatican, Rome, Italy

The early sunlight illuminated his city. As the sun rose, it gave the town a vibrant glow. It made it come alive. It told him that his God was pleased. The pope stood on the terrace of his home at the Vatican. He stood there every morning as the sun rose. He liked to be alone. He wanted to talk to his God in solitude. Somehow, he knew, or thought he knew, that this was when he got all his father's attention, his God. Today, he did not pray. Today, he did not ask for any favors. He knew he had done too much of this in the recent past. He wanted to let his God realize he had the faith to solve the problems independently. He knew faith was the tool he needed to go forward. The bishop of Rome, the Holy Father of all Catholic people, also knew he needed more than faith. That was why he had sent for the man he was waiting for, the man who would help the Catholic Church make peace in the Middle East.

North Africa, an al-Qaeda training camp

The young Arab knew about the man, the leader of the Christian world, for whom the man had sent. He did not know why the Vatican wanted to see this man, but knew he was the most dangerous. The man had been trained by the best, and he had been taught to find and kill terrorists. He knew he had to stop this man before he met with the pope. He had no plans. He and his people only reacted. Yes, they had been told to plan to go hiding and wait for the right moment.

But he had no patience. He had seen how many of his parents' terrorist groups' well-conceived plans had gone awry. They had been exposed, and he thought he knew why. Their plans took too long to develop and put them into action. This gave the enemy time to prepare and find what they were ready to do. He was not about to make that mistake. He would strike quickly when he thought it was time.

The young al-Qaeda recruit had only a few followers, but they were well-trained. Al-Qaeda had taught them how to fight. He and his men were ready to leave al-Qaeda because they had grown impatient. They wanted to strike now. He had grown tired of all the waiting, the planning, the changes of targets. And he knew al-Qaeda's next target. He was determined to get there first. He would show them all how to please Allah.

Positano to Rome, Italy

The black Mercedes left Positano and raced toward Rome. Adam was now anxious to reach his destination and find out what the pope wanted him to do. He had used automatic controls to push his seat as far back as possible to accommodate his six-foot-two-inch frame. The backrest of his seat was tilted back as far as the controls allowed. He was almost lying in his seat, which was the way he liked to drive. Adam seldom used cruise control. He always had to dictate the tempo, and the car was no exception.

Again, Adam wondered why the Vatican had sent for him. He knew he had specific skills that few others possessed, skills he had learned at the expense of the American taxpayers. Not long ago, he had hoped never to use these skills again. How could his skills, training, and experience help the Vatican, the symbol of love and peace? He did not know the answer but was anxious to learn it.

Adam stepped on the accelerator of his powerful Mercedes. He was now ready to reach his destination and learn the answers, to find out about the mission the bishop of Rome wanted him to fulfill. Adam had speculated that his mission had to do with the Middle

East. Had the Catholic Church and the pope decided to get involved in the conflict? Adam strongly believed that the only path to peace in the Middle East was via religion, for it was clearly a religious war, and only religious leaders could make peace. Had the Holy Father in Rome decided to lead the way? And why did he need a trained killer to help him make peace? Adam could not wait to find out the answer.

Stanford, California

He ran. He had done it most of his life. At first he had run barefoot. Later, as he won most of his races, someone did not remember who— had given him a pair of shoes. It was not that he could not afford to buy shoes. He could. His father had been a wealthy man. Ali Muhammad Nasral ran and broke all the records at his college, Stanford University. Soon he also became the American record holder in his two events: five thousand and ten thousand meters. Only two months ago, he set the world record in his favorite race, the ten thousand meters. He was the favorite to win a gold medal in the next Olympics.

Ali had been raised in the United States, but he had been born in Lebanon. His Lebanese father, a devout Shiite Muslim, had worked for a large oil company and had spent most of his time in the US. This was where he had met his wife, the young runner's mother. She was a beautiful woman of Italian descent, a religious Catholic, who hailed from Sonoma, California. Their one child had been born during the It was the only trip she had ever taken to her husband's homeland, but father and son had often traveled back to the Middle East. That was where Ali had met his grandfather. The young runner adored the man. When he visited, he never wanted to leave. As he grew older, he knew that his grandfather was an incredibly special man respected by everyone in Lebanon, with much authority and wealth.

The CIA knew all about the young Stanford runner. They knew he was no ordinary man. They knew about his mother, his father, and all the trips he had taken to the Middle East. They knew that his training was not just focused on running. They knew he had been trained to shoot a gun, make a bomb, shoulder a missile, and shoot to kill. But they did not know when he would do these things, for they did not know his mission. They did not even know which faith the young runner believed in. They knew he had an American passport—and many more. And they did know about his grandfather, the secretary-general of Hezbollah.

Tuscany, Italy

Ali Muhammad Nasral, the young Arab man from Stanford, had followed the black Mercedes sedan since leaving the Positano garage. His grandfather instructed him to follow the man and not lose him. *He is heading for the Vatican. We need to know why. It is not just I who asks you, but Allah.*

Ali was deep in thought as he followed the Mercedes sedan. He was thinking about his religion. He often heard his grandfather speak about the pre-Islamic religion of *Jahiliyya* in Arabia during the Dark Ages. He knew this religion insisted that it was Islam and was best called *jihadism*. For many years, Ali, the grandson of the secretary-general of Hezbollah, did not believe in jihadism. He did not believe that any *kafir*, or nonbeliever, should be killed. He had thought that interpreting the Qur'an advocated peace and nonviolence.

But his grandfather had convinced him that he was wrong, reminding him that the Prophet Muhammad had allowed the Muslims to raise arms and defend themselves at Medina. If they had not, they undoubtedly would have faced elimination. His grandfather had argued that the infidels were trying to destroy Muslims. The *Qur'an* also stated, and his grandfather often pointed out: "Fight in the name of your religion with those who fight against you. Kill the *Mushrikun* (disbelievers) wherever you find them. Fight against those who do not believe in Allah. Only forgive their past if they cease from fitnah (disbelief)."

It did not take Ali long to change the meaning of his readings from the holy book of Islam, the *Qur'an*. He trusted his grandfather and knew he spoke directly to Allah. Now he was convinced that all infidels had to be killed, and only if they changed their belief and made Allah their God would their past be forgiven. Ali had the black Mercedes in sight. He would not lose it. He knew he was following the right path—the path Allah had chosen for him.

The two men in the Fiat also believed in God, but their God was not Allah. These men were Jews, and they worked for the Mossad. Israel's renowned intelligence agency knew about the man the Vatican wanted to see. They knew many others were interested in the Americans who had come to Italy from the United States.

Twice the Mossad had tried to stop this man, and twice they had failed. Miraculously, the American had survived the Mossad's. An assassination attempt on the yacht he boarded in Miami Beach. The Mossad also knew about the stop the American would make in Berlin and tried to stop him then, but they had only been moments too late. Unfortunately, an older man of God had paid the price for their mistake.

The Mossad knew about the small splinter group of al-Qaeda following the Americans. They had also been informed about the other Arab, the young Stanford man driving a Volkswagen Passat, and they knew about the CIA woman the American had left behind on Capri. Surely, the Mossad men thought it would not be long before the CIA was in Rome.

The Mossad driver left the Autostrada and drove his Fiat deep into the city. He had been told to go to one of the safe houses in Rome and wait for further instructions. He knew the message would not be conveyed over the telephone, not even his cell phone. The message would be relayed in a much more conventional way, a way they could trust that no other parties would hear. They would meet with another man, or a woman, who would tell them what to do and where to go. The Mossad did not make any mistakes. They did not have the luxury of doing so.

Capri, Italy

The sun was shining high over the *Golfo di Napoli*, engulfing the island of Capri in its bright light. There was no cloud in the sky. Rays of sunshine filled the bedroom of the apartment she was sleeping in. She rolled over and looked at the clock on the table next to the king-size bed. It was almost 11:00 a.m.

Immediately, she reached out next to her. She felt no one. He was gone. Then she smiled, remembering the evening and the lovemaking, and recalled all the tender words he had whispered into her ears. She also recalled that he had asked her to stay at his place in Capri and not to follow him. He had told her that his mission could be dangerous and that he wanted her out of harm's way. He wanted to be sure she would be there when he returned to Capri.

Nicole had a slight headache and felt as if she had a hangover. But they did not drink much alcohol last night. They had not even touched the champagne. Their night had been filled with lovemaking.

She now realized that he had drugged her. He had wanted her to be fast asleep while he was leaving for Rome. He wanted, at all costs, to keep her out of danger. But she had a job, and danger was her way. That was the job she had chosen.

Nicole got out of bed, quickly showered, dressed, and entered the street to find a public telephone. She had to call her boss. She needed instructions and to be told what to do now. She needed to know what was going on.

CHAPTER 12

Berlin, Germany

THE MINISTER OF INTERNAL AFFAIRS AT the Reichstag, Prince Albert von Hohenzollern, the cousin of the president of the EU, sat in his office in Berlin's parliament building. He leaned back in his leather chair as he lit another cigarette. He was a chain smoker, and the more the pressure, the more he smoked. Today, he smoked more than usual. He was responsible for the men assigned to follow the American the pope had sent for. He knew about all the others following him. Most did not concern him. Most, in his estimation, were amateurs. But not the Israelis; they were the best. The Americans were there too. But he knew how to handle them.

What concerned Prince Albert most was how the other governments would react when they found out what he and his cousin, the EU president, already knew: the reason why the Holy Father in Rome wanted to see this American, who was a former spy and a trained killer. The thought of using force, of killing to get one's will, was not alien to the minister. But had the Vatican decided to use force? It certainly was not alien to them or the others, for they all had done some more, some better. But Albert also knew that force was not the answer.

Did the Holy Father in Rome have a different solution? Had the bishop of Rome sent for the man for another reason? Albert—and his boss and cousin, Prince William—had to be the first to know that reason. When it came to the Vatican, Prince Albert was always best informed.

Rome, Italy

Adam left the Autostrada and headed straight for his hotel. There was no need for diversions. He knew his followers would always find him, at least for now. He drove directly to his favorite hotel, the Hassler-Villa Medici on the Piazza Trinita dei Monti at the top of the Spanish Steps. He wanted to be here tonight and recall the night he and Nicole had spent here not long ago. He always wanted to be close to her or close to places they had shared. He did not know why. He thought he was in love with her, but he was not sure.

He had dated many women and slept with many of them. Some he had become friends with. A few had rejected him when he told them he was dating others and was not ready to commit. Nicole was different. She wanted to have fun. She wanted to enjoy it. She did not ask for a commitment. He was afraid she never would.

He entered the suite he and Nicole had shared only days ago. He carefully checked the slicks and the hiding places the spy agencies used. He was now alone, no longer with the NSA or the Mossad. The thought of being alone relaxed him. It made him feel easier, reminding him of the Bahamian sea, the waves, the sun, and the ocean's vastness. He had been alone then, and he had survived. He now knew that his destiny was not dependent on others. He knew he had been asked to complete a mission, and he did not know the nature of the mission. But he knew the Vatican thought he was the best man to do it.

Adam picked up the telephone on the table next to his bed and called room service. He was hungry and had a craving for American food. He knew he should eat Italian. Usually, he did, because he loved Italian food, but to enjoy an Italian meal took time to sit back, relax, and enjoy each course. Adam ordered a medium-rare cheeseburger with American cheese, tomatoes, onions, and no French fries. Now he was anxious to find out about his mission. He wanted to move on, to get back to Capri, and his stomach wanted American food.

Room service at the Hassler-Villa Medici was prompt. He had just stepped out of the shower when he heard the knock on his door. His naked body was dripping wet as he quickly put on the lush robe of the hotel. He went to the table beside his bed and picked up his gun. The silencer was firmly attached to the barrel. The Beretta had become his gun of choice since the Mossad had trained him.

With the gun in his right hand, he slowly opened the door with his left. He saw the tall man in the white tuxedo jacket and black pants. He was familiar with the attire, the uniform of the staff of the hotel. The man stood behind the tray table, carrying Adam's ordered food. He smiled and asked the man to enter his suite. That was when he noted the shoes. The man did not wear the black-laced leather shoes the staff of the hotel wore. He wore black- and-white Adidas sneakers, and he had a white towel draped over his right hand.

Adam did not hesitate. He had been trained by the best. He fired one shot into the forehead of the young, anxious terrorist from North Africa, and four more into the dying man's body—the Mossad way. The man's gun, which had been hidden under the towel, fell onto the floor of the vestibule. The door to Adam's suite was still open, and Adam looked down at the long corridor. He saw no one. He dragged the dead man's body into his suite and left him lying in the entry hall.

He pushed the service table with his lunch into the room. Then he shut the door. He was hungry. He sat on the expansive sofa and ate the cheeseburger for which he had longed.

When he would finished, he walked over to examine the dead body. The man was lying prone. Adam used his feet to turn himself. The dead man had the complexion of a man from the Middle East. Adam leaned down to search the pockets. He knew he would find no clue. He was right. It was time to get rid of the body.

Adam placed the dead man on the serving table and covered the body with the tablecloth and towels. Then he left his suit and walked down the long hallway. He knocked on the door of the last room on the floor. It was located next to the ice machine. There was no answer. He knocked once more, this time with more force. Again, there was no response.

He picked the lock, opened the door, and entered the room. A double bed occupied most of it. A single dresser was to the right of the bed, a night table to the left. A small artificial Persian rug covered the area between the bed and the door. The door to the bathroom was to his left. He quickly walked into the bath. It was empty. The room was not occupied. This, he thought, was the proper resting place for the man he had just killed.

He walked back to his room to retrieve the serving table with the dead body. Then he pushed the table down the hall and placed it and the dead man in Room 606, the room at the very end of the hallway.

Adam slept peacefully. He always did. He loved to sleep. It made him forget. It also made him remember. In his sleep, he only recalled the moments he wanted. Tonight, he dreamed of Positano and Capri. He dreamed about being with her, dreamed about her touch, her smile, her tender kiss. He dreamed they were in heaven. She was an angel assigned to him, an angel never to leave his side.

When the sun began to illuminate the Holy City, he was sitting on the terrace of his suite. He did not know that a short distance away, another man was watching the sun rise over this city. He was there every day. It was his city. It was the man who had sent for Adam: the bishop of Rome, the Holy Father of all Catholic people, the pope.

Adam's appointment with the man from the Vatican was scheduled for 1:00 p.m. He did not know who he was going to meet. All he knew were the words of his pastor and the telephone number he had called. The instructions were to be at Via della Lupa 29/b at 1:00 p.m. on August 27.

Adam was familiar with the address, for he knew the restaurant. It was located off the Piazza Nicosia. He had dined there and ordered pasta e fagioli, bean soup, fegato alla veneziana, and liver with onions. Adam loved liver. He especially loved *Berliner Art*, served with apples, onions, and bacon, as his grandma had always prepared it.

No one should know about this meeting. He would make sure he was alone. He would leave his hotel two hours before the meeting. He also knew it did not really matter. The game was not won or lost in a car chase. Some still believed it was in the old world of spying. And some of those characters were still at Langley. He smiled at the thought. Would they ever learn?

Once more, he looked over the magnificent Spanish Steps. He turned and left the balcony to enter his suite. It was time to get ready for his meeting with the man from the Vatican. He stepped into the shower and let the hot water relax his muscular body. The small, old wooden crossed around his neck, the necklace that had saved his life, clung to his hairy chest. It would not let go. It would protect him from all evil.

Adam left the hotel as planned, two hours before his meeting. He knew that many people wanted to know where he was going, his mission, and why the pontiff, the father of all Catholic people, had summoned him. But he needed to be alone with the messenger the Holy Father would send. Adam used all the skills the NSA and the Mossad had taught him, skills he had developed to perfection. There was no one better at the spy business than he. The Arab men tailing him lost him easily. The men from Israel were more difficult. It took him a good fifteen minutes to be sure they were no longer there. After all, he knew their methods.

The Americans were also difficult. This surprised him because he knew their procedures, but it had been tough to shake their surveillance today. He thought there was a new guy in charge, someone with fresh ideas. It took another thirty minutes before he felt at ease, convinced he was alone.

But he never really was. He remembered the men from the European Union. Not once had he seen them. He hoped they, too, had lost his trial. He had used all the tricks he had ever learned. Surely no one could have followed him. Nonetheless, he felt uneasy as he entered the restaurant at 1:00 p.m.

Berlin, Germany

Prince Albert was at a party committee meeting at the Reichstag. He was the chairperson, and he did not like to be interrupted. But he had left strict instructions. When the man from Rome called, the prince would be told immediately. Prince Albert left the conference room and stepped into his office to take the call. Here, he knew the line was secure. No one else was listening.

"He is at a restaurant off the Piazza Nicosia," said the calm voice of Carlo DeFino, the pope's closest advisor. "I have not yet met him." "Good," the man at the Reichstag responded. "Keep me up to date." He hung up the telephone. He was always well informed about the goings-on inside the Vatican. His lover, Carlo, made sure of it. Prince Albert also knew that a second source, one for reassurance, was always necessary. This he had learned when he had worked for the former East German intelligence. The Stasis had never trusted. anyone.

The prince stroked his bald head with his right hand. It was a habit he had developed when his hair was still full, brown, and curly more than twenty years ago. Only last week, he celebrated his sixty-fifth birthday. It was to be a wonderful celebration, just the two of them. They had rented a cottage on the island of Sylt in the North Sea. But at the last minute, his lover had called to let him know he could not be there. His boss, the Holy Father, needed him in Rome. Something important was going down. As soon as he knew the details, he would let Albert know, and he had promised to make up for it all. He promised he would do something incredibly special.

The bald, short, heavyset man hastened back to the conference room to chair his meeting. The events about to take place in Rome would require all his time and attention. But to be effective, he had to keep up his image. Prince Albert had little choice.

CHAPTER 13

Capri to Positano, Italy

THE FERRYBOAT LEFT CAPRI AND SPED toward Positano, parting the calm, deep-blue waters. It was a beautiful day, and she stood in the stern of the boat, letting the wind play with her long black hair. She had undone the ponytail to allow her hair to flow more easily. The short, white summer dress she wore accentuated her beautiful body. She had put her small, elegant traveling bag next to her feet. She looked back at the island; she did not want to leave. She loved Capri, and she loved all the days she was now leaving behind. As tears formed in her eyes, she prayed that the memories would never leave her—and she promised she would come back.

When the boat docked, Nicole quickly walked toward the small parking lot at the base of the hill in the small town of Positano. She identified herself to the heavyset Italian man who handled the automobile rentals. He took her driver's license and credit card and walked into his small office at the bottom of the garage. Fifteen minutes later, he emerged with papers and keys in his hands. She signed what she had to. Margaret Nash was renting a silver Alfa Romeo. The fat man at the rental agency handed her the keys and asked whether she needed directions. She smiled and told him she needed none. The man watched as she raised her short skirt to enter the car. She put the manual shift lever into first gear and entered the road. She winked at the man as she left. He stood frozen, clearly not knowing how to react.

Rome, Italy

The maitre d' at Via della Lupa immediately recognized the man from the Vatican. He bowed slightly as he welcomed him to the restaurant, quickly leading him to the room's far corner. Adam was sitting at a table there.

Carlo, the young man from the Vatican, did not wear the cloth of the church. Instead, he wore an elegant, dark-gray, pin-striped suit, a white shirt, and a dark-blue tie. As he approached, Adam rose. Carlo was tall, almost six feet. He had jet-black hair, thick black eyebrows, thin lips, straight white teeth, and a warm smile—the looks of a movie star. He smiled and extended his right hand in greeting. Adam took his hand. The grip was firm.

The two men took their seats and began a cordial conversation: How was your flight? Did you enjoy the drive? Did the hotel meet all your needs? The young man then called the waiter. They did not need to study the menu. Adam knew the dishes he was going to ask for. Adam asked for the bean soup and the liver with onions.

"You must have eaten here before," the man from the Vatican said. "You ordered the best dishes, all my favorites." Carlo said to the waiter, "I will have the same. And bring us a bottle of my friend's favorite white wine, Santa Margherita, Pinot Grigio."

Well, the Vatican had done its homework. They even knew the wine he liked, Adam thought with a smile. He was very anxious to find out what else they knew. But it would not happen today. The young man from the Vatican spoke to him as a new acquaintance would. He asked about Adam's background. He talked about his own. They talked about sports, movies, and briefly about politics. They even talked about girls. This surprised Adam, though he did not know why. The young man was an excellent conversationalist and a great listener as well. The food was outstanding. Adam was enjoying himself. He liked the man the Vatican had sent.

But Adam was also a professional and knew this was no casual meal. He knew the man facing him had not been sent to make idle conversation. The young priest had been sent to evaluate the man whom the Vatican was about to ask to join them in their quest. The young man held a PhD in psychology; he was even a psychiatrist. He would never let anyone know. All he showed Adam was that he was an emissary sent by the Vatican, a host to make sure Adam was comfortable in the city of the pontiff, the bishop of Rome. Neither man ordered dessert. Both men were fit and always watched their diets. Sure, occasionally, they splurged, but not today. They both asked for an espresso.

The young priest sipped the hot coffee and looked up at the man whom his Holy Father, the bishop of Rome, had chosen. He smiled. He had never understood how the pope always chose the right people. Today, Carlo had been sent to make sure, and again, the bishop of Rome had made the right choice. Once more, he had followed the light, the path only God knew, without reservation— the path of Jesus Christ, which the Father in heaven had paved for all humanity to follow to eternal life.

"I had a wonderful meal," Carlo said with a smile. "I also enjoyed your company very much. I always like making new friends. I hope to see you again."

"I, too," Adam responded. He enjoyed the meal. The food had been excellent, and he liked the young man from the Vatican. But

Adam had expected more. He had not come from Miami to have a delicious meal with an emissary from the Vatican. In fact, he had expected to meet the pope himself. Still, he did not know what was going on. He had not seen the game and had to find out more.

But he was not sure how much he still cared. He remembered Capri, remembered her, and wanted to go there to be with her. His thoughts confused him. He needed time to think. That was when the young man from the Vatican handed him an envelope as they left the restaurant.

"I want you to know I came here to make sure," the pontiff's man said. "The Holy Father does not want to make a mistake. He always wants to be sure. That is why he sends me. I am not a psychologist or a shrink. I know people. The pope trusts my judgment. I enjoyed our lunch. God be with you."

The man shook his hand, smiled, turned, and walked away. Adam was surprised, not by the events of the day but by the fact that the eighty-plus-year-old bishop of Rome, the man who ran the Catholic Church and was revered by millions of believers, trusted the judgment of such a young priest.

Adam opened the envelope as he sat back in the taxi, taking him back to his hotel. The envelope contained a small piece of paper—no message, no address, only a phone number. Adam recognized the number at once. It was the same number in the envelope the concierge at the Adlon Hotel in Berlin had given him.

The two men the Mossad had assigned to follow Adam Bergman sat in a small sidewalk café off the Piazza Nicosia. They were both sipping on a glass of Pinot Grigio. The assignment had been easy.

They had been told to follow the man and make it look good. Then let him lose you. They had done precisely that. They were sure that Adam Bergman thought he had outwitted them.

The Mossad paid Carlo, the young priest who had earned the trust of the Holy Father, handsomely. The cleric lived beyond his means. He took many weekend trips and stayed at expensive hotels. Berlin was one of his favorite destinations. The Mossad knew he had a lover there. They did not yet know who it was, but they would find out that it was certain. No matter. They would pay him if the information kept flowing.

Adam returned to his hotel suite to make the phone call he had been anxious to place. He let the phone ring many times. When there was no answer, he hung up and felt dismayed. Why was there no answer? What was going on?

He thought he had done everything correctly and had been careful with his plans. He had not wanted to appear too anxious. But he had been too casual, he thought. Immediately, he dismissed that idea. No, he had done it the right way. He had courted her, not just to the best of his ability but with passion. He had courted her from the heart. Why did she not pick up the phone in his apartment on Capri? After all, they had become lovers. They had shared intimate thoughts. For a few hours, they had become one. Their lovemaking had been tender, giving, sharing. He had left her a note indicating that he would return soon, and he had been sure she would wait for him.

Obviously, he had been wrong. Had her sense of duty won out over his charm? He was disappointed. But he knew he would see her soon. After all, that was her job. Nicole Jefferson had been instructed to fall in love with him again.

CHAPTER 14

Lazio, Italy

THE SILVER ALFA ROMEO LEFT THE Amalfi coast and headed toward Rome. Nicole had lowered the black convertible top when she left the Positano rental agency. She loved the feel of the wind rushing past her, catching her hair, face, and imagination. When the wind engulfed her, it reminded her of her childhood—of sailing on the Great Lakes, the Bahamas, the Virgin Islands, and the Greater Antilles—and the vacations she had taken with her family.

Now she thought only of the last few days she had spent with him. All she recalled was his touch, his lips, his caress, his lovemaking. No other man had ever been so sensitive, gentle, or giving. No other man had ever understood her needs, her desires. No other man had ever wanted to know who she really was, the person deep down she did not even fully understand. Adam wanted to know it all. He cared. He wanted to know her, wanted to love her. He wanted them to be ones with no secrets.

Nicole had heavy feet. The sleek Alfa Romeo two-seater sped through the Lazio countryside. She loved to drive and speed. She laughed as she stroked back the strands of hair that caressed her face. She loved the sun and the wind. She also thought she loved

Adam. The days she had just spent with Adam on Capri were some of her life's best. They were meant for each other. She knew it was time before he would come to her. No, she did not know, but that was her wish.

While on Capri, they had had many conversations about politics and world peace. World peace was an obsession with Adam. He spoke to her as if it were his mission in life. Too often had they discussed the acts of what Adam now called the demons—the power people who only wanted to profit—and he had told her it included many world leaders. Each world leader had their agenda.

Adam felt strongly that peace in the Middle East was essential to peace on earth. He had also shared with Nicole his conviction that peace had to come through religion. He had talked to her about many of the world's political leaders—about their myopic views, their desire to be demagogues and control the world, and their lack of understanding when it came to religion.

And he had spoken to her about the president in office: a woman who lacked confidence, who had trouble making decisions, who was dishonest, who had no idea about the cause of the war in the Middle East. She was a president who insisted that the American way was the only way.

Nicole had listened to her lover, and he was right. She knew there were ways other than the American way. She also believed that the only way to make peace in the Middle East was to pay attention to religion. However, her agency, the CIA, thought differently. They believed that the United States should dominate all and rule the world.

Nicole was a true American. She loved her country, but she also knew when her country was wrong.

Nicole and Adam had had lengthy discussions about the Middle East and the war in Iraq. He did not believe in the current US policy, which he felt was at times too closely aligned with that of the Israelis. He also told her about the "Jews," the nickname the Iraqis had given the American soldiers. He believed a growing number of Arab Muslims perceived a new enemy, the JIA: "Jews, Israel, and America." Adam deeply believed in America and in Judaism. But he did not believe in JIA.

Often during these discussions, he had asked her to join him. Leave the CIA and the services of the US government, he had urged. They would make a perfect team, and they would be together. She did not dismiss the idea. She had become disappointed with the agency and her country's leadership.

Nicole believed in much of what Adam had said. Her country was clearly on the wrong course in the Middle East, and she felt the conflict was distracting the United States from other important foreign, domestic, and longer-range issues such as those in China. While her country was using many resources to try to bring peace to a region where peace was unknown, it ignored a sleeping giant awakening rapidly, a giant to be reckoned with. She knew the Middle East was essential to world peace. But China could be far more important. It was a matter of priority, and Nicole thought her country was not choosing the right ones.

The two lovers had also talked about their past, her upbringing, and his. She always pointed out how plain and simple her background was. Both her parents had been born in the United States. Her dad was of Italian origin, and her mother was Irish. Both were of the Catholic faith. She was fascinated that Adam had been raised as a Christian and a Jew.

He had told her about his past—his early years in Germany, attending church, and being raised a Christian. They had talked about the time. His family decided to move back to the United

States. His dad had authored several books on German history while teaching at the Freie Universität in Berlin and had become an authority on the subject. Soon he was offered the position to which he had always aspired. Stanford University had asked him to take the chair of history and be a tenured professor. Adam's parents had not taken long to decide. His mother knew this was the position for which her husband had worked extremely hard. She also wanted Adam to experience life in the country where his father was raised. And she was excited about living in California.

Adam told Nicole about his trip back to the United States. His parents had stopped in Miami to leave Adam with his grandma. Then his parents went to California to get the job his dad had worked so hard for, the position he had always wanted. Then there was the plane crash that had killed both of his parents and ended their dreams. Adam told Nicole how his grandmother raised him to believe in the Jewish faith. Once, as she and Adam lay naked in each other's arms overlooking the blue waters off the island of Capri, Nicole asked him what religion he believed in. He answered without hesitation: "In God. One God."

Most of all, Nicole wanted to be with her lover. Nicole had promised Adam she would consider his offer, but she wanted time to believe it. As Alfa Romeo entered the outskirts of Rome, Nicole decided to call Langley and resign from the CIA. She would join Adam. She left the Autostrada and drove directly to the Hassler Hotel at the Spanish Steps. She knew he would be there.

CHAPTER 15

Beirut, Lebanon

THEY, EMBRACED, HUGGED, AND KISSED. The young man had to lean down to kiss the other man. He did not mind. He remembered years ago when the older man had to pick him up to kiss and hug him. They had formed a special bond. The older man was more than just a grandfather to him. He did not just love him; he adored him. No, he worshipped his grandfather. One day, Ali prayed that he would be just like him. But he knew it could never be. His grandfather was the secretary-general of Hezbollah. He was their leader.

The young, slender man had received the message to come and meet with his grandfather only two days ago. Ali had finished his daily run on the track at Stanford University in California. He had walked into the men's locker room to take a shower. When he opened his locker, he saw the note. It was computer-generated in English. "Come see me, Grandpa." He and his grandfather had decided a couple of years ago, when the young athlete had enrolled at Stanford, to use this line of communication.

The secretary-general of Hezbollah did not want his grandson to be a target. He had hoped to keep his grandson out of the conflict in the Middle East. He had made that promise to himself after his son,

Ali's father, had died on a mission he had sent him on. Never again, he had pledged, would he ask another family member to be placed in harm's way. Today, he knew he could never abide by his pledge. He had to follow Allah's wishes.

Both men stood in the cool underground cave in South Beirut. The older man still had his hands around his grandson and did not want to let go.

"Son," he said in a husky, emotional voice, "I did not want to call on you. I did not want you to be involved. I know you are training for the Olympics. I am terribly sorry. But Allah needs you." The older man looked directly into the green eyes his grandson had inherited from his American, Californian mother.

"Grandpa," he replied. "I love you, and I love Allah. I will do whatever you think is right. I will always follow you, and I will always follow Allah."

The older man picked up his cane and walked to his large desk in front of the fireplace he could never use. He sat down in his leather Polo chair. As he did, he looked around the large room. He saw all the candles, giving the light he loved so much. He saw all the luxurious rugs, the expensive furnishings. He saw all the wealth of his country. He knew they all wanted his wealth. They all wanted his oil, the vast offshore oil and gas reserves close to his country's shoreline.

"Ali," he said, pointing to one of the chairs flanking the mahogany desk, "please sit down. I know you are tired. You have traveled long and not had much sleep. Ali, do you know why you and I must meet in a cave? Do you know why we are at war? Do you know what we are fighting for?"

"Grandpa, we are fighting for Allah."

"Son, you are right. We believe in Allah, our God, in one God. But so do our enemies. They also believe in one God. They believe in all the messengers we believe in. The Christians believe Jesus Christ was the final messenger. We think it was Muhammad. Does it matter if we all believe in one God?"

"No, it does not matter. Grandpa, where are you going with all this? Have you completely changed your mind? I always thought you believed that we had to kill all the infidels. That is what you have always insisted on."

"I have not changed my mind. All infidels must die. But we must gain their trust by telling them that belief in one God is all that matters, that it is the basis of peace. Once we have gained their trust and convinced them that we want peace, we strike. Only then will we have gained the advantage we need. I received an invitation. The Holy Father of the Catholic Church wants me to come to the Vatican. He has invited all the church leaders. He believes religion is the only way to make peace in the Middle East. And I agreed."

"But Grandpa, how do the world powers feel about being left out?" "Well, they don't like it," the old man replied. "Particularly the president of the United States. She knows nothing about God, about faith. But I do not need to tell you how perverted US society is. It reminds me of ancient Rome. You may recall that they, too, tried to conquer us. They failed. As you know, true peace will only come. when all the *kafirs,* the nonbelievers, have died.

"Son, I have asked you to come here and join me because I need your help. Soon, I will be at the Vatican to bring the Trojan horse and to let all believe we want to make this peace. I know everyone will watch my trip. Many parties will never want to see me reach the Vatican, and not just people from the outside. Many of us own people, the Muslims, do not want me in Rome, for they do not know my true agenda. I need protection. I need someone I can trust. I need someone of my own blood. I need you."

"Grandfather, I will be there for you. You are the leader of our people. Many will die for you. You need to have no fear. Allah will protect you."

"I know," the old man responded as he put both arms on the large desk and sighed. "I know. Still, I like to know you are behind me, just in case."

"Grandpa, I will not go back to the United States. I will stop my training. I will not compete in the Olympics. I will assemble a team to protect you so you can fulfill Allah's wishes. This is my wish too. It is why I was born: to help you, to help Allah."

The older man was silent. Tears were forming in his dark-brown eyes—the tears of Allah.

Ali knew how to protect his grandfather, the secretary-general of Hezbollah. He had trained in the desert and learned all the methods of terrorism, and he knew how to fight. But he also knew that he could only use family and people he could trust to protect his grandfather. He would assemble the best team. They would all be family, cousins, and uncles. In the desert, bloodlines prevailed.

Ali had listened closely to his grandfather. All the religious leaders who believed in the prophet Abraham preached would meet in Rome. Each believed in only one God. Sure, they all believed in different prophets or the importance of each. To Ali, a man of a Christian mother and a Muslim father, the differences appeared to be trivial. He believed in only one God. And so did the Jews, the archenemy of the Arab world. Finally, they all would meet in Rome to make peace among the children of Abraham, a peace his people would use to win the war against all the infidels.

He admired his grandfather, and he loved the plan. He knew that killing all the infidels had to be done through deception, winning their trust, and bringing the war into their own ranks. Ali thought Jerusalem, not Rome, would have been the more appropriate city for the meeting. Well, it was only the first meeting. He felt sure there would be many more. But the final agreement had to be executed in Jerusalem. He knew his grandfather would insist on it.

Ali also knew the other church leaders—the pope, the chief rabbis of Israel, the grand ayatollahs of Iraq and Iran—had hired people to protect them. He decided to learn all about them. He wanted to get to know his adversaries.

Berlin, Germany

Heavy gray clouds covered the sky. It had not rained yet, but it soon would. Prince Albert von Hohenzollern sat behind his large desk at the Reichstag in Berlin. He hated these gloomy days. He loved sunshine, loved the beaches of Spain. Most of all, he loved being there with his lover, the young man at the Vatican.

Prince Albert thought his cousin, Prince William, the president of the European Union, had given him the job in the interior ministry because he knew about his lover. Prince William always wanted to know what the Vatican was up to. Unlike most modern politicians, who had ignored the Vatican and most of the other powerful religious institutions, the leader of the European Union had not. He was a student of history, and he understood the power of the church, the power of faith.

The short, bald man picked up the telephone. He pressed but one button. He did not have to dial a number to speak with his cousin, the president of Europe.

"Yes," was the immediate reply.

"He is in Rome. The girl is with him. Others are coming. The Arab went to see his grandfather. The CIA is sucking hind tit."

"I want to know all the details about the meeting at the Vatican. Why can't you find out?"

"I will. Give me some time."

"I need to know before the Americans do. Understand?" "No problem. They do not know what is going on."

Prince Albert placed the telephone into the receiver on his large desk. He stood and slowly paced through his office. He went to the large window and looked down on his city. Small raindrops had begun to fall lazily on the streets below. It was only drizzling. He loved to stand in his office and watch the weather change. Most of all, he loved to see a rainstorm move in, the gray clouds pushed by the wind, the trees first calm and then move with anticipation. He loved the smell of the fresh air. He loved change.

Prince Albert knew that his cousin, the president of the European Union, also liked change. But he did not like unanticipated change. He liked to be in control, always wanting to know everything before anyone else. Short, heavyset Albert knew that he had to call his lover at the Vatican to get the details his cousin had asked for. He knew he could not wait until they met again on one of their weekend excursions. He had to find out now what the Vatican was up to.

Brooklyn, New York

The rabbi walked slowly toward the old oak tree, a walk he took every day. His routine never changed. He wore black robes and he had a long gray beard and held the words of God and Moses in his right hand. It was a hot, humid day, and perspiration covered his face. When he reached the bench under the tree, he placed the book of

God next to him, reached into his black robe, and extracted a white, well-used handkerchief.

He wiped his forehead and looked at him. The small park in the Garden Heights of Brooklyn was almost empty. It usually was this time of the day, midday. He always came here during the day's heat because no one else would be in the park, and he liked solitude. All would seek sanctuary in their air-conditioned homes. His home had no such comforts. His small loft was on the top floor of a five-story building, and his large ceiling fan hummed day and night.

The rabbi turned and picked up God's book. He randomly opened a page as he always did. He never left a bookmark to remind him of what he had read last. It did not matter because he knew all the words. He had read the book for more than fifty years. Yet each day the words had new life, new meaning. The book, he thought, was always alive.

Suddenly, he felt a vibration next to his thigh—his cell phone. Earlier, the old rabbi had been to the synagogue and had turned off the ring mode. He put down the book and fumbled with his black robe, for he did not remember which pocket his phone was in. He looked like he was having convulsions as he urgently tried to locate the phone. Fortunately, the park was empty. No one saw the old rabbi struggling with himself. He retrieved the phone before its last ring and pushed the talk button.

"Your brother-in-law needs to talk to you."

There was an audible click—there was no chance to respond. The rabbi checked his cell phone to see if the number was recorded. It was not. Slowly, he put the phone back into one of the many deep pockets of his black robe—after he had changed the setting of the phone to ring. He was not sure what to make of the phone call. Only a few days ago, he had received another long-distance call, and when he had returned the call, there had been no answer.

The old rabbi had not spoken to his brother-in-law in many years. It was more than forty years ago when his sister married the man. The two men had never liked each other. It was not a matter of religion, because both were Ashkenazi Jews. Both of their families had their roots in Germany. It was all about his sister, the rabbi's twin. He now knew that it was his own fault. He had always wanted to be with her, never to let her go. They had grown up as one. When their parents had died in an accident, the two of them were only eleven years old. They had lived in a foster home and pledged never to leave each other. When she was nineteen, her new husband had taken her away. He would never forget that moment. And he would never forgive his brother-in-law.

The old rabbi thought about it, thought about returning the telephone call. He really did not want to talk to the man who had taken his twin away from him. But it had been over forty years, and he had not had the opportunity to get even. His God was now showing him the way. After more than forty years, it was time to get even!

The rabbi stood and picked up God's book from the old wooden bench under the large oak tree. He decided to call his brother-in-law but would not use his cell phone. The public phone booth was only fifty yards away. It was located at the entrance to the park, straight down the paved walkway. He never used the paved walkway. Today, he walked straight toward the entrance to the public telephone. Today, he used the paved walkway. Today, he was on a mission.

He picked up the black receiver in the old glass booth. Graffiti covered each glass pane, but he did not see it. His eyes were focused as he dialed the number. A recorded message responded.

"Take a limousine to JFK airport. Go to the El Al Israeli Airlines counter and pick up your ticket. All has been arranged. You will be in Tel Aviv soon. Your sister will meet you."

CHAPTER 16

JFK Airport, New York City

THE MAN WAS READING *TIME* MAGAZINE. His attention was focused on the Vatican. The article's author had been to the Vatican, and he wanted to know whether there was any truth to the rumors that the pope had initiated a plan for peace in the Middle East. The man was oblivious to his surroundings, or so it seemed as he leaned back in his chair in the first-class waiting lounge of El Al Israeli Airlines at JFK airport. But the man noticed all. He was a professional, a *katza*, an officer of the Mossad, Israel's intelligence agency.

The katza put down the magazine and stood to straighten his gray slacks and brush off the crumbs of the Pringles he had been munching on. He tucked the dark-blue polo shirt back into his trousers. Then he briefly ran his right hand over his shortly cropped black hair. He never looked at the man he had been assigned to bring back to Israel, yet the old rabbi never left his peripheral field of vision.

His boss, Maza, the head of the Mossad, had sent him to Brooklyn to find the old rabbi. The rabbi was family, Maza had instructed his katza, the twin brother of his wife. But the rabbi had not communicated with him or his sister for over forty years. The rift had started long ago when Maza had first begun to date the rabbi's sister. Siblings had been close, growing up in an orphanage after both parents were killed in a car accident. When Maza had taken her away to Israel, the rabbi had pledged never to forgive him, to cut all ties, and to love his sister in his daily prayers.

But now the head of the Mossad wanted to talk to the rabbi, his brother-in-law, to learn more about the American the Vatican had sent for—the old rabbi's adopted grandson. The katza had arrived in the United States with instructions to bring the rabbi to the Hadar Dafna building in Tel Aviv, the headquarters of the Mossad.

The katza smiled. He did not have to coerce the old rabbi to accompany him to Israel. The man was going there of his own free will.

Langley, Virginia

William Davis, the DCI, put down the telephone receiver in surprise. He had not anticipated this. He should have. That was where the agency needed help. They needed to understand their people and their motivation. From now on, he will make it a top priority. But he also knew he should not have been so complacent. His people were the best, trained to protect their country. But his people also needed to be better informed. They had every right to understand the reasons. He knew that they had only been told to follow orders in the past. He would change this and make sure they always understood why. The DCI, the director of central intelligence, did not want to lose another officer. He had not wanted to lose Jefferson.

William knew that his boss, President Drew, had a keen interest in the affairs of the Vatican. His boss wanted to be center stage regarding peace in the Middle East. The president had decided to She would make peace in the Middle East with her legacy. She would not let any other leader get in her way and would use all the power she had at her disposal. William knew he was only one of the president's many resources, but he was determined to be the one to make the difference. He would ensure the president got what she wanted, no matter the price.

The DCI knew that Nicole Jefferson had been his best bet to stay close to the man the Vatican had sent for. He also knew that the Vatican was the key to peace. Now he had lost Jefferson, the woman who knew Adam Bergman well. The DCI needed to replace Jefferson with someone who could get close to Bergman. His instincts told him it should be a woman. He sensed that Adam Bergman had a weakness. He did not feel it; he had thoroughly studied the agency's dossier on the man. The CIA knew all about the man. After all, he had worked for them—or the National Security Agency. Still, he had worked for the exact cause, the same government.

Bergman had made a few mistakes in his career, or only one. But he had shown vulnerability. Although he was a trained killer, he had a soft spot for beautiful women. It had only gotten him into trouble once, on a mission in South America. There, he had narrowly escaped disaster. Now he had obviously fallen for Jefferson. The DCI needed to replace her quickly. He needed someone like her: a trained, attractive female agent who knew the ways of Adam Bergman.

Since the DCI had studied Adam's file, he especially remembered Adam's last assignment, when he had worked as a double agent, infiltrated the Mossad, and prevented the assassination of the president of the United States in Berlin. William vaguely remembered that another woman had been involved, not one who worked for him, but as a friend. He picked up the white telephone on his large mahogany desk. "I need to see the Adam Bergman file as soon as possible. Send it."

A few minutes later, he looked at the file on his computer. Yes, he had been right. The Israelis had used a beautiful woman to work with Adam on his last assignment. In that game, she had been his fiancée, and Adam had become infatuated with her. Her name was Lisa.

Tel Aviv, Israel

The phone rang only once. It always did on his private number. He either answered it, or there was a voice message. Maza Sharef did not believe in wasting time—his or anyone else's. Maza picked up the black receiver of his telephone as he stood in front of his small desk in his office at the headquarters of Israel's intelligence agency. He was naked, and water was dripping from his muscular body. Although he would celebrate his sixtieth birthday next year, he looked much younger. It was not only his regular and strenuous daily workout routines but also his diet that kept him young.

The phone rang as he exited his shower. He had picked up the receiver seconds before his recorded message could kick in.

"Yes," he said. "What's up?"

The operator at the switchboard of Mossad's headquarters in Tel Aviv had already traced the call.

"The call is from the director of intelligence in the United States. Should I put him through? Should I follow the procedure?"

"Of course, do both," Maza responded, slightly annoyed by the operator's question. The following procedure meant recording the conversation. Later, it would be dissected. There would be analyses of the voice, tone, and inflections to determine if it was the DCI. The recording would be studied for many hours.

"Maza, how are you? I have not heard from you in weeks. What are you up to?"

"William, nothing much ever happens here in the Middle East. All is as usual."

Both laughed aloud.

"Well, I knew it. That is why I called you. You need to get more involved. You need more action. You need to expand your horizons."

"Thanks, William. Not interested. Right now, my horizon is all. I can handle."

The DCI hesitated. "Maza, I need a favor. It involves the Vatican. I am sure you have been on top of this."

"No," the man from Israel lied. "What are you talking about?"

"Well, we are not sure. The pope intends to go out on his own to make peace in the Middle East. He wants to keep us out, and obviously, you as well. He wants to make this a religious peace among the Jews, Christians, and Muslims. My boss, the president, does not like it. She wants to be involved and head this peace initiative.

"How can I help?"

"The pope hired a man we believe will play a pivotal role. You may know him. You once trained the guy. Bergman—Adam Bergman—is his name. Regardless, we had one of our best agents on his tail, but we lost her. We need someone else. He has a weakness. He is soft when it comes to beautiful women."

"Why did you call me? I am sure there are thousands of beautiful women in the US. I have been to South Beach."

"I don't need just any beautiful woman," the DCI continued. "I need a beautiful woman trained as an agent who knows the guy and has seen how he operates and thinks."

"You know this woman?"

"Yes, she is one of your agents. Her name is Lisa Petterson, and she worked with him on his last assignment. You need to know that

Bergman no longer works for the US government. He went out on his own."

"Okay," the man from Tel Aviv responded. "These are the terms. We work as a team. You will share all your information with us. The minute I find out you have screwed me, the woman quits and comes back home."

"I agree."

Both men ended the telephone conversation that no one else could listen to. The CIA had lost its edge and needed to return to the game.

The man in Tel Aviv smiled. The world's most powerful government had come to him for help, and they had an agreement. He would abide by it, but only by the letter of the agreement. Still smiling, he picked up his in-house telephone.

"Please ask Lisa to come to my office."

Rome, Italy

Adam put down the telephone receiver when there was no answer at his apartment in Capri. He was disappointed, but he knew he would see her soon. He knew her sense of duty would bring her back if all his charm and their lovemaking had failed. It was only a matter of time. Yet he felt unsure, and he did not know why. His reasoning was sound, but his heart was uncertain.

Adam was tired and hungry. This had been a difficult day. His meeting with the Vatican man had not been what he expected. And there had been no answer at his apartment on Capri. He decided to he would have an early dinner at a nearby restaurant, then return to his hotel and enjoy a good night's sleep.

"Please, a table for one at the Ranieri," he told the hotel's concierge. He hung up the phone. He had chosen this restaurant because it was a short walk from his hotel—and because of the *mignottes, alla Regina Vittoria*, veal with potatoes and an eight-cheese sauce.

Adam took a quick shower and dressed casually in a white Armani shirt, a blue Zegna blazer, beige Armani slacks, and dark- brown Gucci shoes. He also used his favorite cologne, Tabak. He hesitated as he stepped into the foyer of his suite. Then he put on his shoulder holster and placed the Beretta into it. He knew he would not need it but was also on a mission. The best intelligence agencies had trained him in the world. He would not make any mistakes. He would always follow the protocol ingrained in him at the best spy agencies in the world: the NSA and the Mossad. It was a beautiful evening in Rome, the city of eternal love. Adam strolled along *Via Condotti* toward the restaurant, which was located on *Via Mario de' Fiori*, a small side street. When he entered, he noticed the damask-covered walls, the crystal chandeliers, and the old paintings adorning the walls. The restaurant was crowded. There was much chatter, and Adam could hardly hear the maitre d' as he greeted him and asked for his reservation. The maitre d' smiled when. He heard the name. His demeanor changed, Adam thought.

Adam was now on full alert. He followed the man closely, walking only inches behind him as the man from the restaurant showed him to his table. He would be the shield if Adam needed one. Adam's right hand was already inside his jacket, touching the fabulous butt of his gun. That was when he saw her. She looked more beautiful than he remembered, than in his dreams. She looked like a gift from God. She wore a plain white dress. Her dark tan accentuated. Her beauty was breathtaking. Her black hair flowed freely down her shoulders, and her green-blue eyes sparkled. Adam fixed his eyes on her, and he knew he loved her.

When he reached her table, Nicole stood. She placed both arms around him and pulled his body close to her. She kissed him on the mouth. Their tongues met and caressed. He did not want to let go. He felt intoxicated and wanted to go on. Nicole slowly eased away from him. She kissed him lightly on his lips, his nose, his cheek.

"I missed you—missed you so much."

"I too," he whispered. "Never, ever leave me again." "I will not. Not until I die."

"I want you to be part of me. I want us to be one. I want to know you are always there for me. I want us to be a team."

"Adam, let's sit down and talk over dinner."

They both sat at the table in the remote corner of the restaurant. She had asked for privacy.

"How did you know I would be here tonight?" Adam asked.

"The CIA trained me. I know everything," she responded with a large smile.

"Nicole. Be serious."

"Okay, I got lucky. I knew you were staying at the Hassler. After all, that is your favorite hotel in Rome. When I approached the concierge's desk, you must have been on the phone with him. I heard him say, 'It is confirmed, Mr. Bergman. Six thirty at the Ranieri.' So here I am. But Adam, please order for me. Let me warn you, I am very hungry. I drove all day."

"No problem. We will have my favorite dish. You will love it." He called for the waiter and ordered a bottle of wine, an appetizer, a salad, and the veal.

"Adam," she said, "I resigned. I left the CIA."

"Great. Now we are a team. Nicole, this is the best decision you have ever made. We love each other. Now we can work as one. You just made me the happiest man on earth."

He leaned over and kissed her. The waiter approached their table and opened the bottle of Pinot Grigio that Adam had ordered. He filled their glasses and left.

"Adam," she said, "I must learn so much. I need to know about your new assignment. I need to learn all the details. I want to help. I want to be part of the team."

"Yes," he responded. "Tomorrow we will sit down and discuss every detail. I need you. I need your expertise. But not tonight. Enjoy dinner, return to the hotel, and make love."

"Making love with you always sounds good to me," she responded as her hand moved up his thigh.

CHAPTER 17

Vatican City, Italy

THE YOUNG PRIEST THOUGHT HE HAD handled Adam Bergman well, but he was not entirely sure. The man was hard to read. He was a professional. Carlo knew all about Adam. He had done his homework; he had to because that was his job.

He knew about Adam's upbringing. First, he had been raised as a Protestant and then as a Jew. He had been born in Berlin, Germany. His father was an American Jew; his mother was a devout German Protestant and Lutheran. When Adam was young, his family moved to the United States. There, he went to the best schools and earned an MBA from Harvard and a law degree from Yale. Adam was bright, but he was also an athlete.

The CIA had wanted him, but Adam had joined the NSA. He had also become a double agent working for the Mossad, but Israel's intelligence agency never knew. That was how good he was, and the young priest knew it. More importantly, the Holy Father knew, and he wanted Adam to be by his side. The pope had told the young priest that he wanted the man from the United States at all costs.

The negotiations had been short. Adam had outlined his terms, and it was clear he would not negotiate. Carlo, the young priest, had tried hard but to no avail. Adam had insisted on his terms, and the deal would go his way. He was to be paid thirty million Euros—fifteen to be deposited now in his Belgian account, and fifteen more when the job was done. The fee Adam had promised was all-inclusive. No matter how many he had to kill, the price was fixed.

Carlo had finally agreed. Fifteen million Euros had been wired to the Belgian bank account the next day. The balance of the money would be paid when the job was done, after the pope, the other religious leaders, the chief rabbis, and the grand ayatollahs met. The pope wanted to make sure the meeting would take place. He knew many intended to stop him—not just the many splinter groups of the Islamic terrorists, but also the right-wing Israelis and the Palestinians who believed that Israel had no right to exist.

Yet these were not his only enemies. The pope understood his more formidable enemies were the two Western world leaders, the presidents of the United States and the European Union. Each wanted to make peace in the Middle East for different reasons and had a different plan for achieving that peace.

The American president's motive, the pope thought, was based on ego, on America's compulsion to dominate, and Monica Drew was determined to make it the legacy of her presidency. Although America seemed to be making an effort to solve the conflict peacefully, the pope knew that eventually the United States would resort to force. After all, that was what America was good at; it was the American way to solve problems. But the pope was convinced that force would only result in a band-aid solution. It would not result in lasting peace. It never had. But bandage solutions were American policy regarding foreign affairs—something his young advisor, Carlo, had always pointed out.

Still, the pope could not ignore Monica Drew, the American president. She had power and military strength. She was the bully on the block, although like her predecessor, she had no clue about the actual cause of the conflict.

The actual threat, the pope was convinced, was the president of the European Union. He did not offer a bandage solution for peace in the Middle East. Instead, he challenged the very existence of religion, calling religion the cause of most wars—and indeed the war in the Middle East. Unlike any other statesperson, Prince William insisted he had the answer to lasting peace: remove the cause, and you end the war.

But the pope believed in his God, who had assured him that a meeting with all the religious leaders would result in peace. The Holy Father also knew he needed help to ensure the meeting would occur, and that expertise was not commonly available. That was why he had decided to send for Adam Bergman.

The bishop of Rome slowly got out of his chair on the balcony overlooking his city. He always spent time here watching the sun disappear in the west. This was when he reflected, preparing for final decisions on the many issues confronting him. By now, he had received the input of all his advisors. He had studied the data carefully. He always wanted to be alone to make the final decision— not alone, but with his God. His God, the Almighty, always gave him the answer.

The Mossad's two men assigned to the Bergman surveillance made a mistake. They knew that the young priest at the Vatican was on their payroll. He was to give them all the information about the man the Vatican had sent for, but the head of the Mossad had instructed them not to follow Adam Bergman, to stay out of sight. That was why they had abandoned the car surveillance and driven straight to Rome. The

Mossad men had been told that Bergman would be there soon and would check into the Hassler Hotel. However, when Adam did not arrive in the city after two days, they became impatient and decided to resume direct surveillance. Upon Adam's arrival at the Hassler Hotel, the Mossad men learned he had made a dinner reservation for two at the Ranieri restaurant that night. They did not know who his dinner partner would be, but they intended to find out. That was a mistake that almost cost them their lives.

Adam Bergman noticed both Mossad men as soon as he entered the restaurant. He could pick them out a mile away. Yes, they were the best, but they had trained him. He knew their methods and their looks. He knew all he had to know. The two Mossad men sat at separate tables, each accompanied by a beautiful woman. A costly night for Israel's intelligence agency, Adam thought with a smirk as he made his way to his table.

The phone call was brief. The young priest Carlo had left Vatican City and gone to a public telephone near Ponte Sant'Angelo, the ancient bridge that crossed the Tiber River. He called his lover in Berlin to let him know he now had more information and details his lover had asked for. Carlo told Prince Albert that the pope wanted the American to protect him. Yes, the Holy Father was well protected, particularly within Vatican City. But the bishop of Rome had realized that this was a different game. Too many influential people wanted to stop him from making peace in the Middle East. The pope had told the young priest that the only way to prevail was to use his enemies' methods. That was why he needed one of the enemies' best.

Prince Albert, the minister from Berlin, wanted more. He needed names, places, dates, and information that the young priest in Rome had no access to. When the man from Rome assured him that he would convey all the details and data as soon as he received them, Berlin's minister was satisfied. He trusted his lover. He was sure he would never betray him. Then Albert told Carlo how much he missed him—his smile, touch, and lovemaking. He told him he could not wait much longer. He wanted to meet him this weekend at his cousin's home in Mallorca. The two had spent memorable days there in the past. Carlo immediately agreed. He would be there on Friday before sunset.

"I wish it were today," the heavyset German noble said. "Me too." Then there was a click, and the phone went silent.

JFK Airport, New York City

The old rabbi sat in the first-class El Al Israeli Airlines lounge at JFK Airport in New York City. He wore his usual attire: dark pants, white buttoned shirt, short suit, tie, black hat, and his *tallit*, the Jewish prayer shawl with the *tzitzit*, specially knotted tassels attached to the four corners. He clung closely to the small bag he had brought. It was a carry-on, yet it contained all his belongings except the Bible. That book he held in his right hand as he nervously looked at him.

He had never traveled. He had taken the subway a few times to Manhattan, the Lower East Side, or Midtown, but he had never gone to the Bronx or Yonkers. On a few occasions, he had visited Queens, primarily for bar mitzvahs. He loved his Brooklyn Heights home and never wanted to leave. He never thought he would get into an airplane to fly to Israel.

But he loved his twin sister, who had married the man now head of the Mossad. He did not know the man well, for they had met only shortly at his sister's wedding. Then he had not liked the man but decided not to pass premature judgment. But his gut had told him that his first impression was correct. It had been said to him that this man would be in trouble one day. *Why am I going to Israel?* he wondered. *Why me? Why does my powerful brother-in-law want me to come—me, an old rabbi from Brooklyn?*

When the announcement was made for all first-class passengers to board the plane, he did not react. An attractive blonde flight attendant approached him with a smile. "Please, follow me," she said reassuringly.

The flight attendant showed him to his window seat in the first-class cabin and asked him to let her put his small case in the overhead compartment. He refused and held on tight. There was no way he was about to let go of all he owned. The rabbi placed the small suitcase between his legs and the Bible in his lap. Small beads of perspiration were forming on his head, perspiration caused by anxiety and the unknown.

The old rabbi did not notice the man who sat in the seat behind him. That man did not perspire. He had traveled more than just on New York subways. He had been to Yonkers and the Bronx, Tokyo, Rio, Tehran, Beijing and other places. He had been everywhere his government wanted him to be. His job was to follow the rabbi and bring him to his boss in Tel Aviv.

Rome, Italy

Adam needed to know if Nicole could be his partner. The CIA had trained her, so she had all the qualifications. But could she? Kill in cold blood? He had to find out as soon as possible, and tonight he had the perfect opportunity.

As soon as he had joined Nicole at their table at Ranieri's restaurant, he had kissed her lightly and whispered into her ear. "Nicole, I am being followed."

"I know," she said. "Two guys, Mossad, each with an expensive hooker."

"You're right." He now knew that she was the person he wanted to cover his ass. "Let's take them out."

"Why?" she said. "They will only send someone else. I think we should ignore them; pretend we do not notice. Besides, I want to go back to your suite and make love. Peace in the Middle East can wait one night.

He knew she was right. But he also knew he had to find out if she could kill.

South Beirut, Lebanon

Ali Muhammad Nasral left the comfortable bunker where he had met with his grandfather, the secretary-general of Hezbollah. Ali understood what was at stake. He would not disappoint the man he had adored all his life. He was ready to devote all his energy and life to his loved one. And he understood that his grandfather always followed Allah's will.

Ali was an educated man. He had received his undergraduate degree from Stanford and had been completing his graduate studies there when his grandfather had summoned him. Ever since he was a child, he had thought about religion. His mother was Catholic, his father a Muslim. Their different nationalities had never mattered much to him; his mother was an American, his dad Lebanese. To him, it did no matter what countries his parents were born in. What *did* matter to him was their beliefs. He loved his mother, and he respected her belief in Catholicism. But he believed in the faith of Islam. He always had. He did not know why. He thought it was because of his grandfather. When he was young, he only visited him a few times. Those were always the most exciting times of his young life, the mystique of the luxurious bunker, the servants, all the people revering in his grandpa. Even as a child, he had always wanted to be like him.

As Ali grew older, he and his grandpa had many long conversations. His grandfather had told him to read all the books of the children of Abraham to understand the Christians, the Jews, and the Muslims. He wanted his grandson to come to know why Allah was his God. He wanted him to make his own decision. His faith was so strong that he was convinced his grandson would choose Allah. And he had been right. His grandson had become a devout Muslim, and Ali had decided to fight for his faith. He had gone into the desert to learn to be a terrorist. He had learned to shoot any weapon, make bombs, and kill all the infidels.

Although Ali had learned all the methods of killing, he was not convinced that war was the way to make peace in the Middle East. He understood that peace in the Middle East was essential to the plan that his grandfather and some of the other Muslim leaders had designed to annihilate Israel and establish a caliphate that would once more be a world power.

Then the pope called and asked all religious leaders to meet in Rome to make peace in the Middle East. It was just as his grandfather had predicted. It all was going according to his grandfather's plan— Allah's. Ali smiled. Allah would once again triumph. Ali would take care of the nuances and prevent any flies in the ointment. He would take care of the man the pope had sent for.

CHAPTER 18

Rome, Italy

THE YOUNG, BEAUTIFUL WOMAN WAS STANDING in the aisle of the Swiss Air first- class cabin, flight 1754, had just arrived at Rome's Fiumicino Airport from Geneva. Lisa Petterson did not carry much luggage, only a small carry-on, which she had stored in the overhead compartment. The kind, older man who had sat next to her had helped her to retrieve it from the small compartment above her seat. A smile was all she needed to thank the man, a smile from a beautiful woman.

She ran her hand through her long blonde hair and then turned on her cell phone. When the jet's doors opened, she walked quickly out of the plane and down the long terminal. She followed the signs indicating public transportation. She ignored the baggage claim signs, for she had carried all her belongings. She was a commuter who regularly traveled from Geneva to Rome. But she had taken a much more complicated route, a trip that had been carefully planned, which had taken her to Berlin and then to London. There she had spent several days. Lisa had taken the train to Paris from London, and then she had driven a rented car to Geneva. At each of her stops, she met with business partners. She was an investment banker, or so surely seemed.

As Lisa left the terminal of Rome's Fiumicino Airport and stepped onto the curb just behind the taxi stand, a small Alfa Romeo sedan pulled up next to her. The driver reached across the seat to open the passenger door. Lisa flung her carry-on into the back of the car and sat in the passenger seat. The car had hardly stopped. Now it left the airport in haste and headed into Rome. Lisa and the driver did not say a word. When they left the Autostrada and entered the town, the driver pulled over. A black Mercedes limousine pulled in front of them. Lisa retrieved her Gucci carry-on, stepped out of the Alfa, and entered the Mercedes. The limousine drove directly to her destination, the Hassler Hotel at the Spanish Steps of Rome. Lisa knew this was where she would find him.

The White House, Washington, DC

Monica Drew, the president of the United States, sat in her office alone. It was late, just before midnight. She sat there often late at night, and this was when she reflected and planned. President Monica Drew always thought the Oval Office was the place to make decisions, and many of her predecessors had done so.

Tonight, she felt ill at ease. She knew about the pope's initiative to make peace in the Middle East, as her DCI had brought her up to speed. She had learned about the role of religion in the war, about the Sunnis, the Shiites, and the many terrorist groups. She knew the EU was involved but did not know how much. She had been told about the man the pope had sent for, who had once been one of their own.

Monica Drew's DCI had also informed her about the woman that he and the Israelis had decided to send into the midst. Yes, she thought, it truly was a chaotic situation, one without a leader—a The

Moment she could cease to assume that role. It was the moment she had waited for all her political life.

President Drew's advisors informed her that the world's religious leaders were convinced peace in the Middle East was spiritual. Each of Abraham's religions—the Jews, the Muslims, and the Christians—believed that only their leaders knew how to make peace. They were convinced that peace had to come through religion. Like her predecessor, President Drew had no clue about the real cause of the conflict, and she did not care. All she cared about was getting credit for making peace in the Middle East—it would be the legacy of her presidency—even if the peace only lasted long enough to make it her legacy.

Monica Drew had watched her predecessor trying to manage the conflict. He had negotiated, set red lines he never enforced, underestimated his opponents, called ISIL a JV team, and never listened, even to his closest advisors. He had been arrogant and aloof, alienating his closest allies, spying on them, and never formulating a strategy to deal with the war in the Middle East. But Monica Drew knew America had the firepower. She would put American boots on the ground if push came to shove. Only she could force peace in the Middle East.

Berlin, Germany

More than three thousand miles to the east, another man sat in his prestigious office. He, too, was concerned about the role he would play in the battle for peace in the Middle East. He, too, was the president of a world power, a power that was challenging the United States. Prince William von Hohenzollern, the president of the EU, had no interest in establishing a legacy. He wanted peace—not a bandage peace, but a peace everlasting. To establish that peace requires bold action. It required the elimination of the very cause of the conflict.

The president of the European Union got out of the antique swivel chair behind his desk. He stood behind the chair and gently ran his hand across the back. He reminded himself that other leaders had sat in this chair, and some of them had been forebears who preferred war to peaceful negotiations to satisfy their goals. But Prince William was different. He believed in peaceful negotiations, tolerance, and self-determination. He thought no one had the right to force his will upon another, no matter how right one thought he was.

Prince William walked toward the large window of his office and looked over the city from which he now ruled the European Union, where he had been born. As he looked over the sunlit skyline of Berlin, he again wondered why the US president and the American people did not understand his people, the Europeans. In a way, they were all family. Most of the American ancestors had come from the continent. He knew it did not matter. America had grown to be too strong, too independent. With that position came arrogance. To Americans, there was only one way: the American way. Had they already forgotten the way the British had treated them? Had they forgotten that arrogance?

He ran his hand through his full black hair. He had always thought that trying to make peace in the Middle East through war was a mistake. His predecessor and his contemporary leaders in Europe had agreed. For that, America had admonished them. He recalled watching American television and ignorant commentators calling the French and his fellow citizens cowards and traitors. They had a different opinion because they did not believe in war. They did not believe in forcing their will, their ideals, or their beliefs on other people. He mused that America had come a long way since 1776—one hundred and eighty degrees.

History has finally impacted Europe. Prince William recalled another man who had tried to force his will not long ago. Europe had been determined not to let it happen again—not from anywhere else, including 100 Pennsylvania Avenue.

Prince William fumbled with his bow tie. He always tied himself but was never satisfied with the results. He wore a black tuxedo for the opening of the Berlin Opera season. A reception was to be held at Schloss Bellevue. He had invited his good friends, the leaders of France and Spain. After the reception, they would enjoy The Marriage of Figaro at Staatsoper.

The prince had always thought the US president did not understand the fundamental issues involved in the Middle East. Publicly, the American leader was a religious woman, attending church regularly. Yet the president knew little about religion. She knew little about history or other parts of the world and their beliefs, needs, hopes, and dreams. She thought it all should be the way it was where she had grown up—like America.

The EU president did not mind that the Americans disagreed with him about waging war to force their will and interests to extend their imperialism and control all. But he knew this was not the right way. Many leaders in the past had tried force, and all had failed. Europe did not want any part in this or any other war. Europe had experienced too many wars and knew that this war would fail. Yes, there was no doubt that some victories would be won on the battlefield, for the Americans had all the firepower. But victory lay in the hearts of the citizens. America would never win that war. Europe had seen it. Europe had fought many wars on its soil. Europe knew.

He looked at his watch. He had to leave his office. He could not be late for the cocktail party at Schloss Bellevue. He never made a friend wait.

Rome, Italy

Adam Bergman stood in the lobby of the Hassler Hotel. It was early, 7:00 a.m. Today, he could not follow his daily routine. His morning run had to come later. Nicole was still asleep in his bed in the luxurious suite. He smiled as he recalled the evening and their lovemaking. She was the best he had ever experienced and had known many. Nicole was different. No, he thought he was different. He felt differently than he had felt at any other time. That was why it all felt special, like never before. He wanted to always be with her. Standing in the lobby waiting for his car, he already missed her. He wanted to go back to his suite to be with her.

"Mr. Bergman," the valet said as he approached Adam. "Your car is parked at the entrance. The keys are in it."

"Thank you," Adam replied, handing the young man a generous tip.

"Gracie."

Adam walked out the door and headed for his car. That was when he noticed her: a beautiful blonde woman about to get into a yellow Ferrari parked in front of Adam's car. As he approached, she turned. She had just opened the door to the driver's seat of her automobile.

"Adam, Adam Bergman!" Lisa Petterson shouted. "What a surprise. Remember me? We once worked together in Berlin."

Adam recognized her at once. How could he ever forget? On his last assignment, she had been his fiancée. Then the action had been fast and furious. He had never had the time to get to know the person to whom he was engaged. He knew she was Israeli and that she worked for the Mossad.

"Lisa," he replied, "of course I remember. How could I ever forget?" Now she had decided not to enter her car. Lisa shut the door of the Ferrari and walked briskly toward him. She smiled. Her long blonde hair flowed freely over her shoulders. She wore a short, navy-blue skirt and a white sweater. The short skirt showed most of her shapely legs, and the white sweater emphasized her beautiful breasts. There was no makeup covering her face, and no need. She had full red lips, blue eyes, and long, dark eyelashes. Her smile was seductive and confident. "Adam," she said as she approached him, "I have thought of you often since Berlin, our last assignment together. How have you been? I have heard so many rumors and stories about you. I want to know which ones are true."

"Lisa, let us stop the bullshit. I have an appointment to keep. I know you are here on assignment. Beautiful women do not just leave Ferraris to say hello to me. Tell me what is up. Tell me what you want to know."

"You are right. I am on assignment. I think you will find the players interesting. We need to spend some time together. How about dinner tonight?"

"It works for me. Eight o'clock at the Ranieri."

"Eight o'clock." She smiled as she stepped close to him. She kissed him on the mouth.

Adam did not want to be late for his appointment. He knew he had to be there on time. The freighter from South Africa was due to arrive at 9:00 a.m. in the harbor of Rome. Adam's package would not be required. The use of any of the many cranes at the waterfront.

His small package would easily fit into the trunk of his rented S550 Mercedes. Adam had to board the ship and meet the captain to get his package. He had only paid a deposit when he struck the Miami Beach deal. The deposit had been half of the fare: ten thousand dollars in cash, half at the bar in South Beach, half in Rome a few weeks later.

The Ranieri restaurant was crowded. Adam had called ahead and asked for his favorite table, a table tucked in a corner of the restaurant. It was near the kitchen. He realized there would be more traffic and a little more noise. But in his business, both helped. And there was the other exit, the exit through the kitchen.

Adam had just sat down, his back against the kitchen wall, when Lisa entered the restaurant. All heads turned. She was beautiful. She wore a loose pantsuit that hid the beauty of her body. Everyone was staring at her face. She had the looks of a movie star.

When Lisa reached the table, he exited his chair and leaned toward her. She kissed him lightly on the mouth. Then she sat down. She did not choose the chair opposite his but sat down next to him, the other chair against the wall—the chair that would save her life.

"Adam, I don't know what has happened to you," Lisa lied. Adam knew the Mossad and the CIA had provided her with all the information, that he had left his government's services, that the Vatican had hired him, and that Nicole had become a team member. Adam knew that this particularly irritated Lisa and made her feel second-rate.

The waiter approached their table and handed each of them a menu. Strange, Lisa thought, that he did not hang around to explain. Regarding the menu, tell them about the specials, or ask if they want a drink. The man appeared nervous. Lisa sensed tension. She reached down to her ankle and pulled the gun out of her holster. As she did, Adam overturned the heavy wooden table and pulled her behind it. A split second later, three bullets lodged in the wood.

Adam pulled his gun as soon as the waiter left. He fired two shots at one of the three hooded men who had entered the restaurant with their weapons blazing. One of the men fell to the floor. Lisa aimed at one of the other men, and she did not miss. The third man was shot before Lisa or Adam could pull their triggers again. That man fell forward; his head no longer attached to his body. The woman behind him put the gun back into her purse and rushed toward Adam. "Let's get out of here!" Nicole shouted. "There may be more!" "Through the kitchen," Adam responded. All three rushed out of the back entrance of the restaurant into a small side street.

"Forget our cars," Adam instructed. "They are being watched. Let us find a taxi." They ran up the alley toward the Piazza Nicosia. Adam knew they would find a taxi there.

In the Ranieri, all hell broke loose. People were screaming and rushing out of the restaurant. Tables were kicked over, dishes flew through the air. Three dead men lay on the floor in the middle of the eatery. Blood was running from their bodies. A hooded head lay two feet in front of its lifeless body, shot from behind at close range. The three Arab terrorists would never see their homeland again.

The taxi took Adam's party to the Majestic Hotel on the Via Veneto. None of them spoke a word. Adam knew they should not return to the Hassler Hotel. Not tonight. Tomorrow he would find out who had tried to kill him. Or was Lisa the target?

He knew the Majestic was an excellent hotel that served fantastic Italian cuisine, and Adam was hungry.

CHAPTER 19

Rome, Italy

THREE ASSASSINS HAD TAKEN THEIR SEATS in the comfortable restaurant of the Majestic Hotel.

"Honey, thanks for covering my ass," Adam said as he kissed Nicole. He now knew that Nicole could kill.

"Thanks for covering mine, too," Lisa put in.

"I am sorry. I plain forgot," Adam said. "The two of you have never met. Please forgive me. Sweetheart, this is Lisa. And Lisa, this is my partner, Nicole." He turned to Nicole. "I met Lisa on our last mission in Berlin. Lisa works for the Mossad."

"Actually, we were engaged then," Lisa smiled.

"It was just a cover," Adam said quickly. "Lisa, Nicole used to work for the CIA. She decided to go independent and joined me. You should think about it, Lisa. We could always use another good partner. The Italian food at this place is great."

When the waiter approached to present the menus, Adam asked for the concierge. The man approached their table within a minute. "I would like to book two luxury suites with king-size beds for the evening." Adam handed the man his credit card.

"Of course. I will be right back with the keys."

The food was as good as Adam had expected. None of them wanted dessert. All were anxious to go to their rooms. Adam wanted to be with Nicole and make love to her. He knew he would always like it. He decided he was in love with her. He decided he would ask her to marry him.

As they entered the elevator to their rooms, Adam suddenly wondered what had happened to the other two Mossad agents who had followed him, the guys he and Nicole had recognized when they had had dinner at Ranieri's. Had Lisa replaced them, or were they still on the job? And why had the Mossad chosen Lisa? He needed answers to these questions, and he needed them soon.

Nicole wanted to talk. She tried to understand, and she needed to know Adam's mission. After all, she was now part of it, so she had every right to know. As soon as they entered their suite, she wanted to talk. Adam had wanted to make love, but he knew she was right. He had to speak to her.

The suite Adam had rented for the night was luxurious. There was a bedroom, a large bath, and a comfortable sitting room. The sofa in the sitting room was a love seat covered in white silk. Two chairs sat opposite, separated by a small mahogany coffee table. Adam knew they needed to talk. He believed Nicole had joined him because she was in love with him. And she had just experienced his way of life, a life of danger and intrigue. Nicole, too, had been exposed to that life. But there was more. It was time for him to explain why he had left the NSA and gone alone. He needed to convince her that he had made the right choice.

"Nicole, the pope sent for me. He needs protection. He wants the leaders of the three religions of Abraham to come to the Vatican and make peace. But he only wants religious leaders. He does not believe this to be a secular issue."

"What about the president of the United States and the president of the European Union?" Nicole asked.

"They are to play no role. This is not a secular issue. It is a religious one."

"Adam, I need to know more about the current struggle in the Middle East and the papacy's role in this war."

"Okay," Adam said. "I will give you a crash course, but not tonight."

He went to her and gently touched her face. He brushed back her black hair and put his right hand behind her head to pull it close. He kissed her on the mouth. Both opened their mouths, and their tongues met in fury. Nicole felt his erection as his penis rubbed against her thigh. He lifted her body and carried her into the bedroom.

Room service was prompt. At 7:00 a.m., breakfast was delivered to Suite 1006 in the Majestic Hotel. Adam barely heard the knock on the door. He had already showered and dressed, but Nicole was still asleep on the king-size bed. Adam had asked for breakfast on the terrace overlooking the city. Then he kissed Nicole, kissing her cheek, forehead, and nose. He whispered into her ear and gently stroked her face. He was about to return to bed when she stirred, lifted her head off the pillow, and smiled. It was the smile he loved.

"Honey," he said gently, "breakfast is ready."

Nicole turned and buried her head into the soft down pillows. She was not ready to get out of bed and face the realities that lay ahead. But Adam had reminded her she had to. She turned and kissed him on the mouth and jumped out of bed, put on the luxurious robe of the hotel and walked onto the terrace to join her lover for breakfast. Adam knew Nicole had many questions, and she wanted answers to all of them.

Nicole was Catholic, and Adam had been raised as both a Protestant and a Jew. His CIA records did not indicate apostasy, but she did not know what religion he believed in now, and she wanted to find out.

Nicole had always been fascinated by religion. When she was only six, she told her dad she wanted to become a priest. Her father had told her that only men could join the priesthood. Nicole had not understood this as a child and did not understand it now. She could become a nun, she remembered her father saying. But Nicole wanted none of that. She wanted to be a priest and have her own parish, flock. She majored in theology when she went to college at Georgetown University, a Jesuit school. Her minor was history. Nicole wanted to get a master's degree in theology, but her dad convinced her to pursue his career and attend law school. The sun was shining brightly over the city of the Pope. No cloud was in the light-blue sky to challenge the sun's rays. Adam was dressed casually as he sat at the table on the terrace to have breakfast with Nicole. A single long-stem red rose adorned the center of their breakfast table.

"Thank you," Nicole said, pointing to the rose as she leaned forward and kissed him.

"You are welcome." He smiled and added, "I love you. Nicole, I have a crucial meeting in a couple of days. Now that we are partners, I wanted you to come along. But the people only want to see me. Follow me and cover my ass, okay?"

"Of course. I love your ass. It is the best I have ever seen. If I am around, no harm will ever come to it."

They laughed and kissed.

"Adam, I still need to understand why you left the NSA to go out on your own," Nicole pressed. "I need to know our mission, who the players are, all the details."

"Nicole, I will tell you more as soon as I find out," Adam replied. "All I know is that we are to protect the pope whenever he leaves the Vatican, and only up to and during his meeting with all the other religious leaders. I do not know all the details yet. I have no idea of his itinerary is. I do not know when or how often he will leave Vatican City. But I have a hunch we will never know much in advance. They will keep us at our toes. We will have little time to prepare, hopefully a few hours. That, Nicole, is why we are getting paid the big bucks. Half of the money is already in my bank account." "Half of what?" she wanted to know.

"Half of thirty million Euros."

"Thirty million Euros just for protection?" she asked, surprised.

"Just about," he replied. He did not want to tell her about the killings. Not now. He knew there would be a better time.

The man from the Vatican had been brief. The meeting was at Bracciano, on Lake Bracciano, just north of Rome. All were to meet at his small cottage on the lake. Was the Pope to take part in the meeting? Adam wondered. Carlo had not said who "all" meant. Adam decided to change cars before driving to Bracciano. He turned in his Mercedes and rented a beige Audi A8 L. The large Audi sedan had been introduced to compete with other luxury sedans. Nicole also changed automobiles. She no longer drove the Alfa Romeo she had rented in Positano. She liked the midnight-blue Porsche Carrera she had chosen.

The sleek Audi sedan sped north toward Lake Bracciano. Adam looked through his rearview mirror. He never saw her, but he knew she was there, covering his ass. Adam thought about his team. He had two good shooters, but he knew he needed more. He needed a spotter, two. Every sharpshooter was much more effective using an experienced spotter, someone next to him adjusting range and windage to help make the kill. He would contact Lisa and ask her to become part of his team. She had expertise. The Mossad had trained her, and she was one of their best *katzas*.

But he wanted her for another reason. He knew she was a well-educated religious Jew. He wanted her perspective to help him make the right decisions. He tried to listen to all his confidants. He knew it was wrong that Nicole should be the only one. She was his only love, and that would never change. But when it came to making business decisions, he wanted diversified input. Now he decided he needed a team, though he had not previously required one. But he needed to be sure when his kill could affect world politics. Although he had killed several times in the past, the stakes had never been as high as now. This time, he wanted to be sure—not only sure of the kill but sure that he was doing the right thing. Sometimes, he thought getting a consensus was only a way to minimize the guilt he might experience for killing. Getting more people to agree provided a dilution factor. Yet he had never felt guilt or remorse after a kill.

The Porsche followed the beige Audi sedan, but not close enough to be in sight. There was no need. Nicole had placed a homing device under the large sedan's rear bumper. That was all she needed. The Audi would always be within her reconnaissance.

As Nicole drove toward Lake Bracciano, she knew this mission was about the Middle East. She believed the key to peace there was through religion. Nicole had loved her studies in theology at Georgetown University, and she had often wished she had not gone to law school—although she had done well there, graduating close to the top of her class.

But she had had no intention of following her dad into law. She loved theology and foreign affairs. Her dad had often asked her how the two complemented each other. It had seemed to him that she was going in two different directions. No, she had told him many times that the road to peace in the Middle East was through religion, the religions of Abraham, and the religions that believed in one God: the Muslims, the Jews, and the Christians. She had told him that this needed to be the immediate goal.

Nicole had studied the conflict between the Jews and the Christians. Ever since Christ, the conflict had been called inevitable by many. When she had attended her first class in theology at Georgetown, she had asked two questions that had been on her mind since childhood. What was religion, and why did it exist?

She was told religion consisted of rituals and beliefs that tied humans to God. Religion existed to bridge the gulf between creatures and the Creator. She had accepted these definitions and even thought they were right on the mark. She felt comfortable being religious.

Then Nicole had gone on to learn that Jesus was not perceived as the Messiah by most of the Jews. The Pharisees, the rabbinical Jews, had resented him. She had learned that Jesus had committed a crime, in the temple that Solomon had built, which was the center of the Jewish cult. He was arrested and executed. The Jews had asked for his death because he had offended them, and the Romans had been the executioners. He had died on the cross, the Roman way of death for non-Roman citizens. "My God, my God, why have you abandoned me?" Those were his last words. "God, into your hands I place my spirit."

Nicole's thoughts were interrupted when Adam's car pulled into a small gravel driveway adjacent to Carlo's cabin on Lake Bracciano. Nicole did not follow Adam's car but drove to the small marina only a few hundred yards past the cottage.

Adam and Nicole had visited the area around Carlo's cottage two days earlier. They had studied the region, the access, the terrain. Since Adam's role was to protect the pope, he needed to know where a potential assassin would take his best shot. Nicole and Adam had decided that the lake was the only spot anyone could view the cottage. This was where they decided that Nicole should be stationed.

Adam felt a little uneasy having only Nicole as his backup. He wished she did not have to be on her own. Nicole could do it, he knew, but he still thought Lisa should be part of his team. A sharpshooter needed a spotter to be most effective. As soon as this meeting ended, he promised to hire Lisa, no matter the cost.

The cottage was a small cabin on the lakefront of Lake Bracciano, surrounded by dense woods. Adam could not get into the cabin but could get the floor plans. The cabin was for sale, and he had acted as a potential buyer who wanted to know the layout.

The house was small: three tiny bedrooms, a kitchenette, a great generous room with a large window overlooking the lake, and a deck. He knew that was where they would meet and talk. The deck and the great room needed to be protected, for this was where the pope would be exposed. That was why Adam had decided on the boat. Nicole would be on a fishing ship on the lake close to the cabin. She would not be alone. She would have Adam's favorite companion, which had been delivered to him on the freighter from North Africa: The Savage Anschutz .223 sniper rifle.

CHAPTER 20

Lake Bracciano, Italy

CARLO, THE HANDSOME MAN FROM THE Vatican, loved the small cottage on the lake he had owned for several years. He did not have many possessions or large bank accounts. His treasure was his cottage on Lake Bracciano. When he had first bought the place, it had been his hideout, his place to escape. No one knew about it except his lover. He had not bought it himself. His lover, Prince Albert, had. The prince had given it to him on their third anniversary.

Never would he forget that day. His lover had flown to Rome, and they had rented a car. "Let's drive and enjoy the beautiful countryside," Prince Albert had said. Let us have a wonderful weekend." Then he had driven the young priest to Lake Bracciano, the beautiful cottage on the lake. There was a bottle of chilled champagne on the small kitchen table. As the prince had poured the sparkling wine, he handed the keys to the young priest.

"It is yours," he had said. "No longer do we have to hide. This is where we can meet. This is where we can love." Then he had stepped forward and kissed the young priest on the mouth. They had made love all weekend—the best weekend the young priest had ever had.

Nicole sat in the small rowboat three hundred yards off the shore. It was a calm day. The sky was blue, with no clouds to hide the sun's brilliant presence. Nicole pretended to be fishing but continuously surveyed the small cabin and its surroundings.

Nicole was not alone on the lake near the cabin. Several other small fishing boats were anchored near to where she sat in the rowboat she had rented for the day. She also kept a close eye on these boats. After all, this was where Adam had told her he would position himself if he were an assassin trying to kill someone in the cottage. Nicole had rowed more than a few hundred yards from the small marina where she had rented the boat to be close to the cabin. The old, kind man at the marina had told her where to fish. He had pointed out his favorite spot—one he never shared with anyone, he had said with a smile and a wink. "Well, to be honest, I only share it with pretty ladies," he had told her as he handed her a small brown paper bag filled with worms, which he had instructed her to use as bait. The older man had also asked her to bring the fish back to him, saying he would clean and fillet them. Nicole had given him a seductive smile and thanked him. Then she had put the small bag of worms into the bucket she had brought with her, picked up her fishing pole, and went to the boat.

Nicole's fishing pole was leaning against the side of the boat as she watched the small cabin nestling among large pine trees. She had not put any bait on the hook, as she did not want the distraction of a bite. After three hours, when she and Adam had agreed, she reeled in the hook, put the fishing rod next to her, and rowed back to the quaint marina. Nicole had noticed no activity at Carlo's cabin. When she returned the boat, the older man at the marina was surprised she had not caught any fish.

"You did go to the spot I told you about?" he asked, and she nodded. "I cannot believe it," he exclaimed. "I always catch fish there." He would have none when she reached into her pocketbook to pay the man for the bait and boat rental. "No fish, no pay," he said with a smile. Nicole thanked and kissed him on the cheek as she slipped a fifty-Euro note into his jacket pocket.

Rome, Italy

When Nicole entered the suite at the Hassler, she knew Adam was already there. The sound of a soccer game filled the large living room, and she knew Adam loved soccer. He liked all sports, but soccer was his favorite.

"Honey," he said, "please sit down. This is a great game. It is over. I will get you a glass of wine."

"Thanks," she answered. "That would be great."

Nicole sat on the couch facing the large plasma television set. She had many questions, but she knew they had to wait until the match he was watching was over.

"Here," he said, handing her a glass of wine. "You look beautiful." He sat next to her and kissed her on the mouth. "It is a tie, two to two. You should have seen great goals, all of them. There are only three minutes to go and then some extra time. There should not be much stoppage time, a minute or two."

Nicole did not mind. She liked watching soccer. She had played it in high school, and her brothers had played in college.

"I can't believe it," he cried out. "A penalty kick with only thirty seconds left! That is the game." He was right. The goalie dove to his left, and the ball hit the net in the opposite corner. "What a game! I wish they were all like this. Nicole, did you catch any fish?" He grinned. It was the teasing, boyish smile she loved so much.

"No," she quipped back, "did you?"

"No," he answered as he turned off the television and leaned back on the large, soft couch. He picked up his wine glass and swirled it. He looked at the floor the way one does to gather thoughts. He nodded his head. His head was still bent forward when he continued.

"It was strange." He straightened and looked her in the eye. "I cannot explain it. Usually, I am good at reading people, at figuring out what is going on. But not this time."

"Maybe I can help," Nicole interrupted. "Tell me exactly what happened."

"You are right. I need someone else's perspective on this. Okay, as you know, I went to the cottage. Before I got to the door to knock, a man opened it. The young priest from the Vatican, Carlo, is the guy I had lunch with. I told you about him."

"Yes, you did. He must have been watching the street to await your arrival."

"I guess so."

"Who else was there? The pope?"

"No," he answered, disappointment in his voice. "There was only a college kid, an American, although he looked like someone from the Middle East."

"What happened?" Nicole pressed him.

"I am not sure. We all sat down and had a glass of red wine, even the kid from the Middle East. We made small talk. We talked about soccer and the World Cup in Brazil. We got along well. I like both guys. They are honest and straightforward."

"What happened next?" Nicole asked impatiently.

"Really, not all that much. The priest changed the topic, and we started to talk about religion. He told us why he had entered the priesthood. We talked about our religious backgrounds."

"Did you tell the truth about yours?"

"Of course I did. Do you think the Vatican hires someone with the bucks they are paying unless they know all about him? Not a chance." "I agree. You did the right thing. They would never trust you again, had you lied."

"Well, when the kid learned I had been raised Protestant and Jewish, he was fascinated. He wanted to know all about it. He could not hear enough. It turned out that he, too, was raised under two religions. His mother had raised him as a Catholic. His father was a Muslim. I am not sure, but his father may be dead."

Adam left the couch and went to the wet bar to fetch the bottle of wine he had opened earlier. He turned to Nicole. "Unlike me, I think the kid has decided."

Nicole stood, picked up her wine glass, and walked toward Adam. "What do you mean, he made up his mind?"

"He chose the Islamic religion. And he is a devout Muslim, a fanatic. I am not sure."

"What makes you think so?" Nicole wanted to know. She handed her wine glass to her lover, and he poured her another glass of Bordeaux. Then he filled his own. He put his right arm around her waist and kissed her.

"Are you with the CIA? You ask too many questions."

"Yes, I am. And if you do not answer them all, I will have to take you into the torture chamber.

"The same one we were in last night?" he asked, smiling as he pointed to the bedroom.

"Yes," she said, "but tonight you will suffer much longer. Before I punish you, tell me why the young Arab is a fanatic?"

"I did not say he was. I said he could be. His words were passionate when he spoke about the Islamic religion."

"How did your meeting end? I think you still do not know any specifics about your mission?

"You are right. I have no clue. The meeting ended a little abruptly. The kid and I were getting along well. The priest mostly just listened. He nodded and encouraged us to talk. Then he suddenly stood up and let us know the meeting was over. It was like he had heard enough, like something had been confirmed. He was very polite, to be sure. But I knew it was time to go."

"Strange," she said. "What's going to happen next?"

"I have no idea," Adam replied. "I think we should sit tight and wait. And now I am preparing for the torture chamber.

He went to her, picked her up, and carried her into the bedroom. Then the phone rang, indicating he did not have to sit tight and wait long. But Adam decided not to answer his phone. Torture was on his mind. All else could wait until the morning.

The phone rang again at 7:00 a.m. It woke him, as he had been fast asleep. He and Nicole had made love through most of the night, and he had not had much sleep.

"What is it?" he answered in a grumpy, sleepy voice as he leaned on one arm and held the phone in the other.

The man on the other end ignored Adam's tone. "The Holy Father wants to see you today. I will pick you up at your hotel at 3:00 p.m. Please, do not be late."

The telephone conversation ended with a click. Adam recognized the voice—it was the young priest from the Vatican.

Adam put down his telephone receiver. Today, he would meet the pope, the father of all Catholic people. Today, he would find out why the bishop of Rome had sent for him. Today, he would know whether he had made the right decision to leave behind his comfortable life on South Beach and once again become the assassin he had trained to be, and had his decision to follow the calling of the bishop of Rome been the right decision?

He rolled onto his back and stared at the ceiling. He was wide awake now, and his adrenaline was flowing. He was anxious to share the news with Nicole, who was fast asleep beside him, but he decided not to wake her. Quietly, he slipped out of bed, put on his white satin robe, and entered the large sitting room. Eggs over easy and sausage were what she liked. He would serve her breakfast in bed. Later, he would tell her about the phone call. He picked up the telephone and called room service.

Nicole was not as deeply asleep as she seemed. She had heard the phone ring, listened to the brief conversation, and noticed her lover getting out of bed. She had heard him call room service and order her favorite breakfast. Why interfere with the process? Breakfast in bed seemed like a clever idea to her. And she knew he would tell her all about the call. In fact, she knew he could not wait to do so.

Nicole made him wait, pretending to be fast asleep when he entered their bedroom, approached her, leaned over, and kissed her gently on her lips. At first she did not respond. But when he stroked back her lengthy, black hair and whispered, "I love you," she succumbed. She kissed him on the mouth, a passionate kiss. Then she pulled him onto the bed beside her and held him close.

"Let's make love again," she whispered.

"Now?" he asked.

"Yes."

"We can't," he replied. "I ordered breakfast. The eggs are getting cold."

"Breakfast?" she asked. "Breakfast in bed? You are right. Let us have breakfast first. Then we will make love."

"That's why I love you," he said, laughing. "You understand priorities."

Adam got up, went into the small kitchen of his hotel suite, and retrieved the tray filled with the breakfast he had ordered. The aroma of hazelnut coffee filled the suite.

CHAPTER 21

Rome, Italy

THE HOLY FATHER, THE POPE, SAT in his spacious, wood-paneled study in his home at the Vatican. This was where he always did his research. This was where his advisors met him to discuss all the alternatives. This was where he always made his decisions—but not the final one. For that, he always walked onto his large balcony overlooking Rome. There he knelt and spoke to his God. Then he reentered the study with his answer—no, with God's answer.

This afternoon, the bishop of Rome would meet with a man he had studied thoroughly. Yet he felt uncomfortable. He did not get the sense that he really knew the man. He knew all about his background, that he had been raised as a Christian and then as a Jew. The Holy Father shook his head at the thought. There were so much the two religions had in common, yet there was so much that divided them. He was anxious to meet and speak to the well-educated man representing both religions.

Carlo, the young priest he had sent to meet with the man from abroad, was sitting opposite the large wooden desk. The pope had always liked the young man, and not only because of his impeccable credentials—Harvard undergraduate studies, Yale Law School, and a Harvard MBA. The young priest was also fluent in several languages. His native tongue was Italian, but he also spoke French with a Parisian accent, and English American English—fluently. He was also well-versed in Spanish. But his favorite language was German. Carlo knew several of the dialects to perfection. His favorite was the dialect of Berlin. He loved that city more than his own place of birth, Rome. It was the city in which his grandparents had been born.

"Holy Father," the young priest said as he sat in the pope's library awaiting the arrival of the man they had hired. "How do you always know? How do you always choose the right people?"

"I don't," the pope answered. "God does."

Adam Bergman was ten minutes early. The pope smiled. He would not make him wait. He asked to have the man brought directly into his study.

When Adam entered the library, the pope knew this was a man sent by God. Adam wore a plain gray suit and a white shirt buttoned to the top. He wore no tie; an old wooden cross hung loosely around his neck. The pope looked only briefly at the man's attire and quickly focused on his eyes.

The eyes, the Holy Father knew, were the window to the soul. This man's eyes were like none the pope had ever seen. They were open, exposing an endless sky. They were magnetic, and the bishop of Rome could not escape their spell. Their stare lasted only a second, less. The pope now knew that he—no, God— had chosen the right man.

Adam approached the bishop of Rome, knelt, bowed his head, and kissed the pope's hand.

The Holy Father was dressed in his usual white robe and wore a small white cap. The holy man appeared much older and feebler than Adam had anticipated. Yet his voice was strong, and his eyes still had the sparkle of youth.

"Please, son, take a seat next to me. I want to talk to you. My hearing is not what it used to be, and my English is passable. But I want to hear your voice—not through interpreters but through you, through your soul."

"Yes," Adam replied as he sat next to the pope. "Your Holy Grace," the young priest said, "should I leave?"

"No, please stay." The pope turned to Adam. "Why do you think I asked you to come to me? I am curious to learn your thoughts."

"Let me be direct, Your Excellency. I do not mean to offend. I know you speak for all the Catholic people. And you say you also speak for God. Others do too. I also know you want to be the creator of peace in the Middle East. Many others have the same ambition, others who have much influence and secular power. They all have their own agendas. I need to speak to you about how that peace will be established. It will not be through war by killing a few opponents. Peace must come through *shalom*, a balance of understanding."

The man who occupied the chair of St. Peter smiled. He was now sure he had chosen the right man to help him.

"My son, you are right. Peace in the Holy Land will only come through religion. We should be able to resolve our differences with ease. After all, we—the Christians, Jews, and Muslims—all believe in one God. Our prophet is Jesus Christ. The Muslim prophet is Muhammad. The Jews reject Jesus as the Messiah and are still waiting for the savior. Do you realize how many wars have been fought, how many people have died over this difference in belief? It all started long ago when our Lord Jesus died on the cross. The time has come to resolve our differences."

"Why," Adam asked, "can't we treasure our beliefs and not force them on anyone else?"

"You are a wise young man," the Holy Father replied. "I wish it were all that simple. Yet, in a sense, it really is. We all believe in God. He is our Father. And our God has spoken to me. He wants me to make peace. He wants all of us to leave the past behind—our hatred and our differences. He wants peace for all humanity. And he has asked me to do it! Many others have tried and are still trying, but he has chosen none. Only I can fulfill his wish, his command. He has chosen me. It is the command of our God, the Holy Father, that I must be the one."

"Your Holiness," Adam replied, "I have always believed peace could only come through religion. And I know God has chosen wisely. Only you can make his wish come true. But how do you intend to accomplish it, and why do you need me?"

"My dear son," the pontiff responded as he nodded to the young priest sitting beside him, "that is what my monsieur will discuss with you. Thank you for coming, and God be with you."

All three men rose, and the holy man strolled out of the office. Silence, an air of peace, lasted for several minutes. No one spoke. Then the young priest put his hand on Adam's shoulder and smiled. He knew the Holy Father had once again added to his flock. He now knew that Adam was committed to the Vatican's cause to be the leader to make peace.

"Tomorrow," he said to Adam. "Tomorrow we will meet and discuss all the details. I will let you know when and where."

CHAPTER 22

Rome, Italy

ADAM BERGMAN AND THE YOUNG PRIEST from the Vatican met the next day. They did not meet at the Vatican. The man from Rome had suggested they meet at Adam's suite at the Hassler Hotel. Nicole had ordered a light lunch: a shrimp salad and a bottle of Pinot Grigio.

The pope's man was punctual. Carlo was dressed in a dark blue business suit, no doubt Armani, and a white shirt with a blue-striped tie. As he entered Adam's suite, he carried a large bouquet of fresh flowers in his right hand. As Nicole met him, he kissed her lightly on both cheeks and presented her with the flowers.

"You should not have done this, but the flowers are beautiful. Thank you so much," Nicole almost whispered because Adam was on the phone as the priest entered their suite.

Adam quickly ended his conversation, hung up the phone, and greeted the priest with a warm handshake. He had thought to hug the man for an instant but decided not to.

"Please," Nicole said, "let's all sit down on the balcony and have a light lunch and a glass of Adam's favorite white wine."

No one objected. Yet it was apparent that Carlo had not come to relax. They were all sitting on the large balcony, a white umbrella shading the table. There was no cloud in the sky, and the sun dominated all. When he began the conversation, Carlo barely took a small sip of his wine.

"Adam," he said, his voice calm, measured, and almost calculated—how diplomats speak when they need help. "Adam, the Vatican never told you why the Holy Father sent for you. It is all about the Middle East. The pope's initiative, desire, and mission to make peace are most controversial. Many people oppose it—not only people here at the Vatican, but many other religious leaders. Yet the Holy Father insists on it. He has convinced all the religious leaders that we are all one and believe in one God. All have agreed. He has the support of all the important religious leaders, the ayatollahs, and the chief rabbis. All will come to Rome to join the pope. Together, they will stand on the balcony of the Vatican to proclaim peace among all religions. Adam, we have finally made peace that has eluded humanity for thousands of years." The young priest was emotional. Tears covered his face.

Nicole wrapped her arms around him and comforted him. The young man quickly regained his composure.

"I am sorry," Carlo said." It is just something I have prayed for since I became a priest. I never thought that I would see it in my lifetime. But now that it is happening, it overwhelms me. Please excuse my emotions." He lifted his wine glass and emptied it. Nicole filled it again. All three began to eat their lunch in silence. A soft breeze ruffled the large umbrella under which they all sat.

"The shrimp salad is outstanding, Nicole," Adam said as he helped himself to another serving and broke the silence.

"I agree," the priest responded. "It is the best I have ever had."

"Okay, where do I come in?" Adam asked.

"Adam, please," Nicole interrupted. "Can't we wait until after lunch?"

"It's okay," Carlo chimed in. "After all, that is why I am here. I have told you that all the religious leaders have agreed to make peace. And clearly, this is a spiritual war. But not everyone sees it that way. Many other people—from no countries—do not want to know about this peace. They have a different agenda. These are powerful countries that want to control and run the world. They have the mindset that only their way is the right way. And when it comes to the Middle East, they want the oil. They do not care about peace or the people. They care about money!

"The pope understands. He truly knows all the agendas. That is why he is a man of God! But he is determined not to let their greed for power, domination, arrogance, and sense of superiority stand in the way of peace. He will not let it happen! That is why he needs you."

"I am following you. Still, I do not see my role."

"Adam, the pope has put me in charge of his security. He realizes that some powerful countries do not want this peace. They will use all their resources to prevent it. They will stop at nothing, and they will try to kill the pope. I hired you to protect the pope—outside the Vatican, since we already have a fine security force inside the pope's residence. Nonetheless, just in case, I would like you and your team to be there. We want to create a security force for the Pope and all the religious leaders. The peace announcement will be announced on the balcony of the Vatican, and that will be when we are most vulnerable." "Okay," Adam responded. He was excited and liked the challenge of protecting the pope. It was the kind of mission he had always dreamed of. "I need all the details—each move he makes, all the clothing he wears, his speech, the identity of all people within two hundred yards of him. I want air clearance, no flights above, and much more. Give me his diary tomorrow. I need time to study it. All three of my team members need to know all the details."

"Three of you? I thought there were only two," Carlo said, surprised.

"No," Adam responded," we needed one more. It is like sharpshooting. You need someone who takes the shot, but more important is the spotter. He determines the windage, the distance, and even the humidity. You cannot take an accurate shot without a spotter." "Okay," the priest said. "So, you added a new member to your team. Who is it?"

"Fortunately," Adam replied, "I was able to find one of the best. I have worked with her before. The Mossad trained her and is one of their best. But now she works for me. The three of us will make sure the pope is safe."

CHAPTER 23

Rome, Italy

THE BISHOP OF ROME RAISED BOTH hands as he stepped out onto the balcony of the Vatican to greet all people—not just his own people who had always believed in him, but also the people of other faiths: the Jews, the Protestants, the Islamists, and all the people who believed in God. He wanted to silence the enormous crowd gathered in St. Peter's Square. He wanted all of them to hear God's Word and celebrate the new peace.

He hesitated for a moment to let the crowd's roar subside. He smiled. Now he knew he was doing what his God had always asked him to do: unify the people to make peace on earth, to believe in finally but one God.

The roar of the crowd silenced the shot. The bullet hit the pontiff between his eyes. He fell backward; his hands still raised in prayer to the Lord. He would never know he had not achieved everything his Father had asked. He would never know that peace on earth was gone, that it all had to begin again.

Adam was in disbelief. He had meticulously planned and made sure the pope was completely protected. There had been no chance for anyone to fire that shot. He rushed onto the balcony where the Holy Father lay. He surveyed the surroundings. There was no way anyone could have taken that shot. The security had been airtight; he had made sure of that himself. He had placed his people, Nicole, and Lisa, in the only places where a shot could reach the pope.

Adam looked to his right, where he had stationed Nicole. He quickly concluded that the shot that had killed the pope had not come from there. There was no doubt that it had come from the opposite direction, the spot where he had positioned Lisa. Had someone overcome her? Unlikely, he thought. Lisa was one of the best. Adam now raced to where he had asked Lisa to be. There was no sign of her or any struggle—and no shell.

Surely this was the work of a professional. There was only one person who could have taken that shot. It could have been no one else.

As soon as the bullet had struck the Holy Father, Adam, who had stood only feet away, instructed the Swiss guard to seal the entire area, call the police, and declare it a crime scene. But Carlo had overruled him. No one was to find out that the Holy Father had been shot. The public was to be informed that the bishop of Rome had died of a heart attack, the priest insisted. He instructed Adam to pursue his investigation in secret. He insisted on it.

Adam needed to meet with Nicole and needed to confirm his suspicions. All three—Lisa, Nicole, and Adam—had agreed to meet at their suite in the Hassler Hotel as soon as the meeting of the religious leaders had ended. Adam was now determined that he had to get there as quickly as possible. The hotel was near to where the religious leaders had met. He decided to run there. As he did, he thought about the shooting. As he got closer to the hotel, he knew only Nicole would be there. There would be no Lisa.

And he was right. Nicole was already in the suit when he entered, sweat dripping from his forehead, breathing rapidly. "Nicole, what happened?"

"I do not know. We had the best security. Covered all the angles. But where is Lisa?"

He went into the bathroom, retrieved a towel, and wiped the sweat off his face.

"Nicole," he said. "I made a big mistake."

"A big mistake? What are you talking about?"

He lifted the towel in his right hand and shook it in frustration. "I trusted Lisa. She took the shot."

"No way," Nicole responded. "She is one of us. I do not believe it!" Adam now put the white towel around his neck. He walked toward the large couch in the living room, but he did not sit down. Nicole sat in one of the plush chairs opposite the sofa. He looked at her.

"Nicole, why is Lisa not here? We all agreed to meet in this suite."

"She was held up. She will be here soon."

"No way, Nicole. No one else could have taken that shot—the angle, the position, the way the pope was struck. It came from where Lisa was stationed."

"Wait, I cannot believe it. Are you saying that Lisa killed the pope?" "The shot came from where Lisa stood. Could someone has overtaken her and then taken the shot? I thought about it, but there is no chance. Lisa is the best. No one surprises Lisa. And even if someone did, I saw no evidence—no dead Lisa, no signs of a struggle. And I found no shell—clearly the work of a professional. But when we recover the bullet, we will know."

"But why would Lisa betray us and shoot the pope?" "I don't know, but I certainly will find out!"

Again, he had made a mistake. He had done it once before, and it had involved a beautiful woman then, too. That mistake had almost cost him his life. He remembered now. It was one of his first assignments with the NSA in South America. He had vowed never to let it happen again. But surely beautiful women were his weakness, even if he had no other.

He sat back on the large, soft couch in the suite's living room. He sat opposite Nicole but did not look at her as he put the white towel over his head. Now, he needed to think.

All his thoughts were focused on Lisa. Where had he gone wrong? He had collaborated with her in the past. He knew the Mossad had trained her and was one of their best. The NSA had given her a green light: she was clean.

He had trusted the NSA. They rarely made a mistake, so he had taken their word for it and had not thought to check further. He wanted her on his team. She was beautiful, so he was attracted to her.

But now the game had changed. Now he needed to do the homework he should have done long ago. Now he needed to know all about Lisa.

All the world leaders attended the funeral of Pope Leo XIV, and more than one hundred thousand faithful lined St. Peter's Square. All had come to pray for the holy man and pay their respects. It had been told that the leader of the Catholic church had died of a massive heart attack just as he was about to give a speech that would change the world, a speech that would unify all religions and pave the way to peace on earth. First, the grand ayatollah from Iran took the stage. He called the pope his brother, his best friend, his right hand in the struggle to unite all religions. Then he asked that the fight to unite continue. It is what the pope had wanted, for what he had prayed. It had been his mission. "Let us honor the pontiff," he urged. "Let us follow the path he has shown us. Let us all be one under one God!"

The chief rabbinate from Jerusalem, one of the leaders of the Jews, spoke next. He was an older man. Arthritis had forced him to walk with a cane years ago, and now his vision had begun to fail him. He barely managed the two steps to the podium. It was not just his arthritis and failing vision that made it difficult for the rabbi to conquer the steps. It was the tears streaming from his failing eyes.

He attempted to speak when he reached the podium, but his voice was a whisper. He struggled to gather himself, but he was overtaken by emotion. Finally, he asked God to give him the strength he needed. And God answered. With a strong voice, one the old rabbi had not used in years, the man from Jerusalem addressed all who had gathered in the square to honor the pope.

"Let us all say a silent prayer," he said. "Let us all remember the Pope as a man of God sent to us to make peace. And let his efforts not die here with him. Let his death be our inspiration to make his dream, wish, and goal come true. Let there be peace on earth!"

The crowd in the square of the Vatican erupted with cheers. "Peace on earth! Peace on earth!" they all shouted at the top of their lungs. The cheer did not subside. It continued as the crowd dispersed and made their way home. The cheer was infectious.

The reaction of the secular world was quite different.

CHAPTER 24

Washington, DC

CROSS THE OCEAN, THE PRESIDENT OF the United States had decided to send her vice president to the Pope's funeral. Monica Drew had no intention of giving too much importance to the pope's efforts to make peace in the Middle East. After all, that was to become the legacy of her presidency, and she was determined that no preacher, as she liked to call all religious leaders, would spoil her mission.

"Does the pope's death mean that the peace in the Middle East is also dead?" she asked her chief of staff.

The president's man nodded. "It does indeed."

"Did we play a role in this?" the president asked.

"No, absolutely not," her chief of staff responded.

"You are certain. No surprises."

"None," the man responded.

"You checked with all, even the NSA?"

"Yes, ma'am, I have assurances from all. We were not involved."

"Very well," the president responded with a smirk. She leaned back in her chair behind the large desk. Well, she thought, now that the religious leaders had failed to make peace in the Middle East, she had been given another opportunity. Peace in the Middle East could still become the legacy of her presidency.

Berlin, Germany

The leader of the European Union was well informed about the events in Rome. His cousin's lover, the pope's confidant Carlo, had shared all the details. The pope had not died of a heart attack. Instead, he had been shot by one of the people he had hired to protect him. No one knew the assassin's identity, but as soon as he found out, he would let his lover, Prince Albert, know.

The EU president had always known, or thought he had known, that the religious leaders could never make peace in the Middle East on their own. All of them were fanatics who believed too much in their own religions. Their deep faith would never allow them to compromise.

Only through compromise could there ever be peace, and compromise was his strength. After all, had he not united much of Europe, countries that had fought each other for centuries, people who spoke different languages and had different values and cultures and believed in different religions? He had learned how to get people to sit at a table to talk. Most importantly, he had learned how to listen. And he knew the actual cause of the war in the Middle East. He knew that he alone could make peace and making that peace had become his obsession.

South Beirut, Lebanon

The full moon and stars in the black sky lit the unending sand in the desert, but only candles illuminated the luxurious bunker. In that desert, the home of Hezbollah's secretary-general, only two people occupied the opulent bunker's sitting room. The older man, the secretary-general, sat in his chair, the place he always preferred when deciding. His grandson, in contrast, sat next to him on the floor.

"Grandson," he said, "I want you to speak first. I want to hear what you think. The pope is dead. Is peace dead as well? Have we succeeded? Where do we go from here?"

Ali Nasral, the grandson of the secretary-general, was surprised. Never had his grandfather asked him to speak first, to give his opinion without restraint.

"Grandpa," he responded, "peace is dead for now. You always taught me peace will only come when all humanity believes in Allah."

The secretary-general smiled and reached for his grandson, and they embraced.

Tel Aviv, Israel

The head of the Mossad was concerned. It seemed that one of his agents—or his former agent—had pulled the trigger on the weapon that had killed the pope. Surely it would not be long before the blame would be placed on the Mossad, in Israel. Yet his agency had had nothing to do with it. But who would believe it? Once more, the Arabs would blame Israel, and the rest of the world would follow. The Americans would not be as direct; they never were. They would do it more subtly, the American way. He needed a way to defuse the issue, to distance his agency from what had happened.

He struggled for an answer as he paced his office in the Hadar Dafna building, the center of Mossad operations. Yes, Lisa had been a Mossad agent, which he could not deny. Then she had left the agency and joined a private group. She had severed all her ties to the Mossad.

But who would believe that? It was his job to make sure the Mossad and Israel looked clean. But how, when all fingers were pointing at Israel? He reached his desk and pounded his large right fist on the mahogany table. It hit so hard that the glass of water he had been drinking fell off the desk and shattered into many pieces. Again, he began to pace through his office nervously. He wished to consult with someone, but he knew he could not. This was his job. It was up to him to produce a solution.

Frustrated and desperate, he sat in the swivel chair behind his desk. He leaned forward, both hands supporting his head. Now was the time when he needed his God, he thought. And suddenly an idea flashed through his mind. He raised his head. Had God just answered him? Had he come to help him? Slowly, he scratched his forehead, a gesture he often used when he was deep in thought.

Yes, the rabbi from Brooklyn, his brother-in-law. Could he be the answer?

Maza had sent for him to learn all about Adam Bergman, the man the pope had decided to protect. His brother-in-law had been Adam's rabbi while Adam was growing up in New York. Maza knew that Adam and the rabbi had developed a close relationship, a bond. And then the rabbi had adopted him as his grandson. Maza Sharef, the head of Israel's intelligence agency, needed to know all about Adam. He thought Adam was the key to the pope's assassination.

JFK Airport, New York City

The old rabbi from Brooklyn Heights had suddenly decided not to fly to Tel Aviv. He had had an uneasy feeling, a premonition, something telling him not to go. He quickly retrieved his small bag beneath his seat, grasped his Bible, and left the large El Al airplane as the doors closed. He rushed out of the plane. He wanted to go home.

The Mossad agent assigned to bring the old rabbi to Tel Aviv was surprised. He quickly left his seat and followed the older man from Brooklyn. Both escaped the plane before the doors of the jumbo jet were closed. The Mossad agent reached for his phone and followed the rabbi heading to the airport's exit. The Katz called Tel Aviv.

"The man left the airplane," he shouted into his phone. "It seems he's going home."

"Relax," was the response from the Mossad headquarters. "Just follow him. He will come around."

The rabbi hailed a taxi as soon as he left the terminal at JFK. He had never used a cab before, and he had little money. But today he wanted to get home as quickly as he could. He did not know why. All he knew was that he wanted to be home, where he was safe, where he felt at ease. When the taxi reached the rabbi's home in Brooklyn Heights, he had to give the taxi driver all the money he had. He did not mind. Now he was safe and thanked his God as he clutched the Bible with both hands.

The Mossad man had followed the rabbi's taxi. He took notice of the apartment building the older man had entered. It was late, close to 9:00 p.m. A small, run-down motel was only a block from the rabbi's home. The Mossad agent had noticed it as his cab followed the rabbi. The katza decided to take a room there. No doubt, his target would not go anywhere tonight.

The katza was right. The following morning, he followed the old rabbi on his daily walk to the large oak tree in the park. He watched as the older man sat. The Mossad man watched the rabbi on the bench and reads his Bible. For three days, the katza called Tel Aviv.

Every day, he was told to be patient and assured that the rabbi would eventually get on the plane and fly to Tel Aviv.

The Mossad was right.

The old rabbi was not sure why he had left the plane. It had been an impulse, a fear of the unknown. Sitting under the large oak tree and holding his Bible each day, he was unsure what to do. Indeed, he was afraid of the unknown and comfortable in his environment. Yet he wanted to see his sister one more time before he died, and he knew there would not be many opportunities to do so. After three days of prayer, contemplation, and reasoning, he decided to go to Tel Aviv.

JFK Airport, New York City

The rabbi from Brooklyn Heights held tight to his Bible, both hands clamped onto the Holy Book as the plane landed. For hours, he prayed, only taking a brief nap during his long trip to New York. He had declined any food or drink. As the plane landed, he became even more uncertain. Why had he left his home? His hands trembled as he held the Bible, the book that meant all to him, his reason for life.

The captain of the large airplane turned on the signal for all passengers to disembark. The rabbi did not move. His hands continued to grip the book he believed in. When one of the pretty airline attendants asked him to depart the plane, he shook his head. He would wait to let all the others get off the plane first. He wanted to stay on the plane and go back to New York, back to his Brooklyn home.

He had brought only a small suitcase that had fit easily in the overhead compartment. The flight attendant helped him retrieve his carry-on bag. All the people had left the airplane. He was the last one. He felt unsure and did not want to go, afraid of what lay ahead. Yet he knew he had no choice.

His right hand pulled his carry-on, and his left held his Bible. As he entered the concourse, two men immediately took charge. Both were large men, six foot two and muscular, and neither smiled. One took the rabbi's rolling suitcase. The other just asked the rabbi to follow him.

As they stepped outside the airport, two Cadillac SUVs, their motors running, were waiting. Two more men occupied each car. No words were spoken. The rabbi was almost pushed into the rear seat of the first car.

They had no sirens, but they were oblivious to any traffic rules. Both cars raced toward a destination they knew: the home of the head of the Mossad. The rabbi's hands were still shaking when both vehicles entered the compound. One of the men opened the door of the bulletproof car. He helped the old rabbi take the two steps to leave the vehicle.

The rabbi had barely exited the car when she came to him. She did not walk; she raced to embrace him. They hugged. It lasted a few minutes. The sister he had thought long lost was his again. When they hugged and kissed, he dropped his Bible, but he did not mind—not now with his sister in his arms.

CHAPTER 25

Berlin, Germany

I T WAS AUTUMN. THE SUN WAS alone in the bright-blue sky, and the trees in the Tiergarten, one of Berlin's many parks, were showing their magnificent fall colors. It was the time he most enjoyed in Berlin, the city of his birth. His office in the Chancellery overlooked the park where German royalty had gone to ride and hunt centuries ago. He loved his city. After all, God had placed it in the middle of the world, at least so a popular Berlin song said.

Prince William von Hohenzollern slowly walked toward the large window of his office. He often did so. He loved looking at his city and knew he could never live elsewhere. Now he remembered his days in grammar school here in the suburb of Dahlem, his days at the Arndt Gymnasium, his schooling at the Freie Universität Berlin, and his boyhood days at the beach at the Wannsee, Strandbad Wannsee. No, he would never leave Berlin.

He had worked hard to make the EU a reality. Many had opposed it. He knew them all and would never forget. But now the EU had become a world power. He had always liked to downplay it, but he did not know why. Was it because of the history of his country? He always wondered.

Nonetheless, he became the president of the EU, and the EU became a powerful union worldwide. The process had not been easy; making peace never was. Yes, there had been setbacks, particularly Greece's inability and refusal to make its debt payments. The Greeks had lived lavishly on borrowed money they knew they could not afford to pay back. Unlike others, Prince William had never thought that Greece's departure from the eurozone or the EU would mean uniting Europe had not worked well. He was convinced that a united Europe was better off, with or without Greece.

But now he had to look forward. Europe needed the oil from the Middle East. The Americans needed it too, but they tried to do it their way—with a gun at their hip, shooting away. He guessed that was how America had been created long ago. They did not know that times had changed.

Prince William understood that Middle East oil was essential to the European Union, but more importantly, he wanted peace. His desire to prevent a third great war had driven him to form a united Europe. Now, peace in the Middle East had become his obsession, and he knew only he could accomplish it. Only he had the pedigree of peacemaking. He had united countries that had fought each other for centuries, and only he had understood that to make peace, you had to remove the cause of war. And only he understood the actual cause.

He turned away from the large window that overlooked the Tiergarten and slowly walked toward the large portrait that adorned one of the walls of his expansive office. It was an oil painting of one of his forebears, Kaiser William II, holding a Bible as he was proclaimed Kaiser more than a hundred years ago. Now that the very Bible rested beneath the painting on an ornate wooden table. Prince William picked up the holy book and placed it into the bottom drawer of the table.

Sochi, Russia

Dressed only in his Speedo bathing suit, the most powerful man in Russia stood on the beach of his favorite resort, the place he had built: Sochi.

Yes, the Olympics, his games, had been a success. He had shown the world that Russia was a world power once again. He knew there had been a few glitches during the games—the shooting of all the stray dogs, the failure of all the Olympic rings to light up during the opening games. He particularly viewed the latter as an insult to his homeland, Russia. But he had taken care of the engineer who had betrayed Mother Russia. He had had the man brutally murdered in his hotel room. The president of Russia had no remorse. It is what the man deserved for betraying his country.

Vladimir Pavlov picked up another stone and threw it into the sea. Russia had won more medals than any other country. That made him proud. But he had also defeated his archrival, the United States. He smiled, stroking his head with both hands, a gesture he often used when pleased.

He picked up another stone and threw it as hard as he could. It skipped over the water more times than on his previous throws. Now he knew he had made the right decision. His aides had advised against it, but the Russian president had insisted. He had argued that America should once again be involved in a conflict that cannot be resolved. Let American lives be lost. Russia would stay out of the conflict in the Middle East, at least for now. He knew he needed to wait.

But he had not waited to invade Crimea, a territory that had once belonged to his Mother Russia. Just like Adolf Hitler, a man Vladimir Pavlov admired, he had invaded the Ukrainian region under the pretense of protecting the many Russians who lived there. Hitler had used the same excuse in 1938 when he had occupied the Sudetenland, where many Germans lived. Like Hitler, Vladimir Pavlov had used the invasion as a test to determine the enemy's resolve. He had expected a vigorous response, but there had been little. Now that the Olympics in his homeland were over, the Russian Federation president was ready to take competition to the next level. Crimea had only been the first step. Syria was next.

Politics reminded him of the sport of curling. It was a sport of tactics, fitness, and anticipating your opponent's next move. But it also required precise execution. During the game, many stones were thrown, and tactics were changed. Each stone could change the game. Now he smiled. He did not often smile in public, but he smiled when he was at ease. Yes, he thought, curling and politics were so much alike. At times, whoever threw the last stone had the best chance of winning. And he intended to do just that in the Middle East.

Vladimir Pavlov, the president of Russia, loved his country. He believed it should once more be a world power. All the territories that had belonged to Russia needed to be returned to it. Russia should once more be as it had been under Catherine the Great.

Rome, Italy

Nicole watched Adam as he sat on the large white loveseat in their suite at the Hassler Hotel. He was clearly distraught because he knew he was responsible. He had been hired to protect the pope, and his team had failed. For many hours, he had relived aloud the moments that had led to the pope's death, but he still had no answer.

"Nicole," he said, "we need to find Lisa. I do not care what it takes. We need answers. Why did she betray us? What was her motive?

For whom does she really work? And let us do a comprehensive background check. I never really made a mistake. I should have done it. But I thought that if the Mossad had cleared her up, she would be okay. Now I know better. Let us get on ASAP. If you need help, let me know."

Nicole nodded in agreement. She also felt guilt, for she had trusted Lisa, although at their first meeting, she had been jealous. She knew Adam and Lisa had worked together in the past on an assignment in Berlin. Then, they played the role of a couple engaged to be married. Nicole often wondered if it was just a role, but she had never asked Adam about it.

Nicole knew that finding Lisa would not be easy. She had been trained by the best, the Mossad. And now Nicole did not know who she was working for—the Mossad, the NSA, the EU, the Russians, the Iranians, the Iraqis? It surely was someone who wanted the pope dead, who wanted to end all the peace talks in the Middle East. But that did not shorten her list of the many suspects. To find out why Lisa had done this, Nicole needed to find out all about Lisa to learn every detail of her life. And that was what she would do.

"Adam," Nicole asked as they both lay in bed, their naked bodies touching after they had made love, "is there anything significant you can remember about Lisa? Anything at all?"

He rolled over and kissed her on the mouth. His right hand caressed her face. "I cannot believe you. We are making love, and you are still thinking about the job."

"No," she responded, "lovemaking was over a minute or so ago. You have asked me to do a job, and I need information. What do you know about Lisa's past?"

"Well, I've told you before about the Mossad training, I don't know much more."

"Please, think. Did she ever mention anything else?"

"Nothing of relevance," he responded. "We never really discussed anything but our assignments."

"She never told you where she was born, her nationality?"

"Yes, she did. We had gone out to dinner while on an assignment. We did not have much to discuss, so we just talked briefly. Then I asked her about her education and family, where she had gone to school, where she was born, and so on. She said she was Swedish and educated at Stanford. She really did not want to talk, but I pressed her. Her mother was quite an athlete and an Olympic cross-country skier from Sweden. She studied in Berlin. Tears formed in Lisa's eyes when she talked about her mother, so I stopped the conversation."

Suddenly, Adam sat up in bed. "Nicole, which is it. That is where you need to go. Find out all about her father and Stanford. I have a feeling that this is where we will find the answer to why she killed the pope."

Adam insisted that Lisa's father and Stanford would give them all the insight. But Nicole wondered why Adam had not mentioned Sofia, Lisa's mother. Female instinct told her to find out more about the mother. This, she thought, could be the key.

Nicole decided to visit Lisa's mother's hometown of Idre in Sweden. There, she met with Lars Petterson, one of Sofia's brothers. He was highly informative. His sister had been a phenomenally successful cross-country skier for Sweden. She had grown up in the small town of Idre, northwest of Stockholm, close to the Norwegian border. Idre—Fjall was one of Sweden's best ski resorts.

Lisa's mother had been the youngest of the four children of the Pettersons, who had lived in Idre for generations. She was the only girl, a tomboy. All her brothers were also competitive skiers. But only she had made the Swedish Olympic team to compete in Sarajevo. As a result, she had had the opportunity to compete all over Europe, to see more than her brothers ever had. Many sponsors of ski equipment had approached her to promote their products.

One of these sponsorships had taken her to Berlin, Germany. It only took Sofia a few hours to fall in love with the city. She loved that there was more parkland than any other European city, and she loved all the waterways, the rivers, and the lakes. But most of all, she loved the Berliners. They were never without an answer; they did not know what to say. The Berliners had endured much, but they were survivors. They knew how not to give up and keep going and had the most positive attitudes.

Lars told Nicole that his sister had arrived at the airport and had taken a cab to her hotel on the Ku'damm, one of Berlin's most famous avenues. The driver had been a *wasch echter* Berliner, a Berliner born and raised in Berlin. As the cab took her from the airport to her hotel, she asked the driver about Berlin's resurgence. In his classic Berlin dialect, the driver had proclaimed that Berlin was the center of the world and that no one could ever challenge that. She laughed. That was typical Berlin *Schnauze*. Berliners were known for their big mouths. She had decided to move to Berlin to study at the Freie Universität. Nicole could confirm that Lisa's mother had graduated with a degree in history, but she needed to know more. She was convinced that Lisa's mother had played a pivotal role.

Nicole dug deep. Lisa's mother, Sofia Petterson, had rented a small room in one of the villas in the fashionable suburb of Dahlem, close to the university. Sofia tutored the young children of the household and lived rent-free. Although most Swedes are Protestant—Lutheran, about 2 percent are Catholics. The Pettersons belonged to that minority.

Sofia joined the parish of a young priest at the St. Bernhard church on the Koenig-Luise Strasse in Dahlem, near to where she lived. Then Nicole discovered that Lisa had been born in Berlin at the Charité Hospital, Berlin's best. Tragically, Lisa's mother had died in childbirth from eclampsia, a hypertensive disorder of pregnancy. The birth records only indicated the name of Lisa's mother—no father. Who was her father? Nicole had to find out.

After Lisa's birth, the young Catholic priest at the St. Bernhard church decided to raise the child, for Lisa's mother and the priest had become close. The priest had hired a full-time nanny to take care of the child. As Lisa grew older, she was not denied anything. She went to the best schools, including Le Rosey, one of Switzerland's most expensive finishing schools, and then on to Stanford. Upon graduation, she received a generous trust account. Obviously, Nicole concluded, money was not a motivating factor.

Nicole decided to learn more about the young priest who had agreed to raise Lisa. Matthias von Meissen was the son of a very wealthy German aristocratic family. He was born in Munich and attended grade school there. Then, his family moved to Berlin, where he attended the Arndt Gymnasium on the Koenig—Luise Strasse in Dahlem. His family was Catholic and had joined the St. Bernhard parish on their move to Berlin.

Matthias loved the parish priest there, Heimar Weider. The priest convinced Matthias to follow him and become a priest. Upon graduating from the Arndt Gymnasium, Matthias enrolled at the seminar at the University of Munich and earned his doctorate there. When he moved back to Berlin, he became a priest. He taught fundamental theology at his old church, St. Bernhard, and as a lecturer at the Freie Universität in Berlin.

Thereafter, he was named Archbishop of Berlin, and only three years later, the pope named him a cardinal. He was one of the pope's closest advisors. When the pope died of a heart attack, Matthias became the immediate choice to succeed the Holy Father.

It took only thirty minutes for the smoke to rise and announce that a new pope had been chosen.

CHAPTER 26

Berlin, Germany

THE EU PRESIDENT LOOKED OUT HIS window as heavy snowflakes began to cover his beloved city. He loved the snow. When he was a child, his parents had taken him to all the winter resorts: St. Moritz, Gstaad, Zermatt, St. Anton—he had skied at them all. Snow was in his blood. He always thought his city looked more magnificent when covered by the white flakes that now fall heavily from the sky. He did not know why.

In the past, he thought the white snow hid most of the history that this city had stood for and endured. It had seemed to him that the snow was a blanket that covered much that he wanted to forget. But now he was not a man of the past; his focus was on the future. Now he saw the snow differently, cleansing all, creating a new beginning. Each flake brought new opportunity, hope, and challenges that meant a new Europe, a continent unified and second to none.

He turned from the window and sat in the large leather armchair behind his mahogany desk. He had closely followed the pope's agenda, the pontiff's attempt to unify all religions to make peace in the Middle East. The president of the EU always had a front row seat. He was always the best informed, for his cousin was the lover of the Pope's confidant, a young

Italian priest. There was never a detail that his cousin, Prince Albert, did not know. Yet the assassination had come as a complete surprise. The EU president knew that the pope had hired a special security force to protect him, and he knew it was the best. The best agencies had trained the man who headed the force: the Navy SEALs, the NSA, and the Mossad.

The head of the EU shook his head. Then he smiled. He knew the pope could never have made the peace, for the pope would never have accepted the proper solution to peace, which was to remove the cause and religion.

Yes, Prince William thought, the pope had been a great man. He had had the courage to enter the world of politics, which he had never really understood, alien to him. The pope had understood the risks. He had known he was a fish out of water. But his faith, his belief, had never faltered. He thought his God would again part the seas and create another miracle. Prince William knew that the Pope's God was a belief, not reality or the truth.

Not long ago, one of the pope's predecessors, Pope Benedict, chose as his episcopal motto "cooperation of the truth." He had said, "In today's world, the theme of truth is omitted almost entirely as something too great for man, and yet everything collapses if truth is missing." Prince William now knew why Pope Benedict had resigned, the first pope ever to do so. It was not old age or ill health. Many previous popes had suffered from those exact causes, but none had left the papacy. No, Pope Benedict had not been able to reconcile religion and truth. He had been the first honest pope.

South Beirut, Lebanon

Hassan Nasral, the secretary-general of Hezbollah, sat in his bunker. He also believed in God, but not the pope's God. His God was Allah.

He and his grandson had just embraced. Both believed peace had to be made in the Middle East and the world. Peace in the Middle East would be the first step. It would create the foundation for peace on earth. But peace could only come when there were no more *kafirs*, nonbelievers. All nonbelievers had to cease from fitnah— disbelief— or be killed. Only then could there be world peace; of this Hassan was certain.

He was also sure that he could never accomplish it alone, so he sent for his grandson. He had two reasons for doing so. First, he needed help because he was growing old and unable to travel and communicate with his brother. He needed someone young to excite his people, motivate them, and unite them to support his cause.

Second, he needed someone with skills beyond those learned in the desert. He needed someone who understood the rest of the world, spoke their language, and could think like they did if the need arises. But he also had to be a person whose loyalty to him and to Islam was unquestionable. He needed his grandson.

Tel Aviv, Israel

Maza Sharef, the head of the Mossad, had asked his brother-in-law to come to his office in the Hadar Dafna building and join him for breakfast between 8:30 and 9:00 a.m. They had agreed to the meeting during dinner the night before—one that his wife, the rabbi's sister, had prepared with much care and love.

She had cooked her brother's favorite meal, and her brother, the rabbi, had begun the meal by breaking the bread, the *challah*. Next, she served matzo ball soup. Afterward, she had presented her brother's favorite, *holishkes*, or stuffed cabbage. She remembered how much he had always enjoyed that meal when they were children.

Often, she had not finished all of hers to give more to her brother. And finally, for dessert, she had prepared Jewish apple cake. She knew dairy products could not be eaten at the same meal as meat under Kosher law. That was why she had chosen Jewish apple cake.

The next morning, the rabbi from Brooklyn felt more relaxed. Seeing his sister and enjoying the home-cooked meal made him feel part of the family. But he was not entirely at ease, unlike how he felt when he went for daily walks to his home in Brooklyn Heights. He missed carrying his Bible. He missed the trees in his small park and the bench he sat on daily. He wanted to go back. But he also wanted to be with his sister. He loved her.

A large black SUV, a Cadillac Escalade with all the windows blackened, picked him up at his sister's house, the house of the head of the Mossad, at precisely 8:00 a.m. Three men occupied the car. All wore dark suits, and all were tall and muscular. None smiled.

Two men in the car jumped out when they reached the Dafna building, the Mossad's headquarters. Two other tall, muscular men dressed in dark suits joined them. All four surrounded the rabbi from Brooklyn, forming a shield.

The office of the head of the Mossad was in the basement of the building. The office had no windows. The rabbi's brother-in-law had always wanted to change that. There was no longer any reason to hide in the basement. Everyone knew where the head of Israel's intelligence agency spent much of his day.

The basement was the past, and Maza knew he needed to change it, but that was his last priority. Now he needed to learn more about the EU leader's plot to make peace in the Middle East, and about the pope's death. The Mossad had briefed him in detail. They had identified all the players and knew all the motives. They knew who was involved and what they wanted to do. But they had no idea how it had come about. That was why Maza had sent for his brother-in-law, the rabbi from Brooklyn Heights.

Washington, DC

The president of the United States and her secretary of state did not often meet in private. They did not like each other. In fact, they had campaigned against each other for the office of the White House. The campaign had been particularly ruthless, each trying to dig up dirt on the opponent, each using no restraint in their speeches to denounce the other. It had been a contest like none before. Many had thought it was an embarrassment to the United States.

But neither candidate cared. All they had wanted was to occupy the highest office in the land, no matter the cost, not only in dollars but in morals, ethics, broken promises, and bribes. "Anything goes" had clearly been their motto, and the one who was the best at it had won.

The president sat opposite her secretary of state and smiled. It had been a shrewd political maneuver to appoint her arrival to that office. She had not thought of the idea herself. In fact, it was not a choice she would ever have made. It was her husband who had convinced her that this was the right choice. He had quoted an old saying: "Always keep your enemy closer than your friends," and he had been right.

"Mrs. President," the secretary of state said, initiating the conversation, "what is our position on the pope's death and peace in the Middle East?"

"To me, the pope's death was a blessing in disguise," said the president. "Do not get me wrong. I regret that he had to die, but he died so that we politicians can make the right peace. The religious leaders could never have done it. Many are fanatics. Only politicians can make lasting peace in the Middle East."

"So, where do we go from here, Mrs. President?" the secretary of state asked, entirely disagreeing with his commander in chief.

"Let it ride."

"Let it ride? What do you mean?"

"We should stay out of it for a while!"

"Stay out of it?" the secretary asked, surprised.

"Yes," the president replied. "Let things play out their way for a bit."

Capri, Italy

ADAM HAD DECIDED NOT TO SPEND the night at his condominium. He wanted to give Nicole a special treat. He booked a suite at the Quisisana Hotel, for Nicole who loved that place. They made love all night there.

Adam rose early, as he always did. The sun had barely appeared on the horizon as he wore his Nike running shoes. His routine never changed: five miles of jogging, and then a light breakfast, followed by an hour in the gym, lifting weights. But three times a week, he added a one-hour swim. Usually, it was in a pool, but he would swim in the ocean here. Often Nicole would join him, but not today. She was still asleep as he brought the breakfast tray he had ordered from room service to her bed. He had asked them to place a single red rose on the tray.

Gently, he placed the tray on the night table next to her. He did not want to wake her. As he left the building to begin his run, he knew he was obligated to fulfill. He had failed to protect the pope, the job he had been hired to do. All his senses told him he had to find the assassin. More importantly, he had to find out the reason for the assassination. This much he owed the dead pope.

He always loved to jog on the island of Capri. It was never flat, and he loved the hills. His run would take him up the steep hill to Anacapri, a run he had done many times. Then he would jog back down to the main marina, Marina Grande, and back up the steep hill to his condominium. Jogging always helped him clear his mind.

But today, all he thought about was the pope and his assassination. Adam was almost sure that it was Lisa who had shot the pope. Why? Lisa had been a trusted member of his team. But now he knew more about Lisa than he should have known. It had taken Nicole only a few days to find out much about Lisa's family. But why had she shot the Holy Father?

Perspiration covered his muscular body as he ran up the steep hill from Marina Grande. It was early, and the streets were empty. The tourist boats had not yet arrived. Then, suddenly, he remembered a conversation he had had with Lisa. They had been together on an assignment in Berlin. They had gone out to dinner at Borchardts at the Gendarmenmarkt. The conversation had been all small talk. He had asked her about her family, but she had deflected his questions, never wanting to answer them. At the time, he had thought it was part of her training, the Mossad way, and that he knew all too well.

When they had gotten up to leave the restaurant, Lisa pulled him close and gave him a light kiss on the lips. "Thank you for a lovely dinner," she had said. "I love being back in my city."

My city? The Mossad had told him that she was from Stockholm, Sweden. Why had she called Berlin her city?

Nicole slept until 9:00 a.m. When she woke up, she noticed the breakfast tray next to her bed. She focused on the red rose and smiled. He had ordered her favorite breakfast: eggs over light, bacon, hash brown potatoes, white toast, and strawberry jam.

Nicole was healthy and disciplined and occasionally indulged in her favorite breakfast. Her standard was cereal with nonfat milk and black decaf coffee.

She rolled over and took a bite of the bacon. It was cold, and so was the coffee. Nicole picked up the phone and called room service. She ordered the same breakfast once again. She would do it the right way if she were going to splurge.

Room service would take twenty minutes, she was told—long enough to take a shower and get dressed. She heard a loud knock on her door as she stepped out of the shower. Surely it was room service, she thought. Quickly, she put on one of the hotel's white Armani robes and opened the door. The man at the door was not from room service, and it was not Adam. It was Carlo, the young priest from the Vatican. His dress was impeccable: a dark-blue blazer, a white silk shirt, white linen trousers, and dark-brown shoes.

"Nicole, please excuse me for the intrusion. I know I should have called first, and I apologize," he said politely as he stood at the door.

The man from Rome had taken Nicole completely by surprise, and she did not know how to respond. She hesitated.

"May I come in?" the young priest asked.

"Of course," Nicole responded as she regained her composure.

"Thank you. May I ask if Adam is available? I would like to talk to you both."

"He will be here any moment. He went for his early morning run. Can I offer you a cup of coffee when room service arrives?"

"No, Gracie," Carlo replied," but please proceed with your chores. I obviously arrived at a tough time."

"No," she said and smiled. "Just give me a minute while I get dressed. Please sit down and make yourself comfortable. I will be just a minute or two."

The pontiff's man had just sat down when Adam entered the apartment. Adam was surprised, but his training told him not to show it. "Good to see you again," he said as he approached the man from the Vatican. Carlo immediately stood up as Adam entered the room. They shook hands.

"Likewise," Carlo answered and smiled.

"Please, sit down and make yourself comfortable," Adam said as he picked up a towel to wipe off the perspiration on his face.

A knock at the door interrupted their conversation. It was room service. Adam instructed the waiter to carry the tray into the bedroom. "Sorry for the interruption," he said to his guest.

"No, I need to apologize," said the priest. "I should have called and told you I wanted to see you. I would very much like you to join me tomorrow. I hired a boat, a *gozzo*. You know the captain. Victorino is the best. He will take us around the island of Capri and serve us lunch. We will be all alone—just you, Nicole, and me. Then we can talk. No one will listen. There is much you need to know."

"I always enjoy a trip on Victorino's gozzo," Adam replied.

The priest smiled. He rose from the chair he had been sitting in and shook Adam's hand. "Till tomorrow. Let us meet at the small marina, Marina Piccolo, at 10:00 a.m. Do not forget your suntan lotion. I will bring everything else."

"Adam," Nicole said as she entered the living room. "Has Carlo left? What was his visit all about?"

"I think we will find out tomorrow. It should be an exciting day."

"Adam, let me tell you all I have learned about Lisa, her family, and her upbringing—all we should have known."

"Please, Nicole, I want to hear it all."

Nicole sat next to Adam on the white loveseat in their hotel suite and told Adam all that she had learned.

"Adam," she began, "Lisa was born in Berlin, not in Stockholm as you had been told. She was born at the Charité Hospital—not at the main campus, Stadt Mitte, where your father was born, but at one of the other three campuses, CBF, Campus Benjamin Franklin, in Steglitz, Berlin. Of course, I obtained my medical records; a CIA badge gives you access to anything.

"Now it becomes interesting. Lisa's mother died in childbirth. She suffered from pre-eclampsia, a hypertensive disorder of pregnancy. Her cause of death was listed as eclampsia. But her birth certificate did not mention a father, only her mother, Sofia Petterson. "Of course, I needed to find out what had happened to the baby, who had taken care of her, and who had raised her. Now, Adam, you must listen closely because the story becomes fascinating."

Nicole stood up and slowly walked toward the bar to pour a glass of Pinot Grigio. She did not want the wine but tried to hold Adam in complete suspense.

"Nicole, please stop it," Adam almost shouted. "No theatrics. You have my full attention."

"Okay, I just wanted to make sure I have your attention," Nicole said with a smile. "Now, where was I? Oh, yes. Who took care of the baby? Who raised her? No relatives showed up, not even Sofia's brothers. I do not know why. Most Swedes are Protestants; very few are Catholic, but the Pettersons were Catholic. Lisa's mother had joined the priest Mattias von Meissen's parish at the St. Bernhard church on Koenig-Luise Strasse in Dahlem, near where she lived and attended the Freie Universität of Berlin. The priest and Sofia, Lisa's mother, had become close friends and shared many interests. Often, Sofia had helped the young priest to organize charitable events. However, I was still surprised when I learned the priest had decided to raise Lisa's baby. The priest had all the means to do so, as his family was one of the wealthiest German families, and he used his resources. Lisa had many nannies and went to the best schools, including the most expensive finishing school in Switzerland, Le Rosey. Then she attended Stanford. "Nicole, please, slow down," Adam interrupted. "Are you telling. Tell me that this priest in Berlin raised Lisa, the daughter of one of his parishioners?"

"Yes, he did. That was what God's men did. That is why they are special. But please, hear me out. The best is yet to come. Mattias von Meissen, the priest at the St. Bernhard parish in Dahlem, soon became the Archbishop of Berlin, the priest at St. Hedwig's Cathedral. Then he was raised to the position of cardinal, and eventually he became Pope Leo XIV."

"The pope raised Lisa?" Adam asked in disbelief. "Nicole, what a fascinating story. You did an excellent job!"

"Not yet," Nicole answered. "I still need to find Lisa's father!"

Rome, Italy

The phone call was brief. The young confidant of the pope, Carlo, told his lover in Berlin that all had gone according to plan. They would all go out on a boat off the island of Capri. That was when he would tell Adam what Berlin wanted him to do. No, he would not just tell him; he would convince him that Berlin's way was the right way, the only way, the way of the truth.

Capri, Italy

It was a beautiful day. The waters of the Mediterranean Sea looked bluer and glistening than Adam had ever remembered. Shortly after he would finished his jog around his favorite island, Nicole reminded him of their date. Both were packed light—shorts, bathing suits, sandals, and suntan lotion.

Adam smiled. Suntan lotion was the only request the young priest made. Marina Piccolo was down the steep hill from their hotel, so Adam took a taxi. It was a short drive, and Adam and Nicole arrived fifteen minutes early. Both the captain and the young priest were already on the boat. They were all greeted like old friends, with hugs and kisses. Even Victorino got into it. Victorino's boat was a classic wooden boat, a replica of the *Bella Latina, a small workboat* from the past.

Victorino had stocked his Gozzo well. As always, there was wine. Much of the food he had grown in his own garden. He always prided himself on his fresh produce, basil, tomatoes, capers, olive oil, and homemade bread. Adam's favorite dish, *ricci*—sea urchin topped with lemon—had been prepared by Victorino that morning.

The gozzo had a huge lounging bed in the bow of the boat. All three relaxed there.

The priest from Rome began the conversation. "Adam, you now surely know that the pope and I had an incredibly special relationship. He trusted me. I was his only confidant. Let me share with you how I first met the pope. It is a story not too many people know. I am Italian but grew up in Berlin, where my grandparents raised me. The Holy Father was but a priest then, and I was ten or eleven years old. I lived in Dahlem, a Berlin suburb near where the pope had his parish.

"Nearby, there was a park, Im Schwarzen Grund, where children would go sledding and skiing in the wintertime—and still do. The hills are small and gentle, but we enjoyed sledding and skiing there as kids. I still remember it vividly. It was the day after Christmas. My Christmas present was a brand-new pair of skis. Naturally, I could not wait to try them out. I went to the park to ski. On my very first run, a young girl on a sled crossed my skis, breaking the tip of one of them. I was in disbelief. I had wished for a pair of skis all my life. I was in tears. The young girl also cried. She apologized profusely. Then she told me to go home and speak to her uncle to see if he could help.

I asked her where she lived, and she told me she lived at the church of St. Bernhard in Dahlem Dorf. It was not too far away from my home. So, I took my broken ski and went to church. It was a Sunday afternoon, and all the worshippers had left the church. I went to the residence adjacent to the church, where I knew the priest lived. I knocked on the door, and the priest opened it. With the broken ski in my hand, I told him the story. He smiled and put his right hand on my shoulder.

"Son," he said, "this is a lesson you should never forget. Do not be angry. Learn how to forgive. And may I use your broken ski as a topic for my sermon next Sunday? I would like you to be there."

The next day, I received a brand-new pair of skis. The following Sunday, I went to his church to hear his sermon. He held my broken ski held his right hand as he spoke about healing, forgiveness, love, and peace. It was at once that I decided to enter the priesthood. Thanks to him, I could follow him to Rome and the Vatican. As you know, I was his right hand, his most trusted person. The pope and I had an incredibly special relationship. I know more about the pontiff than anyone else."

"What do you mean, you know more than anyone else?" Adam asked.

"Well, that is why I am here. I can no longer bear the burden. I need to share. Some of what I know is fact, and some is speculation."

"What is your interest in getting to the bottom?" Adam interrupted. "Is it just curiosity, or is there more to it?"

"There is more. The pope and I always had a special relationship."

"Well, let's start at the beginning," Nicole piped up. "I only see things when I have seen them from the start."

"Okay," Carlo responded, "let us go back and start at the beginning. The pope had asked me to research his birth secretly. He was born on October 15, 1944, at the Charité Hospital in Berlin. He had heard rumors about switched babies that day at that same hospital. But he did not know the time of his birth. He wanted to be sure he was not one of the switched babies. If he was, he was aware of the possible consequences. That was why he had asked me to research in secret.

"The original rumors had it that four boys—Schneider, Rubin, Bergman, and von Hohenzollern—had been born within the same hour on October 15 at the Charité Hospital. Schneider became the president of the EU, and his butler assassinated him, as you well know. Daniel Bergman died in a plane crash in the United States; he was your father, Adam—or not. William von Hohenzollern is now the president of the EU. Rubin later changed his name to Sharef, and he is now the head of the Mossad.

"But my research showed that the original rumors were not factual. Sharef had not born at the Charité Hospital in Stadtmitte. Yes, he was born on October 15, but at another Charité campus, Berlin-Buch. And not three boys but five were born that night at the Stadtmitte Charité hospital. The names of the others are von Claussen and von Meissen, the pope's family name."

"How did you come to all that information?" Adam asked in disbelief.

The priest did not answer Adam at once. He stood up from the sunbath he had been lying on and walked toward the stern of the boat. "Victorino, please hand me a bottle of wine," he said with a smile. Carlo carried the bottle, and the captain handed him to the large sun bed before the boat. He filled Nicole's and Adam's glasses.

Then he carefully put the bottle in the small cooler Victorino had placed next to the sun bed.

"I—obviously with the pope's support—left no stone unturned," Carlo continued as he sat beside Nicole. "The hospital records clearly indicated that all the babies born that day, in the same hour, had been admitted to the nursery. Later, the ward nurses discovered all the babies' armbands on the floor. Martha Bergman had removed all the identification wristlets and thrown them on the floor. She had been in haste and acted out of panic."

"Okay," Nicole said, "let me summarize, and please tell me when I'm wrong."

"No problem," the young priest replied. "I know it is complicated. Please go ahead."

"Okay, thank you. We are in Berlin, Germany, at the Charité Hospital in Stadtmitte on October 15, 1944, early in the morning. Five baby boys are lying in the nursery. A woman sneaks in: Martha Bergman. She is desperate and wants to hide the identity of her baby, for she is afraid the Nazis will kill him because he's Jewish. Am I right so far?" Nicole asked.

The priest nodded.

"Now," Nicole continued, "Mrs. Bergman switches the babies, puts them in different cribs, removes all the names in front of the cribs, removes the identification bands from the babies' wrists, and throws them all on the floor, and leaves in haste. How am I doing?" Nicole wanted to know.

"Perfect," the young priest replied.

"Let me go on, please," Nicole said. "I want to make sure I get this right. Then Mrs. Bergman, the alleged perpetrator, leaves. But someone sees her, someone who knows her—one of the nurses who left the meeting to go to the bathroom. But did the nurse witness the switch, or did she notice the presence of Mrs. Bergman?"

"No," Carlo answered. "All she noticed was that Mrs. Bergman was there—although this had seemed odd to the nurse since it was not visiting hours but late at night."

"Well," Nicole continued, "I agree that it was odd, but there is no proof that Mrs. Bergman did all she has been accused of, correct? And how did the nurse identify Mrs. Bergman? Did she know her?"

"Mrs. Bergman had done much charity work at the hospital, particularly with children," Carlo answered. "Everyone knew her."

Adam was sitting next to Nicole on the large sun bed of Victorino's gozzo. He had not commented but had listened intently to Nicole. He had absorbed every sentence and had not missed a word. After all, this discussion involved his father, whoever he might have been. "Please, Nicole," Adam pleaded, "please go on. You are making it clear, helping me to understand."

Nicole smiled at him, reached for his hand, and squeezed it. She knew this conversation evoked emotions for Adam. Who would not become emotional when learning who one's father's warehouse was not?

"Well, here we are today," Nicole continued. "Three of the five boys are dead: Dr. Schneider, Daniel Bergman, and Pope Leo XIV. Now we are left with two boys born at the same place on the same day at the same time. One is the president of the EU. And the other—what happened to that baby?"

"We have no idea," the young priest replied. "All we know is the name: von Claussen."

"What a mess," Adam said. "Will we ever know who is. More importantly, does it really matter?"

"Whether it matters or not is a different subject for discussion," Carlo replied. "It matters significantly to some, and little to others.

But to your next question, will we ever know—yes, there is a way. And you, Adam, know it all too well."

The priest looked at Adam, not really seeking the answer, for he knew Adam had used the methodology many times before in his profession. He looked into Adam's eyes to see his soul, just as his superior, the pope, had done when he had first met Adam. However, unlike the pope, the young priest could not see Adam's soul. He only saw an endless ocean—calm, without a single wave.

"DNA testing," Adam whispered. He took another bite of the ricci that Victorino had prepared. Then he stood up and faced the young priest. In his right hand, he held a bottle of suntan lotion. Slowly, he covered his body with it. He knew it would cover him from the sun, but it was not the sun about which he was concerned.

"Yes, DNA testing," Carlo said. "The Vatican sent me here to obtain your permission. Of course, we already have the necessary material in our possession. But on my way to Capri to meet with you, I received new instructions. I was told by the Vatican that there should not be any testing, that the whole story about the switched babies should be ignored and treated as a hoax. I guess it would have been difficult for the Catholic Church to admit that Pope Leo was a Jew if DNA tests proved it to be so.

Adam leaned back onto the soft cushions of Victorino's gozzo. He had learned about the alleged switch. Often, he confronted his grandmother to find out the truth. She was always steadfast in her answer: it had never happened. She usually said, there had been a Nazi plot to degrade her family. "Adam," she had always said, "I am your grandmother. Don't you feel it?" And then they would hug and kiss. Then Adam knew, or thought he knew, that he could trust her, that she was telling the truth.

Nonetheless, Adam had often thought about what might have happened to the babies if there had been a switch at the hospital. The possibilities were staggering. Any one of the babies could have been the pope, even a Jewish baby. A Jewish pope? Not a bad possibility, Adam thought with a sneaker. But was it really wishing to find out?

Carlo smiled, because he had another purpose, another reason for coming here to meet with Adam.

His lover in Berlin needed Adam.

CHAPTER 27

South Beirut, Lebanon

ACROSS THE MEDITERRANEAN SEA AND surrounded by miles of sand, the older man gently stroked his gray beard. Hassan Nasral was sitting in his bunker deep underground, a place no one would ever find. He was barefoot as he sat on his chair, which had been placed on one of the many luxurious rugs that covered most of his hideaway. He looked at the large fireplace, the centerpiece of this elegant bunker.

The imam loved fireplaces. He had previously watched the wood burn and the flames change colors and smelled smoke. It always reminded him of the days when he fought the wars, when his people lit a fire in the mountains of his beloved country each night. But today there was no fire; that could never be. The smoke would reveal his secret hideaway, and he could not take that chance. He never took chances. That was why he had survived and had become their leader.

Tonight, the secretary-general of Hezbollah was not alone. His only grandson had come to be with him, to support him during these difficult times. The young man had left his studies at Stanford University to be with his grandfather. For the young man, it had been an easy choice. He had never wanted to leave the desert, his family, his grandfather, his people. But his grandfather had insisted. "You need to be educated," he had said. "Learn all about our enemies, their beliefs, and their thinking. You need to know your enemy to win a war. And I want you to lead the way. Go and study the infidels and learn all about their weaknesses. Then, and only then, can we strike." And his grandson had done so. The imam smiled. He had never expected his grandson to be ready so soon, but the young man had far exceeded his expectations.

The bunker was a lonely place. The holy man never entertained here. Very few people knew its location. And the leader of Hezbollah liked to be alone. This was where he planned and prayed. From here, he would destroy all the infidels and conquer the world for Allah, his God.

When his grandson first entered the bunker, the older man had just completed a prayer. He almost did not recognize the young man from California. He was young, tall, and athletic, and he had a purposeful stride. The older man loved Allah, but he loved his grandson even more. He turned toward him, a large smile filling his face. Then he noticed that his grandson was not alone. A young, beautiful blonde woman was walking next to him. The imam was surprised. No woman had ever entered his bunker. Women were forbidden here, and his grandson knew it too well.

Once they had embraced, the young man from California quickly explained: "Grandfather, I know only incredibly special people can enter this bunker. But this woman is incredibly special. She deserves to be here."

"Let us all sit down, feel at ease, and get to know each other," Hassan replied.

"I agree," the young man from Stanford said nervously.

"Relax, be at ease," the old man said as his grandson and the young woman took a place on the rug in front of the fireplace. "Now, let's hear your story."

"This is Lisa. I met her at Stanford, and we are in love. She used to work for the Mossad, but now she is dedicated to our cause."

"How do you know? How can you tell?" the secretary-general asked softly, not wanting to antagonize his grandson. But experience had told him to be careful, not to trust.

"I know you will agree with me," the young man responded respectfully but confidently. "Lisa did what you asked for. She shot the pope!"

This startled the older man. He had not expected this. Not often was he caught by surprise. "She shot the pope?" he asked, in disbelief. "How did it come about? Please explain."

"I asked her to do it," his grandson responded enthusiastically. "She is the one who fulfilled your wish. She is the one who paved the way for our faith to dominate the world. You wanted me to pull the trigger, but that was impossible. There was too much security. I had to use someone inside who was part of the security. Fortunately, the man the pope hired, Adam Bergman, had trusted Lisa and made her part of his security team. He had placed her in the perfect position to take the fatal shot. Of course, he had no idea that Lisa was working for me. He made a serious mistake, and I took advantage of it."

"You did better than I ever expected," the old man replied, gently stroking his beard. I should have known better, as you consistently exceed my expectations." He leaned over and kissed his grandson. "I am very blessed to have a grandson like you. Allah chose the best for me. And Ali, my son, could I speak with you privately? I am sure Lisa will not mind. I want both of you to be my guest, to stay at my humble home tonight." He smiled at Lisa as he extended the invitation. "There are many bedrooms here. Why don't we have one of the servants show Lisa around and let her choose where she wants to stay?"

"Great, Grandpa. I will go along."

"No," the old imam replied. "I have not seen you for too long. I want to spend a few minutes with only you. I am sure Lisa will not mind."

"Of course not," Lisa answered quickly, wanting to please the old holy man and win him over.

As Lisa left the luxurious sitting room of the bunker, accompanied by a young servant, Hassan asked his grandson to sit close to him. The older man hugged the person he loved more than his God. Tears formed in his eyes. He knew he was about to ask his grandson to make a most difficult decision that would define Ali's belief in him—and, more importantly, Allah. The leader of Hezbollah was short on words, for he did not believe in sugar coating—not when it came to family, nor when it came to his God.

"Ali," he said as soon as Lisa and the servant had left the sitting room, "Lisa now knows too much. Do it tonight. Do it silently. Do it the Mossad way but do it for Allah."

Hassan Nasral barely heard the shots. His grandson had used a silencer. But the older man counted each: five shots, the Mossad way.

Berlin, Germany

Prince William von Hohenzollern was nervous. For days, he had not heard from his cousin. His cousin, Prince Albert, had promised him that his contact, the young priest at the Vatican, would meet with Adam Bergman. He was to convince Adam to resolve the issue of his birth.

No matter the outcome of the DNA testing, William could not, would not be a Jew that he knew. But he needed to hear the results before anyone else. Then he could manipulate the data. He had no choice but to agree to the DNA testing. The Vatican was determined to go through with that. The president of the EU did not understand why. It could show that the pope was Jewish. Would the Vatican take that chance? He did not trust the Vatican; he never had. They had another agenda, of which, he was sure. He was not religious, and when it came to politics, he knew the church should keep out of it. He was convinced that prayers did not resolve politics, diplomacy, and peace on earth. It took more than belief to make peace. But he knew others thought differently. It was his mission to prove them wrong.

Washington, DC

Monica Drew, president of the United States, had changed her mind, as she often did when vital decisions were involved. It had quickly become a signature of her term at the White House. No one ever knew where the president was going from one day to the next. Neither did she. Today, she had decided that she wanted no part in the peace process in the Middle East—not now, after her predecessor's policies had failed miserably.

It was too early to intervene again, she thought. Let the Europeans and the Russians fight it out first. Let them take on the jihadists. She thought she had learned from the mistakes of her predecessor, and she was determined not to replicate his mistakes. She would wait until all had failed to make peace in the Middle East. Then, and only then, would she take the initiative, no matter how many innocent people would be killed by the terrorists.

"Mrs. President," the secretary of state had argued, "if we wait to get involved, we will miss the boat. Attacks may also happen again in America." Both were sitting in the oval office and still disliked each other.

"Mr. Secretary," the president replied as she left the chair behind her desk and walked toward her former opponent, "I respect your opinion, but you are wrong. We will stay out of it. And we will do it until I, only I, decide to get involved. Am I making myself clear?" She said it nonthreateningly but in a tone that left no doubt.

"Yes, Madame President," the secretary replied. "You've made it very clear."

Capri, Italy

Victorino steered his boat gently next to the rocky dock at the Marina Piccolo on the island of Capri. His three guests hugged him as they disembarked. The young priest, who had hired the boat, left last. He put his arms around the captain, whispered to him in Italian, and gave him a large tip.

The three passengers now began the arduous walk back to town. None spoke as they ascended the steep steps. When they reached Carlo's hotel, he pulled Adam aside.

"Please, let us have dinner tonight. I need to talk to you about another matter, and it has to do with Berlin. It is okay if you bring Nicole. I do not mind."

"All right," Adam answered." Let us meet in the lobby of your hotel at 7:00 p.m."

"Fine," the priest said, "and thank you for joining me today." Adam and Nicole had both taken showers and were sipping a Campari and orange juice are Nicole's favorite drinks. They were sitting on the balcony of Adam's apartment overlooking the calm sea. The sky was still blue, and the sun had not yet shown signs of leaving the sky. The breeze was gentle.

"Adam," Nicole said, raising her glass of Campari, "what do you make of all this DNA testing? What was the Vatican after? Why did they drop the idea, or—I guess, more importantly—why did they want the tests in the first place?"

"Darling, I'm not sure," Adam said as he picked up his drink. "It makes no sense. I mean, it could turn out that the pope was Jewish. That might be why they dropped the idea. I have no clue why they wanted to perform the tests in the first place. Why are they not focused on finding the pope's assassin? I cannot figure it out."

Nicole leaned back. She was deep in thought.

"Could it be that one may lead to the other?" she almost whispered. Adam did not respond. It was an interesting thought, and all the possibilities raced through his mind. But there were too many, and He could not make sense of them all—not now anyway.

The young man from Rome took a shower in his luxury suite at the Quisisana Hotel, one of the best on the island of Capri. He always stayed at the best hotels, and Rome paid for it. He had a very generous budget.

Carlo walked out of the shower and dried his slim body. He was glad the Vatican had abandoned the idea of the DNA tests, even though it had been his idea in the first place. Carlo had always suspected that the pope's assassin was someone from within the pope's inner circle, and DNA testing of some of the players could shed some light on who the perpetrator was. But the negative consequences—the pope perhaps being a Jew far outweighed the possible insight into who the pope's assassin was. Besides, Carlo already possessed DNA samples of some of the players, and he was not about to ask the Vatican for permission to try to match those samples.

Tel Aviv, Israel

The rabbi from Brooklyn was nervous. He knew his brother-in-law was one of the most powerful people in Israel—and the world. Sitting in the Mossad office thirty minutes early, he wondered why he had come to Israel. It was a chance to see his sister, his last. Ever since she had left Brooklyn to marry the man now head of the Mossad, he loved and missed her. But why, he wondered, would the head of the Mossad need to talk to him? Yesterday had been a wonderful day, the plane ride, the extensive limousine that had taken him to his sister's mansion, embracing his sister, whom he loved so much, and the wonderful dinner she had cooked for him. He would never forget any of it. Only when he saw her, when they embraced, did he know he had made the right choice to come to Israel. He had hesitated, never wanting to leave his home in Brooklyn Heights. But he loved his sister.

At precisely 10:00 a.m., when his brother-in-law had arranged to meet him, Maza entered his office. The rabbi was nervous, and drops of perspiration ran down his forehead. He stood up as his brother-in-law entered the room. The rabbi from Brooklyn wore the traditional robe of a rabbi, and his brother-in-law wore a pin-striped, gray Armani suit.

"Please, Baruch, relax. You wonder why I sent it to you, and you should. But it is not a big deal. Relax. I need some information. You may have it, or you may not. Nonetheless, it was great for you to come. Your sister undoubtedly is enjoying your visit. She wants you to stay forever." The head of the Mossad smiled, clearly wishing to put his brother-in-law at ease. "Would you like a refreshment—a bottle of water, a Coke?" he asked.

The rabbi from Brooklyn shook his head. He did not want any. All he wanted was to see his sister again—and then go back home and sit under the large oak tree where he always said his prayers.

"Okay," Maza continued, "let us get down to it. There was a boy, a young man named Adam Bergman, who was part of your temple. Do you remember him?"

"Yes, I do," the rabbi answered. "I knew him well. He always prayed with me. He and I often walked in my park. You must know I adopted him as my grandson. I love him."

"Can you tell me more? Tell me for whom he worked?"

"No, I cannot. All I know is that he believed in God, a belief that he and I shared deeply."

Now the head of the Mossad realized that the rabbi from Brooklyn had no information. It had been a waste to send for him—but not a complete waste, for his wife would always thank him.

Capri, Italy

Adam had made reservations at his favorite restaurant on Capri, the Aurora, to have dinner with Carlo. The restaurant was small—only a few tables, some outside in the open air. There was no view, but the food was the best. He called the young priest to meet him at 9:30 p.m. at the restaurant. Adam and Nicole enjoyed eating late, and the priest did not mind.

Everyone at the restaurant knew Adam, as he ate there often. When he and Nicole arrived, his favorite bottle of wine was already open next to the table, chilling in ice water. Nicole and Adam were early. They had taken a stroll, a ritual they always performed before dinner. But the man from Rome was punctual. As his German lover had always told him, being on time was important. People respected you when you respected the value of their time. He had always told his lover that being late meant that you believed your time was more valuable than your guest's message you never wanted to send.

Nicole and Adam had already taken a seat at Adam's favorite table. Adam liked to sit outside, and he always enjoyed the sea air, the soft breeze off the Mediterranean Sea. When the young priest approached them, Adam rose. He greeted Carlo warmly, putting his arms around him. The young priest had wanted to greet Nicole first, the customary European way, but Adam had not let him.

After Adam's embrace, the priest hugged Nicole and kissed her on both cheeks. Then Adam handed him a glass of wine. "Salute," he said. "Here we are again. Rome must have given you a full agenda."

"Yes," the priest replied, embarrassed. "Yes, Rome surely did."

"Let's order dinner," Adam said. "Here they serve the best pasta vongole, my favorite dish."

"Mine too," Nicole piped up.

"Well, you have convinced me. I will join you," Carlo said with a smile.

"If peace on earth were that easy," Adam joked, "we would not be here tonight."

"True," the man from Rome replied, "but not everyone likes pasta vongole."

They all chuckled and raised their glasses.

"You're right," Nicole said with a laugh. "That is the problem. Everyone should like pasta vongole."

The waiter approached to take the order. He knew Adam well. He knew the dish Adam would request, and his guests ordered the same: the house special, pasta vongole. The waiter smiled and winked at Adam, who returned his smile.

"Now we will experience my favorite meal," Adam said. "But I know that is not why we are here tonight—although it should be. But I cannot always have it my way." He turned toward the young priest. "You asked to have dinner with me tonight and said you did not mind if Nicole came along. What is on your mind?"

"As I mentioned briefly earlier, this concerns Berlin."

"Berlin?" Adam said curiously. "What is the Vatican doing in Berlin?"

"This is not a Vatican affair. I have a particularly good friend in Berlin— in the government, in fact. He is the cousin of the German chancellor, the EU president. He is Prince Albert."

"Excuse me," the waiter interrupted. "Are you ready to be served?"

"Yes," Nicole replied. "You noticed our intense conversation and did not want to interrupt."

"Si," he said with a broad smile that said he understood. The waiter served their meal. It was the best pasta the man from Rome had ever had. For several minutes, there was silence at the small table at the Aurora restaurant. No one spoke. All enjoyed the meal.

Adam finally broke the silence. "Please bring us another bottle of wine," he said to the waiter. He lifted his glass and finished what had been left in it. As he put the glass back on the table, he stared at the priest."

"Please continue. What does Berlin want?"

"Prince William von Hohenzollern wants to meet with you at his home in Berlin. It should be at your convenience, and the prince will adjust his schedule."

"Carlo, do you know the reason for the meeting? Why does the prince want to see me?"

"No, I do not, but it has to do with the peace in the Middle East. There are rumors—and you are aware of them—that the prince has a unique solution to the peace."

"No," Adam replied, "I have not heard them. Have you?"

"Yes, I have—at least the rumors at the Vatican. But I cannot speak to their authenticity."

"Carlo, what are they saying?"

"Prince William believes that to stop the war, you must remove the cause."

"Of course," Adam quickly interrupted. "Who doesn't believe so?"

"Clearly, everyone does," Carlo continued, "but that is not the issue. The issue is what the prince believes to be the cause."

"And what is that?" Adam was now anxious to know.

"Religion," Carlo responded as he looked into Adam's eyes and attempted to see a proper reaction. There was none.

"Religion," Adam repeated. "An interesting concept. No one can deny the fact that we are fighting a bunch of religious fanatics. The prince has kindled my curiosity. I would like to know how he intends to remove the cause, remove religion.

"So, do I have your permission to set up a meeting in Berlin?" Carlo asked.

"Yes, indeed, you do. When it comes to peace, I intend to explore all viable solutions. That I owe to Pope Leo."

The man from Rome smiled. "I admire your outlook. I wish the rest of the world would think like you."

They had finished dinner—one of the best the man from Rome had ever enjoyed. All had now been served a glass of Grappa, Adam's favorite after-dinner drink.

The priest took a sip. He was not used to such strong drinks, but he enjoyed the flavor. He took another sip—a little larger than the first one. He smiled. He loved the company of Nicole and Adam.

Adam slept restlessly and turned repeatedly, never gaining a deep sleep. Too much was on his mind. It was 3:00 a.m. At least that was what the clock next to his bed in his comfortable apartment told him. He stretched and removed the down covers from his body. He reached to his right and retrieved the bottle of water he always kept next to him. He took a large drink and returned the bottle to the night table. The water bottle was always on his right. His gun was to his left—not that he was a lefty, but he had learned that if he was attacked, he needed to roll over quickly to avoid getting shot. Then he could grab his gun with his right hand, the hand he shot best with. It was not that Adamcould nott shoot with his left hand; he was a marksman with both. But his right hand was better.

He knew he could sleep no more. He thought about the boys who had all been born on October 15, 1944, at the same time, at the Charité hospital in Berlin. He knew that one of those boys was his father, but he did not know which one—although his grandmother, who had never admitted that she had switched the babies, always insisted that he was her grandson. One of those babies was now the president of the EU, and another had been the pope. Did it really matter what their roots were, whether they were Catholic or Jewish? Wasn't peace more important? He was excited to visit Prince William von Hohenzollern. He wanted to learn all about making peace in the Middle East.

CHAPTER 28

Rome, Italy

THE YOUNG PRIEST, THE FORMER POPE'S confidant, still had not coped with the pope's death. He never would, he thought as he put on his Armani pin-striped suit for another meeting with Adam. But deep in his heart, he knew that his pope had always wanted him to follow the only path to peace the holy man had shown him. It was the path of truth.

It had been fourteen days since the pope had died. Yet no smoke had escaped the chimneys of the Vatican to indicate that a new leader of the Catholic Church had been elected.

The young priest was late for his dinner date. He had been detained at the Vatican. The meeting had taken longer than he had expected. There were questions about the pope's death, security, and every detail of his life. The young priest had tried to answer all the questions and had done well, he thought. But he knew his dinner date would be different. It would not focus on the past.

Adam had suggested Ranieri, his favorite restaurant in Rome. The young priest had agreed. When Adam arrived, he asked for his usual table near the kitchen. He took a seat with the wall at his back, the way of the Mossad and the NSA, the way he had been trained. He smiled, almost laughed. Old habits never die.

Adam was fifteen minutes early. Again, that was what he had been taught to do: be early, survey the stage, and if you are not comfortable, leave at once. He no longer had to think about these routines, for they were in his blood and had become second nature.

He wore a Zegna white dinner jacket, perfectly matching his muscular body. But there had been no room to hide his Beretta, the gun he always carried, even when he was about to meet a man of peace. He had strapped the weapon to the inside of his left leg just above his ankle to make it less visible but more accessible. Adam had no reason to wear the gun tonight, but as he often told Nicole, he felt naked without it. And he only wanted to feel that way when he was with her.

The priest entered the restaurant ten minutes late. He immediately spotted Adam, who rose from his chair to greet the man. They hugged. They liked each other. Adam asked Carlo to sit in the chair opposite him. Always place your opponent where you want him to be another lesson he has learned while training to be an assassin. "Gracie," the priest said as he sat in the chair Adam had pointed to.

"You look exhausted," Adam said. "You need a drink."

"Please, just a glass of Pinot Grigio would be fine," Carlo responded. "And you must forgive me. First, I am late. I am sorry about that, but the business at the Vatican kept me there. Second, the Vatican decided to identify the pope's assassin. We believe you should handle it. Unfortunately, I cannot have dinner with you tonight, but I would love a rain check. My plate is full of the pope's death, and no new pope has been appointed yet. I hope you understand." The young priest rose from his chair. "I believe that there will be an important meeting soon. You should be part of it." He embraced Adam, who was now also standing. The priest kissed Adam on both cheeks, turned around, and hurriedly left the restaurant. Adam sat back in his chair, his back to the restaurant's wall.

He reflected on what the young priest had just told him. First, there was the issue of the pope's assassin, Lisa. He knew it was his responsibility to make things right. After all, she had been part of his team, and he had hired her to protect the pope. He would take care of it. He was still surprised by the Vatican's decision not to pursue the DNA testing. Only a week ago, the Vatican had been intent on learning all about the babies. Adam had never understood their reason. Was it only now that the Vatican understood that the pope might be the son of a Jew? Or was there more to it than Adam knew?

Adam missed Nicole. She was waiting for him on Capri. Adam needed rest and time to think and make things right with the Vatican concerning the pope's assassination.

He left the restaurant in Rome and hired a car to drive him to Naples. There, he caught the last ferry to Capri. He stood on the boat's deck, staring at the star-filled sky. He felt carefree whenever he left Napoli on the ferry to go to Capri. Now he felt like all his burdens had been left behind. It almost seemed to him like he was starting a new life without a past, a life full of new beginnings. Of course, he knew it was but a dream. But it was a dream that lasted a few days with his love on the island he adored, a dream he had always sought, a dream of life.

Lake Bracciano, Italy

They were naked. Both had waited long to make love again. The priest from Rome and the German minister embraced. They caressed. They kissed. It had been several months since they had last met on their secret hideaway on Lake Bracciano.

The German minister, Prince Albert, the cousin of the EU president, rolled over in the king-size bed that overlooked the lake. He and Carlo had just made love. It reminded him of how much he had missed the man from Rome, his young lover. He lit a cigarette for himself and then another for his lover. Both sat up in bed, smiled, and kissed. "Well," the minister said as he inhaled the smoke of his Marlboro cigarette. He did not continue but waited to exhale the smoke. "All is going according to plan. You have not missed a beat. I am proud of you, but more importantly, I love you." He smiled at his younger lover, touched his cheek, and kissed him. "Really," Prince Albert continued, "no one else could have given us the information. We needed."

He tucked a pillow behind his head. He was almost bald, yet he looked much younger than his chronological age of sixty-seven. He exercised regularly, and his body was firm and muscular. "Now all the pieces will soon be in place. Most already are."

The young priest from Rome smiled. He adored his lover, and he loved it when he praised him. His right hand gently stroked the face of the minister.

"I did it only for you," Carlo whispered.

But the man from Berlin was more of a realist. Yes, he loved the man from Rome, but he also knew that the young priest was only a part of the plot that his cousin, the EU president, had designed. Germany was once again the most potent economic force in Europe. But some wounds would never heal. His cousin, the chancellor of Germany and president of the EU, had told him this. "They punished us after World War I," he always said. "They overdid it. They kicked us as if one would kick an animal. There was only one way for us to react: to retaliate. Well, that was World War II. Again, we lost because we had the wrong leadership. There will never be a World

War III. That surely would be the end of humanity." In this way, Prince William had lectured his cousin.

Yet a different World War III was raging right now, William insisted. It was a war much different from the last two world wars. It was a war about a much more powerful cause than nationalism. It was a war whose cause had no boundaries and crossed all national borders—even continents. The reason was religion. For Prince William to stop the war, William had to stop religion. People had to give up their beliefs and accept the truth as the new gospel.

Berlin, Germany

Prince Albert believed in his cousin, and now he knew that the key to controlling the world powers was within his cousin's reach. To change beliefs, the basis of religion, was the key to peace in the Middle East. He and his cousin, the chancellor of Germany, often discussed their country's role in current world politics. The chancellor often expressed his belief that Germany had an outstanding debt to pay for the damage it had caused during the twentieth century. It had been instrumental in starting two world wars, which had resulted in many deaths and much devastation. In his mind, the German chancellor knew he had to repay Germany's debt, and he was determined to do so. He knew he had to achieve only two goals to repay that debt, but he also knew that these goals would be difficult to achieve. There would always be others to compete with, most with agendas much different from their own.

One of the goals was to control the economy, which had come easily, much to his surprise. Germany had become the driving force of Europe's economy, and he had successfully created a united Europe. It had happened despite the United States's efforts to prevent it.

However, the president of the EU, the chancellor of Germany, knew that this power of economic excellence was only one of the ingredients he needed for world peace. The other, he knew, was religion. That was why his cousin, the minister, played a key role. The president of the EU needed to know about the Vatican. He needed to know all about all the religions. He needed to change the basic tenets of their beliefs. He needed to make them accept the truth and understand that belief was not reality, not fact. Only the truth was.

It was time for all religious leaders to accept the truth that there was no proof of a creator, no heaven, no seventy virgins waiting. It was time to bring all the players together and sit at one table to accept the truth, finally, the only way to peace. Only then would he be able to repay the world and make the peace his country owed to the rest of the world.

He had decided to call for a meeting of all religious leaders, for he knew—unlike all the other politicians—that true peace could only be achieved via religion. He had spent weeks finding the perfect place to make peace. At first he had thought that the Bundestag, the German parliament house, would be the right place. But he changed his mind. The proper place to finalize peace had to be a place of history, a place of tranquility, a sanctuary. Then he knew. It had to take place at Sanssouci, Frederick the Great's retreat. The very name meant "without worry." Here the great leader had often retreated to relax. Here the emperor had often spent time with Voltaire, played his music, and thought about peace. And the palace was near to the capital of Germany, only a few miles from the Bundestag in the city of Potsdam. Yes, he thought, Sanssouci was where they would all meet.

He picked up his phone as he leaned back in the large leather chair in his office of the Chancellery. He called his cousin, the minister of

Foreign affairs. "Albert," he said when the man answered, "you have done well. Now it is time to finalize our plan. Don't you agree?"

"Yes," was the reply. "All is going the way you wanted."

"It is now that we should meet with all the players. Now is the time to make peace!"

"Yes," his cousin, the minister, replied. "I agree."

"Then let us all meet. Let us discuss what needs to be done to finalize peace."

"I will arrange it," the minister replied.

"Send me a list of all the people you think should participate," Prince William continued. "I need it soon."

"I will," the minister answered. "Where should we all meet?"

"Sanssouci." There was a click, and the phone went silent.

Sanssouci, Prince Albert thought, was the perfect place. His cousin always made the right choices. Now, he needed to invite all the right people who could make the peace his cousin wanted, the peace his cousin thought Germany owed the world. His list was not long. He knew the people who should be there. He also knew the people who wanted to be there. He decided to create two lists and then let his cousin decide.

He first sent both lists to his lover, the young priest in Rome. He wanted his input, for he respected his opinion. The first list was noticeably short. It included the EU president, the grand ayatollah from Iran, the imam from Iraq or his representative, the chief rabbis, and a representative from the Vatican since no new pope had yet been named. The other list, the longer one, also included the head of the Mossad, the president of the United States, and the President of the Russian Federation.

The young priest recommended adopting the first list, but he decided to add one more name. He wanted Adam Bergman on the

He wanted Adam for his own protection in case the Vatican selected him as their representative.

When the minister at the Bundestag received the response from his lover in Rome, he smiled. He had chosen the same players. It did not take him long to have his cousin, the president of the EU, agree. The date, the place, and the participants were all decided upon. But all had to be secret. All knew that the NSA was listening. All knew that the president of the United States wanted to be involved. The president of the Russian Federation was opposed to the peace altogether. He did not care about legacy. He cared only about Mother Russia. Peace in the Middle East without Russia could destroy his plans to make Russia a world power once more. He would not let that happen. Not after he had staged the best Olympics and had shown the world his determination in Ukraine.

That was why the minister of the Bundestag decided that the invitations had to be delivered by hand. He knew any electronic transmission would be intercepted, for the NSA never missed one. He did not know how. He asked his lover in Rome for advice. His lover told him that only one man could accomplish this mission: Adam Bergman.

Capri, Italy

It was late. Adam had taken the very last ferry from Napoli to Capri. He was tired, but he could not wait to see Nicole. He never sat down during the one-hour ferry ride. Instead, he paced back and forth on the deck of the boat. He was anxious, and he needed to relax. He needed to be in Nicole's arms. He needed to make love to her.

When the ferry anchored at Marina Grande, she was there. She was beautifully dressed all in white, her hair flowing in the wind. Lips full. He had missed her and held her, never wanting to let go. The taxi took them up the steep hill to his apartment.

He carried her into the bedroom, and they made love. Their naked bodies were covered with perspiration. Their lovemaking had been vigorous, and she had several orgasms—more than she had ever experienced. He had only one. He knew how to control himself and give his partner the best. For him, pleasing the woman meant all. It was his ultimate thrill, his ultimate pleasure.

They slept until the sun was at its peak, having made love until early in the morning. Nicole was the first to rise, and she kissed her lover on the cheek, gently shaking him with the shoulder. He moaned and then looked at her. He reached for her face and kissed her on the lips.

"I guess we need to get up?" he said sleepily.

"Yes," she responded as she gave him another kiss. "Let us take a shower and have lunch. I am starving. Aren't you?"

"Only for your love," he answered with a grin. He picked up the phone and ordered lunch. The shrimp salad was Nicole's favorite. He ordered two of them, a bottle of Pellegrino, and a bottle of his favorite white wine. Room service set up their lunch overlooking the beautiful blue sea of Capri.

Nicole had taken her shower and was dressed all in white—a beautiful white Armani top and Armani slacks. As Adam stepped onto the balcony to join Nicole for lunch, he again realized why he loved her. She was the most beautiful woman he had ever met.

Adam lifted the bottle of white wine out of the cooler and poured some into their glasses. Then he put the bottle back on ice.

Nicole lifted her glass and asked Adam to do the same. "Here is to us, to our love," she said. She reached over to Adam and kissed him on the mouth.

CHAPTER 29

Sochi, Russia

H E LAY ON THE BEACH IN a Speedo bathing suit. It was his favorite resort, the place he had built for his people. Pavlov loved Russia. He loved her past and thought that Russia should be a world power once more. It was his mission, his goal, to make that happen. In Sochi at the Olympics, he had shown the world that Russia was a player. Then, he invaded Ukraine to prove his point. He really was not sure how far he could push the envelope.

The head of the Russian Federation did not arrive at his position easily. Unlike his adversary across the ocean, he had to play politics differently. In Russia, a leader without courage and determination who could never decide would never be tolerated.

Russia had lost much of its power and status in the world. But things were changing quickly. Now, Russia was rich. Oil and gas had made Mother Russia a world power once more. And Russia's enemy was weak. The former man in the White House had seemed to have no backbone, had appeared indecisive, and the new president was no different. And the United States never learned from history. It did not learn from Mother Russia's mistakes—getting involved in wars they never should have been involved in, wars they could never win.

The president of the Russian Federation loved America's willingness to fight all the wars and its desire to control the entire world. He had no such ambition, not now. He knew how to wait. His country had been embarrassed, degraded to a minor power that no longer had a say in world politics. His mission was to change all that, and he was confident he could do it.

He was an athlete, a kickboxer, and he had learned when to attack, when to move back, and when to strike again. Mother Russia was not yet ready for an attack. Mother Russia was moving back, preparing for the next move.

Vladimir Pavlov was born in Leningrad, now called St. Petersburg, where he attended the state university before joining the KGB. After he retired from the KGB, he entered politics and rose to become president within a few years. Though he was an orthodox Christian, he was not inclined to get involved in the war in the Middle East. He considered it a regional religious war that could not be won. Never had he bothered to understand all the conflicts in the Middle East. Yes, his country had become involved in Afghanistan, a war they should have never fought. The Middle East was not a war he had any interest in.

On the contrary, he thought, let America become involved. Let them make all the mistakes he had once made in Afghanistan. He was an intelligent man. He knew a war based on religious beliefs could not be won. He would not get involved, not now. But he liked the role that his opponent, America, was playing. They wanted to control the world and be everywhere. In his mind, it was clearly more than they could handle. He knew how to take advantage of America's arrogance.

He also knew that he now had only weak opponents in the White House and a president who could not decide. That was why he had decided to regain territory that belonged to him. Crimea was clearly his, just as Hitler had considered the Sudetenland to be his.

The Russian Federation president smiled as he stepped onto the large terrace of his villa in Sochi. His Olympics had been a success. Once more, he had shown the world that Russia was a world power to be reckoned with.

The White House, Washington, DC

It was telepathy. Six thousand miles to the west, the president of the United States sat in the Oval Office. It was 1:00 a.m., and she was alone. She was designing her bucket list. She had made many promises, few of which she could ever keep. But she knew it would only take one to create a legacy.

She was tired and knew she needed sleep. But thoughts of failing as president—the first female president—kept her awake. She knew she needed to make a difference but did not know how. Decisions were not her forte. She thought she had become the free world leader by default. It had been easy to make promises to the voters who believed in her, telling the country she could change everything and improve their lives. She had made them think that there would be no more wars under her supervision, that she would ensure America was safe. She never spoke about the truth, because belief was a much easier sell—one that most of them heard at church every Sunday.

She stood up and walked around the Oval Office, wondering how many of her predecessors had had to make decisions as difficult as hers. She knew many had, and she also knew that most had been more. She was more decisive and courageous than her. She was a fish out of water. She should never have been in this position.

But she was. She was the president of the United States, the commander in chief. That thought alone frightened her. Never had she envisioned having to make so many decisions. Ever since she was a child, decision-making has been difficult for her. When the American people had elected her, they had asked for change, which she had promised them. Of course, she had been unable to live up to her promises. Yet it did not seem to matter. Her husband had assured her that all the promises she had had to make would be forgotten. After all, he knew this was true.

She was a president with little personality, one who appeared aloof and out of touch with the people. She clearly lacked leadership and charisma. Worse, she never listened to her advisors. She thought she and her husband knew it all. In every speech she gave, she raised her nose at the public, her audience, and her voters. It was a clear sign that she thought she was above them all.

She continued to pace the Oval Office, her sanctuary. All the problems were overwhelming her. Her predecessor had screwed up everywhere: Benghazi, the IRS, the NSA spying, the war in Afghanistan, Iraq, the handling of the Iran nuclear threat, ISIS, the war in the Middle East, Ebola—and the list went on. And she had been part of it, supported it all. She wondered whether the former president had done anything right, and then she decided he had not. To call ISIS a junior varsity team, to announce that Ebola was very unlikely to enter the United States, to appoint an Ebola czar who knew nothing about health care—these were just a few of the many mistakes the former president had made. He had wanted to establish a legacy for his presidency, but it was a legacy of mistakes.

Monica Drew was determined to establish her legacy and would not wait until it was too late. The war in the Middle East, she thought, could become her legacy. Again, she was indecisive. She did not know how to commit American forces. "No boots on the ground," she had promised the American people. But her advisors, generals, and Secretary of Defense knew that a war with no boots on the ground could never be won. Once more, she had not listened, thinking she knew better. Even after her party had taken a severe blow during the midterm elections when America spoke to her, she did not change her mind. She was out of touch—and delusional. She picked up the can of Diet Coke she had placed on her desk in the Oval Office. She had a small drink. She often considered resigning because she knew she was not up to the job. But her husband had dissuaded her. He had said it would be a disgrace, not just to her but to her family—and to all female voters who had cast their vote for her. But now she was alone in her office, the most powerful office in the world. Again, she stood up and walked around. She was president of the United States, the commander in chief, the most powerful person in the world—and she did not know what she wanted to do.

She returned to her desk and sat in the chair where many decisive, courageous presidents had sat before. It inspired her. She quickly forgot all her failures and inadequacies. She felt the energy that many of her predecessors had left behind for people like her. Now her mind was fully at work. She opened another can of Diet Coke and placed it on the desk. Somehow, she needed to make an impact and establish a legacy for her presidency. Her tenure had to be remembered. Indeed, none of her domestic policies would do it. There she had already failed miserably. Her only chance for a legacy lay in foreign policy. Of course, there she had also failed, but she could blame others, blame her secretary of state.

As she leaned back in her chair, she knew her presidency had been a complete failure. But since she was arrogant, a woman defiant toward facts, she would try once more. She decided that her legacy would be to make peace in the Middle East. Of course, she did not understand the struggle, cause, religion, or why. America, she decided, did not care. America just needed to dominate everything.

She quickly forgot all her mistakes. All she knew now was that she was the most powerful person in the world. She never learned from her mistakes; her arrogance did not allow it.

She had received intelligence from Berlin, Germany. The president of the EU had a plan that was entirely underway to make peace in the Middle East. The president of the United States looked at the information given to her by the CIA and FBI. Clearly the EU president was about to beat her to the punch. This she could not let happen. After all, she was the most powerful person in the world, the leader of the free world. Only she should have the right to make peace in the Middle East.

She did not bother to read the brief that explained who the real enemy was. It was not the terrorists, their fighters, their tanks, or their armor. The real enemy was religion. No drone strikes, no air strikes, no boots on the ground could ever defeat that enemy. Religion had to be fought in a much different way, and about this the US president had no clue.

South Beirut, Lebanon

The old Arab, Hassan Nasral, secretary-general of Hezbollah, sat in his bunker in the south of Beirut. He sat in his favorite chair facing the fireplace he could never light. He smiled as he stroked his long gray beard. Finally, all the pieces he had maneuvered for more than thirty years were falling into place—pieces Allah had told him to move. It was but a chess game, the old Arab thought. He always spoke to his God, Allah, when he sat in front of the fireplace. That was when Allah told him what to do.

The plan had been quite simple, yet it had taken many years to implement. The goal was clear. All infidels had to die. Only those who believed in Allah were to live. The old Arab had decided years ago that no conventional warfare, no physical confrontation, would ever result in this goal. He knew that to make Islam the only religion, to destroy all infidels, he had to find a new way. For years he had thought about how to kill all infidels and make Islam the only religion—and Allah the only God.

Finally, Allah had given him the answer. Use two weapons, Allah had told him in his prayers. But to fulfill Allah's wish, the old man needed his grandson. He needed an emissary, someone who could explain his God's message to all Islamic people. He needed someone who could convince the leader of the Shiite people, the grand ayatollah of Iran, that Allah had spoken for all Islamic people. He had asked his grandson, the man from Stanford, to drive to Tehran to speak with the grand ayatollah.

The grand ayatollah of Iran, Iran's supreme leader, listened attentively as the young Shiite Arab explained his grandfather's plan. The goal, the young man made clear, was not for the Shiites or Sunnis to dominate one over the other. The goal— Allah's goal—was to kill all the infidels if they did not become believers. He went on to explain his grandfather's two-pronged attack. Guerilla warfare had been the first of his tactics. After all, major powers such as Russia, France, and the United States had always been defeated by that style of warfare. That was how they had lost wars in Vietnam and Afghanistan.

The grand ayatollah nodded. He liked the young man from Lebanon. The two of them were sitting in the Iranian leader's study. No one else was present. The young man had insisted on it.

"As you recall," Ali said, "years ago my grandfather proposed his idea of guerrilla warfare to fight the infidels. Then he called for the formation of groups of fighters—now called terrorist groups by our enemy. To motivate them, he used religion as their cause. My grandfather also wanted to recruit foreign fighters from within our enemies' countries. He believed that this would have several benefits." Ali smiled. "First of all, fewer of us would be killed. But more importantly, it would help us spread our cause and make more people believe in Allah and want to kill the infidels."

"You are right. I do recall your grandfather's plan," the grand ayatollah responded enthusiastically. "We all implemented it. It was brilliant and look at the remarkable success we are having. And now your grandfather has another plan to kill all the infidels, to make Allah supreme?"

"Yes," the young man replied, now anxious to share all the information with the most powerful man in Iran.

"My grandfather's ideas must be coordinated simultaneously for the most powerful effect. My grandfather's second weapon is deceit."

"What do you mean by deceit?"

"It's quite simple," said the Stanford man. "Our archenemy, the Mossad, has used it successfully for years. Their motto says, 'By way of deception thou shalt do war.' Deceit is our most powerful weapon. We need to unite, even as we let all the infidels think we are still fighting each other. They must believe that we have no common cause or hate each other."

"What good will that do?" the grand ayatollah of Iran wanted to know.

"Much good," Ali replied. "First, it will keep them completely off guard. They will not know who to support. They will choose one side or another, but it will always be us. We will receive their support, weapons, money, and even their boots on the ground." He laughed as he said it, and so did the ayatollah.

"You are a very bright man. Allah has sent you. And your grandfather is no less. I bless you both."

Ali Nasral approached the ayatollah of Iran, and they embraced and kissed on each cheek, which meant they agreed. "I do have one last question," said the grand ayatollah. "When it is all over, when we have won the war and killed all the infidels, who will rule—the Sunnis or us?"

"Allah will rule," the young man replied.

Ali had come from Beirut by car. No one knew about him, and he had not been followed. He was totally under everyone's radar. As he traveled back to the bunker of his grandfather in Beirut, he thought much about the plan to kill all the infidels. He thought much about Allah and about religion. He had heard his grandfather say that their religion had deceived all infidels, that their religion was but a belief and not the truth. There was no concrete evidence of their God. But was there evidence for Allah? Or was Allah also just a belief, an unverified truth?

Washington, DC

The US president had never understood the importance of peace in the Middle East. In fact, she understood little at all about the Middle East, and nothing about its history, the core of the conflict, or the religions. She had never even visited any of the nations. But she had decided that making peace in the Middle East would be the legacy she needed.

Her predecessor's administration was encumbered with more failures than any other: Benghazi, the NSA spying on American citizens and its closest allies, listening to the cell phone of Angela Merkel, the chancellor of Germany and one of America's closest allies, the IRS scandal targeting his opponents, immigration reform, Pavlov's challenge in the Ukraine, and all the promises he had made to the American people during his election campaigns.

And now she had inherited it all. During her campaign, she had done all she could to distance herself from her boss, often denying the truth. Even though most Americans did not trust her, she had been elected. Early in her presidency, she established a legacy so that people would remember that the first female US president had made a difference. And she had decided that peace in the Middle East was her only chance for a legacy. Her secretary of state had taken many trips there, and he would be the one to help establish the peace—the peace she would take all the credit for.

But her secretary of state was no different from her. He, too, had campaigned for the presidency. He, too, was utterly ignorant of the issues in the Middle East, what the people in the streets wanted, and what made them tick. The secretary had met with all the dignitaries and had conferred with them about what America wanted to do. But he never listened. He never learned what the people believed in and wanted to do. He spoke eloquently about what America could accomplish. He never heard the people's voice or understood the war's actual cause.

Moscow, Russia

The Russian Federation president did not care much about the Middle East. He had a very different agenda. He loved diversion, loved the idea that all his enemies were focused on the Middle East. He would use that to his advantage, for he was a man of history and ambition.

Mother Russia had been humiliated, and much of his country had been taken away from him. It very much reminded him of Germany. They, too, had lost much of their country after World War I. And they had retaliated. He thought he had to do the same, and now was the time to act. All were focused on the Middle East, and his number one adversary, the president of the United States, could not decide. More importantly, the people in her country did not want to enter another war. They were already involved in wars they could never win, wars without reason.

Now was the time to strike, to regain some of the land Mother Russia had lost. The opposition would be weak, and America was in no mood to fight back. Yes, he knew they would call for sanctions and try to hurt him economically as they had done when he had reclaimed Crimea. But all he had tried to do was regain the territory that belonged to him, which had been taken away without cause.

His secret intelligence agency had told him about the peace the Vatican had tried to make in the Middle East, but it held little interest. Sure, he would believe it was important to him and Mother Russia. But all this diversion would only allow him to finalize his true mission: to regain all of Russia's territories. Ukraine was only his first step. Poland was next.

He also knew that the US president would allow him to do so. The woman the American people had elected had no courage. Why? Was the world's most significant power unwilling to lead in the Middle East? Why didn't the United States accept the fact that the only way to win the war was to place boots on the ground? *No balls*, Vladimir Pavlov decided with a snicker.

Well, he knew he had balls, and he had decided he would fill the leadership role the United States had left vacant. He would put boots on the ground. No one killed innocent Russian citizens as ISIS had done by shooting down a Russian passenger jet. He, Vladimir Pavlov, would always protect his people and not just make promises.

He stood up from behind his large desk and looked at the map of Europe that had been placed on his desk. All of Mother Russia's territories were highlighted in red—not just today's territories but the territories that he believed belonged to him. He knew it was his mission to make Russia a world power once again. If he had to—and he knew he eventually would—he would use all of Russia's might to accomplish his goal. He was not afraid. He had the balls to put boots on the ground.

The president of the Russian federation was not a reactionary man. He loved to plan, deceive, and keep his enemies guessing. This he had learned during his years at the KGB, Russia's former intelligence agency. Politics, he always told his staff, was no more than a chess game, but it was much more like poker. In chess you had to outsmart the opponent and lure him into a trap. But poker was more his game. He loved to bluff and let his enemy think he was dealing from strength when his hand was weak. And never had he met another opponent who could be bluffed so easily, an opponent who would not raise the ante even if she held the best cards. Pavlov had met the president of the United States on a few occasions. He had looked her in the eye and had known that the woman was not a worthy adversary. His training and his years in the KGB had taught him well how to judge people. Rarely was he wrong. Often, he had put himself in the shoes of the US president. He knew that to be effective in fighting an enemy, you had to know all about him. It was a lesson the Americans had never bothered to learn.

Vladimir Pavlov sat back in the leather chair behind his desk and focused on the map of Europe, but his thoughts were elsewhere. His thoughts were with his enemy, the president of the United States.

Clearly the American people were dissatisfied with her leadership, both domestically and in foreign policy. Domestically, she had betrayed her people. She had not delivered on any of her campaign promises, and she continued to lie about all the blunders committed by herself and her predecessor. Clearly her foreign policy, which she had authored as secretary of state, was also a disaster. The woman had proven not to be ready for the job.

In a way, the president of the Russian federation almost felt sorry for the US president. He smiled as he stroked his right hand over the map of Europe in front of him. He wondered whether his counterpart in the US had created a "bucket list" for her second term. Surely, she must have, and surely it included the success of her health-care bill, immigration reform, and peace in the Middle East, which had to be number one.

Pavlov rose from the chair and strolled to the malachite foyer, a long corridor right off the throne room in the Grand Kremlin Palace, his official residence. The walls were adorned with portraits of Russian kings and conquerors. As he stared at the portrait of Peter the Great, who had expanded the Russian empire to the Baltic Sea, a thought entered his mind. He chuckled. He had an idea. He would send a message to the president of the United States. It would be a simple message: "Perhaps you should change the first letter of your bucket list to an F."

Berlin, Germany

The president of the EU had received two lists from his cousin. They contained the names of all the men who needed to meet to establish peace in the Middle East. First, he looked at the longer list. He smiled when he saw the name of the leader of the Russian Federation, Mr.

Pavlov. Russia's leader was hardly a man who knew how to make peace. His idea of peace was not unlike Hitler's: station all your troops on the border and then negotiate. The president of the EU knew better. That had been tried before and only ended in war, not peace. Germany's leader was determined to make peace. He wanted to repay the world. Now he smiled again. The president of the United States also wanted to attend the meeting. If she could not even make peace in Washington, how could she make peace in the Middle East? He threw the first list into the garbage can. Then he immediately looked at the other list, the concise list that his cousin recommended.

Yes, he thought these were the right players. With their help, peace in the Middle East was possible. He picked up the phone.

"Call my cousin, please," he instructed his secretary. His phone rang within minutes.

"Yes," he said.

"It is your cousin, the minister," the secretary informed him.

"Put him on, please," he responded. He spoke again when he heard his cousin's voice. "I really like your concise list. You did a wonderful job. Let us set the date and make it soon. And it must be at Sanssouci, otherwise Frederick would never forgive me." Germany's leader chuckled.

For the brief list, the minister had thought about who should play a part. Undoubtedly, his cousin had to be there, for he had to preside over the meeting. Then there had to be representatives of all the religions involved: Jews, Muslims, and Christians. Naturally, the Muslims would send leaders of the Shiites and Sunnis. The Christians would have sent the pope, but now that he was dead, they would send a representative. And the Jews would send someone whom the head of the Mossad approved. It would not necessarily be one of the chief rabbinates. Then he thought about Adam Bergman, whom his cousin had also included on the list. Prince Albert had never met him, but his lover in Rome had assured him that Adam was first-rate—and a little extra security, the minister thought, would never hurt. This was the list that Prince William von Hohenzollern approved.

His cousin instructed the minister to keep the meeting secret, and he knew of only one man who could secretly deliver the message to all the chosen participants. He would ask his lover in Rome to instruct Adam Bergman to ensure that only the chosen people knew the meeting's date, place, and time. Adam also had to take care of all the travel arrangements. There should be no pattern, not even one that the Obama spies could follow. Berlin would pay for all.

Tel Aviv, Israel

He had just stepped out of the shower when the bell rang at 5:00 a.m. He was dripping wet and quickly put a towel around his large, muscular body. He walked to the door. He did not have to open it, for he saw the white envelope that had been pushed under it. Only his bodyguards were allowed to ring the bell if it was important.

"Sir," one of the guards texted, "the cleaning lady dropped off this envelope. She said it was important, and it was for you. We checked it. It is safe."

A small field near South Beirut

Goats were all he owned, and they were his life. They had been his father's and grandfather's lives as well. He raised them and loved them. They were his livelihood. Each morning, he would gather them and walk them to the field where they would graze and drink from a small brook. There he would sit in the shade of the trees and nap. And then he would walk the animals back to their home. It was a routine that had not changed since he was a child.

A few months ago, a man had approached him to buy some of his goat milk. He wanted two liters every day, and he came to the oasis to pick up the milk every day. The shepherd did not mind. He needed the money.

But today was different. Early in the morning, another man approached him just before he was ready to walk his goats to the field. This man asked him to deliver a white envelope to the man who always bought the goat milk. The shepherd took the envelope and the handsome money the man handed him. He was told to ensure that the man who always bought the goat milk got this envelope.

Berlin, Germany

Carlo had traveled to Berlin to lay fresh flowers at his grandparents' graves. He did this every year on the anniversary of their deaths, and then he went to the church to pray. He knelt and looked up at the large cross as he prayed to God. Then the priest who conducted the ceremony at St. Bernard, the Catholic church at Königin–Luise Str. in Dahlem, Berlin, asked all to open their booklets to page 86 and sing in unison to praise the lord. As the young priest from Rome opened his prayer book to page 86, and a small white envelope fell out. He quickly retrieved it and put it in his pocket. He did not read it—not now. Now was his time to be with his Lord.

Tehran, Iran

The grand ayatollah of Iran received the small white envelope in a very conventional way: a diplomatic pouch from Berlin, Germany.

South Beirut, Lebanon

The envelope and goat milk were delivered to the secretary-general of Hezbollah in his bunker. The envelope contained an invitation from the president of the EU to a meeting to make peace. It included a list of all who had been invited, a date, the time, and the place. Hassan struck a match and burned the message. He knew he would accept the invitation. He needed no time to think about it.

Tel Aviv, Israel

The head of the Mossad always wanted to know. He craved information, for he believed it was the foundation of his job. The more information he had, the more powerful he was. He did not wait to dry himself as he held the small white envelope in his large right hand. He tore it open immediately, anxious to read the message.

The message took him by surprise. He knew there had been an initiative by the Vatican to make peace in the Middle East. His intelligence agency, the Mossad, had informed him that the pope, the bishop of Rome, had intended this peace to be his legacy. But when the pope died, so had the drive for peace—or so the head of the Mossad had thought. Now he knew he was wrong. He had received bad information.

The head of the Mossad was a decisive man who made decisions quickly. He would not attend the meeting that the president of the EU had called for. He knew the meeting was for people of faith and that his faith had to be represented. It did not take him long to decide who he would send—not any chief rabbinates, for he trusted none. His brother-in-law, the rabbi from Brooklyn, would represent Israel. The rabbi from Brooklyn would go to Sanssouci.

CHAPTER 30

South Beirut, Lebanon

IT HAD NOT TAKEN LONG. EVERYONE had been prepared for this event. All of them had known that the location would eventually be disclosed, but they were surprised it had taken so many years.

He sat on the carpet in his bunker before the fireplace he could never use. He loved fireplaces. The idea of fire had always inspired him. It could heal, warm, and comfort people. But more importantly, it could destroy. Fire was a two-edged sword. It was the kind of sword he believed in and would use at Sanssouci. He would send his grandson and save the sharp end.

Capri, Italy

The gozzo bobbed gently in the Mediterranean Sea only a few hundred yards off the island of Capri. The captain had turned off its engines, letting the boat drift gently into the blue sea. There was but a light breeze and not a cloud in the sky—the kind of day Victorino, the boat's captain, was used to. Today, he had only two passengers, close friends whom he knew well. The man had asked him to turn off the engines and drift in the blue waters. The man and the woman were lounging on the large bed in the boat's bow. Both were enjoying the wine and food Victorino had brought.

Nicole turned to face Adam on the sofa cushions in the boat's bow. "Adam," she said, "I cannot understand it. It seems like the conflict in the Middle East is becoming more confusing. It changes all the time. Can you explain that? What does peace in the Middle East really mean? Peace with whom?"

Adam reached for his favorite Pinot Grigio glass and took a small sip. Then he sat up and raised his muscular, suntanned body to face Nicole. He took off his Armani sunglasses and used the white towel next to his body to wipe his face. "I thought we came here today to relax, eat, and enjoy the drink, the sun, and the water. Then we will go back to our apartment and make love."

"All that is still part of my agenda." Nicole smiled. "But making love is the prize. First, explain peace in the Middle East."

"Okay," Adam replied. "It would have been an easy answer a few years ago. But since then, we Americans have screwed it all up. Let us return to when peace in the Middle East meant peace between Israel and Palestine. Surely, they had their differences in their religions, and they still do. The Israelis are Jews, and the Palestinians are mostly Muslim. But do you know that they have much in common? Most Muslims of Palestine are descendants of Christians, Jews, and other inhabitants of the Levant."

"The Levant," Nicole interrupted. "What is the Levant?"

"Well, do you want me to keep it simple and just give you the big picture, or do you want the details? In short, the Levant is a geographic and cultural region consisting of Cyprus, Israel, Jordan, Lebanon, Palestine, Syria, and parts of Turkey."

"Okay." Nicole shook her head and took another sip of her white wine. "Spare me all the details. Just get down to what I need to know."

"A little detail will help," Adam responded with a smile. He knew Nicole was impatient. "I think you should know that a study of high-resolution haplotypes demonstrated that a substantial portion of Y chromosomes of Israeli Jews, 70 percent, and of Palestinian Muslims, eighty-two percent belonged to the same chromosome pool."

"What the heck is a haplotype?" she asked.

"A haplotype is the group of genes that a progeny inherits from one parent," he responded.

"So, they are all related, have the same blood, and are like brothers. Then why are they fighting?" Nicole stood up and shook her head in disbelief.

"It's simple," Adam replied. "It is all about belief and religion. Only the religious leaders can ever resolve this conflict."

"Adam, please go on. Please explain to me what is happening right now, where does ISIS fit in, and al-Qaeda, and all the terrorist factions. What needs to be done?"

"There will never be peace by military force. Drones and air strikes do not defeat belief. They may suppress it, but they will never destroy it. Peace must come from within all the religions. It must come when we finally all believe in our one God."

"How do we achieve that goal?" Nicole was anxious to know.

"There is only one way," Adam said as he walked to the stern of the gozzo to retrieve another bottle of his favorite Pinot Grigio.

"How can it be done?" Nicole urged him.

He smiled. He knew that peace among the religions was what the pope had always wanted to accomplish. "The politicians will never achieve peace. Peace can only be made by the holy men. They all must meet: the ayatollahs, the chief rabbis, the pope, and all the religious leaders. Only they can make peace. It really is quite simple. To start a war, any war, you need a cause. Look at Russia. Their alleged cause for invading Crimea was to protect Russians who lived there. Hitler used the same excuse on many occasions.

"War is like a disease. You take away the cause to cure the ailment. The cause in the Middle East is religion. It may well be that many of the terrorists fighting in the Middle East are not really committed to their religion. That, however, is irrelevant. They use religion as their cause. It is a cause that is easily understood, one that men will follow, one that arouses emotions, one that people are willing to kill for."

"Are you telling me that religion is just a pretense?" Nicole asked as she sat back on the large sun pad at the bow of Victorino's boat.

"To some degree," Adam replied." Some surely are religious fanatics, but they are not the brain trust. They are only using religion to usurp power. Religion is the cause that rallies the troops. The jihadist leaders fully understand that the Islamic religion is one of peace. But they are the experts in deceit to make people believe differently." He took another sip of his white wine and joined Nicole on the large bed in front of the gozzo. "But can we just relax and not talk about the war in the Middle East?"

"No," she responded." I really want a better understanding. I want to know how you think this can all be resolved."

"Okay, I will answer you only because I love you. The problem is that most politicians do not seem to understand or want to accept that this is a religious war, that only religion can make peace. It will not be easy. Even the Muslims are fighting each other; there is no love lost between the Sunnis and the Shiites. Indeed, they have had differences since Muhammad died in 672 and did not name a successor. But their differences are a minor matter of different holidays and traditions.

"But you know that the Jewish people also have different factions. There are the Ashkenazi Jews from France, Germany, and Eastern Europe, and the Sephardic Jews from Syria, Portugal, North Africa, and the Middle East. They speak different languages: Yiddish, which is based on German and Hebrew, and Ladino, which is based on Spanish and Hebrew. Yet they do not shoot each other. Why can't the Sunnis and the Shiites do the same? Now, let us take a break. Let us take a quick swim to cool off."

Both jumped off Victorino's gozzo, holding hands. The water was cooler than both had expected. Quickly, they returned to the boat, dried themselves, and sat down for lunch that their captain had prepared. The food was always the best, because all the vegetables freshly grown in Victorino's garden.

"Adam, please tell me how you think this will all end," Nicole said as she walked to the boat's bow with a white towel wrapped around her shapely body.

"Before I give you the answer to solve all the problems in the world, I need two things: first, another glass of white wine, and then a kiss." He walked to the stern of the boat, where Victorino stored the wine in a large, worn, white cooler. He picked up a bottle that had already been opened and poured himself a glass.

"Another?" he asked as he looked at Nicole. "No, thank you. I want to hear your answer."

Adam strolled back to the boat's bow and sat next to Nicole. "Actually," he said, "the answer is quite simple. You need to remove the cause."

"Remove the cause? What do you mean?" Nicole asked.

"All the air strikes, drone attacks, and even boots on the ground will never end the struggle. These things may slow down the conflict, but they will never end it. You must stop the cause, and then there will be no more war."

"How do you stop the cause?" Nicole was now sitting up, anxious to learn Adam's answer.

"Simple," he said. "One answer is to get all the religious leaders—leaders of the Sunnis, the Shiites, the Jews, the Catholics, the Protestants, and all other religions—to agree on one religion and eliminate the differences they are fighting about. If there is peace among all the religions, the terrorists have no cause. No one will join them. It is like a plant deprived of water."

"Why are our leaders not pursuing that idea?" Nicole asked excitedly. "It sounds good to me."

"Some do not want peace, and some want to make peace on their own terms and make that their legacy. But real peace can only be made by the religious leaders, not politicians."

"You said that this is the only solution. What is the other? "The other is that you remove religion altogether."

"But so many people are believers," Nicole interrupted, "not all in the same faith, yet they believe."

Victorino had started the engine of his small boat and was steering it back to Marina Piccolo, where Adam had asked to be dropped off. "You are right," Adam said, leaning over and kissing Nicole. "But you are always right." He smiled. "Let us go back to our conversation just a few minutes ago. We both know that religion—at least in its current form—is the cause of the war in the Middle East. Take religion out of the equation, and then no one has a reason to fight."

"How do you do that?" Nicole asked.

"I wish I knew the answer to that question. First, people need to become aware of the evil that religion can cause, all the harm it can do, and is doing. Second, we need to find a substitute for religion, because people want to hope, to believe."

"How do you replace their faith?"

"We all need to find an inner spirit, a spirit of our own that we can believe in—not one dictated by religion but one completely based on facts and truth. I know it will take strength and a belief in oneself, a true belief. Religion was created by a few who wanted to dominate and control people. They realized that people were weak and needed a crutch, a comforting hope for a better life. But religion was used to help a few people gain power. They subject believers to them by telling them of miracles that never materialized, and they went to war with those who did not believe. Christians and Muslims all killed to make believers. Wars will never end until we stop the root of the evil."

"Again, Adam, how do we do that?" Nicole asked anxiously.

"Unfortunately, it will take a long, long time. Religion has been. around for too long, and it has become part of most people's lives. It will be very difficult to change or eradicate. Yet I hope that eventually all the religious leaders will understand the problem. Naturally, they want to ignore it and maintain their stronghold on humanity. Eventually, they, too, will realize that religion must change. The new, progressive church leaders will call for a different spiritual experience, not one based on centuries of lies and deceit but on the truth that each of us is comfortable with. It will not be dictated by the past church leaders or preached every Sunday."

"Adam," Nicole interrupted, "your reasoning makes all the sense. in the world. Why doesn't everyone understand the problem?"

"Fortunately, one man understands it all—a powerful man, who can make a difference. I cannot tell you, his name. But I can give you a secret word you can never reveal to anyone."

"Of course, you have my word," she said. "Sanssouci," was his reply.

CHAPTER 31

Potsdam, Germany

SANSSOURCR, FREDERRCK THE GREAT'S SUMMER The Palace was the perfect place for the meeting, the minister thought. His cousin, the president of the European Union, always seemed to make the right decisions. The palace was in Potsdam, only a short distance from Berlin. The Schloss had been built in the mid-1700s. Here, the King of Prussia, Frederick the Great, relaxed to get away from the pump and ceremonies of his court in Berlin. Often, he meets his friend Voltaire. Here, he entertained the people he really enjoyed. It was a place of peace where he could be alone.

But Sanssouci was no longer a place without worry, a place where the chancellor of Germany could hide or speak in secret to his confidants. The NSA and the CIA heard it all.

The White House, Washington, DC

The president of the United States was infuriated. She had staked her legacy on making peace in the Middle East after all her domestic and foreign programs failed. Now she was left out. But so was her rival, the president of the Russian Federation. Finally, both had found common ground in a common cause: to stop the peace Berlin was about to make!

Both knew that the architect of the peace was the president of the EU. Both knew that there would be no peace in the Middle East without him. But the two uninvited leaders did not trust each other. The US president thought that her Russian counterpart was a bully, a peasant, and a man without class. The Russian saw the US president as a weakling, a woman who could not make a major decision. They traded many phone calls but never reached a common ground. They could not agree.

Potsdam, Germany

It was a sunny day. The gardens at Sanssouci were in full bloom. The minister of internal affairs of Germany, cousin of the EU's president, had arranged for horse carriages to meet all the guests at the estate's entrance. From here, they would be taken through the beautiful gardens to the palace. The meeting was to begin at 1:00 p.m. The president of the EU had decided that the reception should take place in the Marmorsaal. It was the principal reception room, the setting for celebration in the palace.

Carlo DeFino, the young priest from the Vatican, was anxious—in a panic. He needed to speak with Adam Bergman to share a burden he had carried for too long, and he needed to do it now, before the meeting at the Marmorsaal in the Schloss began. Later, it would be too late. Fortunately, he recognized Adam as he crossed the courtyard and was about to enter the palace.

"Adam!" he shouted. "I need to talk to you for but a minute. It is important."

Adam turned and saw the young priest rushing toward him. Carlo seemed nervous and irritable, not as composed as he usually was.

"Adam, please," the priest pleaded, "let us stroll in the garden. There is something you need to know about Lisa."

"Lisa Petterson?" Adam asked.

"Yes," Carlo replied as he gently took Adam's left arm and steered him toward the gravel walkway to the beautiful rose garden outside of Schloss Sanssouci. "It is a secret I have kept inside me for too long, and I need to share it with someone. I must share it now, and only you will fully understand." Carlo was shaking with emotion.

"Relax, Carlo, be at ease," Adam reassured him. "I am your friend, and I am listening carefully. Please, go on."

"The information I am about to give you is only what one other person and I know about. Only the head of the Mossad, Maza Sharef, and I share this secret. But I have decided that you, too, have a right to know. When Lisa joined the Mossad after she graduated from Stanford, Israel's intelligence agency did a thorough vetting and found nothing to prevent Lisa from joining the agency. However, Maza had always been intrigued by her upbringing, particularly her relationship with the priest, allegedly her uncle, von Meissen, who later became Pope Leo XIV. So Maza decided to do DNA testing and asked me to supply a sample from the pope. He had access to Lisa's DNA. I agreed to do it because the result would be shared with me."

Now Adam was listening closely, anxious to learn more.

"Well," Carlo continued, "I will get right to the point: the samples matched."

"The samples matched?" Adam asked, incredulously.

"Yes," the young priest replied, "the pope had a child. Lisa is his daughter."

"Are you certain that only you and Maza know about it? Incredible. So, you are telling me that Lisa shot her father, the pope. Did she know he was her father?"

"Yes, she did." Carlo went on. "When Lisa worked for the Mossad, she discovered her file, a file that only Maza, the head of the Mossad, had access to."

"Why did she kill the pope, her father?" Adam wanted to know. "I do not have that answer," Carlo replied, "but I suppose that when she discovered that the pope was her father, she felt betrayed by years of lies and deceit. She became angry—no, not just angry but hateful. Besides, you must remember that by then she had become radicalized and had become a Jihadist. Her boyfriend, Ali Nasral, had made sure of it while they both attended Stanford. He was the one who convinced her to infiltrate the Mossad, and he was the one who asked her to shoot the pope."

"It's still hard to believe." Adam shook his head. "The pope has a child, and the child kills the pope."

"Adam, please use this information with discretion. It may be best not to share it with anyone. I had promised to keep it a secret, but I could no longer bear the burden and had to share it with someone today.

Adam agreed and promised never to reveal what he had just learned. He did not ask Carlo why he had shared this secret today. Adam's mind was too occupied. But in retrospect, he should have.

As guests arrived at Schloss Sanssouci, champagne was served. Prince William von Hohenzollern greeted each one with a firm handshake and a hug. He wanted all of them to feel like friends. He wanted all of them to know that they were here to make peace. Although the perimeter security was very tight, the EU president had insisted that his guests were to be trusted. After all, he had told his head of security, this was a mission of peace. None were examined for weapons, and no one was frisked.

Prince William valued time and liked to get things done. Once all the introductions had been cordially completed, he asked all to join him in the Marmorsaal. A table had been set up in the middle of the room, and name plates indicated where each guest should sit.

Prince William and his cousin, Prince Albert, stood to allow all the guests to take a seat. All of them did, except for the young priest from Rome. He had not taken a glass of champagne when he had first entered the reception room.

This was strange, thought his lover, Prince Albert. He knew that Carlo loved champagne, particularly the Crystal being served. He also felt that his lover from the Vatican acted nervously. It was just the occasion, he thought. But he was wrong. The young priest walked up to the minister, his lover, pulled a gun, and held it to his head.

"You betrayed me! You have another lover—your cousin!" He pulled the trigger. Brain material covered the young priest's face and body, but he did not care. He wanted justice.

He turned to where the president of the EU was standing in disbelief, only five yards from him. Carlo DeFino took one shot, which struck William in the body. William fell to the floor. Now the young priest from Rome pointed the gun at William's forehead and was about to pull the trigger. But he was too late. The bullet from Adam's gun hit Carlo's eyes. He died at once.

CHAPTER 32

Charitee Hospital, Berlin

THE PRESIDENT OF THE EU, THE Chancellor of Germany, was at once airlifted to his place of birth, the Charité Hospital. There he underwent immediate surgery, and his spleen was removed—the only damage the bullet had done. When he finally awoke, he wondered who he really was, which one of the babies who had been switched on October 15, 1944. Now he would never know. Yet he knew he still had a mission. He had to make peace, and as sure as hell, he would try again.

Prince William rested peacefully in his private room at the Charité Hospital in Stadtmitte in Berlin, where he had been born. It was not often that the president of the European Union and chancellor of Germany experienced much quiet time, but quiet time was what the doctors had ordered. Quiet time, the prince decided to apply only to his body, not his mind. His doctors had no control over that—not yet anyway.

Prince William leaned back on the soft down cushion and gathered his thoughts. He thought he fully understood the war in the Middle East—or World War III, as the Vatican ambitiously called the conflict. The Vatican had a clear interest in elevating the significance of the struggle, because the Catholic Church's empire was directly threatened by Daesh, the Arab acronym for ISIS, a term ISIS resented. The prince recognized the difference between al-Qaeda—a network of autonomous cells that had modern political ambitions but used medieval disguise—and ISIS—a religious crusade adhering to the strictest teachings of their prophet Muhammad and requiring territory, a caliphate, to be legitimate. ISIS could not and would not waver from the rules embedded in Islam by their prophet Muhammad.

The leader of ISIS, Sayed Bagherall, established himself as a true caliph. He met all the requirements laid down by Islamic Sharia law: he was a Muslim adult male of Quraysh descent, of the tribe of the Prophet Muhammad, and he showed mental and physical integrity, honesty, and, most importantly, *amr*, or authority. Authority meant having a territory where he could enforce Islamic law, where all Muslims were obliged to immigrate.

Prince William understood that the caliph, the head of ISIS, was determined to revive traditions that had been dormant for hundreds of years. To be a caliph, he had to. Many now call him a terrorist, but in fact, he was a true believer in the teachings of his prophet Muhammad. He had taught that anyone veering from his strict teachings would be an apostate. Two hundred million Shiite Muslims were marked for death because they innovated, changing some of the traditions taught by the Prophet. To innovate was apostasy. Christians and Jews were exempted from execution if they subjugated themselves and paid the *jizya*, a special tax.

The prince also reminded himself that all Muslims were waiting for the Mahdi, a messianic figure destined to lead the Muslims to victory before the end of the world. A battle would take place at Dabiq near Aleppo, where the army of "Rome," the infidels, would be killed, and the Muslims would go on to conquer the world. William shook his head. Belief was a wonderful thing, but only if it was the truth.

The prince leaned to his right and took a large drink from the glass of water that the nurse had placed on his night table. Then he chuckled as he recalled the former president of the United States saying, "If a JV team puts on Lakers' uniforms, that does not make them Kobe Bryant." Now it clearly was Kobe Bryant in the Middle East. William was also convinced that all the air and drone strikes, and even boots on the ground, were not the solution. Indeed, the United States had the wherewithal to put boots on the ground, destroy ISIS, and take away the caliphate that made Sayed Bagherall, the ISIS leader, a legitimate caliph.

But then what? To invade, kill ISIS, and leave would once again leave a vacuum—only to be filled by another ISIS. But how long can you stay where you are not wanted, a place you do not understand? The prince thought this was not an alternative, and at best it would only be a temporary solution. No, only he had the permanent answer to peace. It was all a matter of belief and truth. Only when all people accept all religions as beliefs rather than the truth would there be everlasting peace!

Or would there be? He once again wondered if religion had been used as a motivating tool just as nationalism had been used in previous wars. Once religion is eliminated, would humanity seek and find another causes for war? What was the actual cause of all the conflicts? Was it the basic instinct humans shared with all animals, the survival instinct? Could there ever really be peace?

Prince William von Hohenzollern now sat in his bed and looked around him. The room was filled with bouquets of flowers sent by dignitaries from everywhere. When the nurse's aide brought in a new bouquet, the prince asked to see the attached card. He read them all.

The nurse's aide knocked and entered the hospital room, but she was not alone. The bouquet was too large for her to carry this time, and two men aided her. The prince asked to have the flowers placed at the end of his bed, the only space available. The card attached to the bouquet was small, simple, and white. But a bold message had been written on it: "Speedy recovery. Truth, not belief, will prevail. Signed, von Claussen."

South Beirut, Lebanon

He was alone, deep in a bunker in South Beirut. He now sat on his carpet in front of the large fireplace. He did not need the chair. He felt rejuvenated, and he smiled. Once again, the infidels had done his job. Once again, he did not have to use the sharp end of his sword, but he knew the day would come when he would use it. He could not wait. Each day, he prayed that Allah would let him be the one to kill all the infidels.

Tel Aviv, Israel

The large Boeing jet lifted gently off the runway at the airport in Tel Aviv, its destination: New York. The first cabin was unoccupied except for a single passenger. He sat in the front row; aisle seat 1 B. Tears were streaming down the face of the old rabbi. He clenched his Bible tightly. Never would he let it go. He wished he had never left his home in Brooklyn Heights, wished he had never answered his brother-in-law's telephone call. As he wiped the tears from his eyes, he saw in his mind the bench under the large oak tree in Brooklyn Heights where he always went to pray. There, every day, he would read the Bible. He could not wait to do it again.